10/21

De Vries, Peter.

The prick of noon

APR 2 2 1985

DATE			

PETER DE VRIES

The Prick of Noon

LITTLE, BROWN AND COMPANY
Boston   Toronto

FIRST EDITION

Library of Congress Cataloging in Publication Data
De Vries, Peter.
    The prick of noon.

    I. Title.
PS3507.E8673P7   1985   813'.52   85-4256
ISBN 0-316-18205-2

BP

Designed by Patricia Girvin Dunbar

*Published simultaneously in Canada
by Little, Brown & Company (Canada) Limited*

PRINTED IN THE UNITED STATES OF AMERICA

Contents

The Prick of Noon

O N E

A Normal Fever

THE TROUBLE with treating people as equals is that the first thing you know they may be doing the same thing to you. Such reprisals seriously disrupt the pecking order, especially in a democracy where the class distinctions are so much more finely balanced than in other systems. The resort to what in the nuclear age is called the second-strike capability results in total confusion, a shambles leaving no survivors amid the rubble of status, though giving some of us upstarts a momentary bit of a gloat.

Something like it may have happened in the case of Cynthia Pickles and me, unsettling an equilibrium ticklishly founded on the principle of a place for everyone and everyone in his place. Her being gracious enough to imply that I was as good as she was ought never to have been challenged by my stupidly returning the compliment, thus forgetting my station in the some think divinely ordained scheme of things: to wit, the fact that the great Butcher upstairs who cuts us up into chops of supposedly equal weight and worth sometimes purposely leaves a little less gristle here, a little more bone or fat there, when He doesn't actually have His thumb on the scale. A prettier metaphor for all this would be that He, let's see, that He must play his tune on pipes of varying lengths or there's no music, one dearer to people benefiting from the master-servant axis than to me, who speaks out less as one with many opportunities to treat people as equals than as underdog biting back.

Worshipping from afar is hard work and long hours, especially if you have to do it close up and with no talent for the pretty verses knights of yore were expected to grind out for snooty ladies who often didn't know they were alive.

My fatal contact began that early July afternoon beside a country club swimming pool asplash with numberless fattening porpoises of the genus *Homo suburbanitis*. The similes with which I flogged my smitten heart would hardly rate as poetry, but they came naturally to one with a brief history in the liquor game. Her eyes, then, were dark as ale while her hair was light as beer, always a smashing combination, right? A fair complexion probably normally the color of tawny port had been deepened by the summer sun into more like that of Jamaica rum. I found the rain of comparisons personally intoxicating, though I would probably wake up with a head in the morning. It remained only for lips of claret, parted in laughter at the moment of first glimpse, to complete the demolition. "You have faultless taste, Teeters," I told myself, "so let's try to hide your tasteless faults. O.K.? *Aspire.*"

Drunk with passion now, tomorrow hung over? Friends and countrymen, six months ago I'd not even have been allowed in this country club, but it had gone bankrupt and been bought by the town, and was now public. No one was admitted either by car or on the hoof who didn't have the requisite six bits entrance fee, collected at the gate by an old

4

codger who often collared those on foot in the ritual known as "passing the time of day," long enough to haul you into the tollbooth and lift his shirttail to show you his tumor.

The princess, or as we say now days target female, had undoubtedly been a member of Rolling Acres before it had gone belly-up, as had the trio seated around a poolside table at which she paused to chat, lightly swinging a racquet, and they all probably considered the club territory invaded by barbarians. Together they made one of those habitat groups, they call them, that so niftily typify a time and place. I mean they could have been kept in dry ice and unpacked for installation in a museum centuries hence, and your gaping narrator with them, to symbolize leisure in ours. We have a rather substantial heterosexual community in Merrymount, Conn., where it's said they can always spot one of us. Your correspondent drooling till he will soon be weak from loss of saliva as he twinkles in a little closer to the habitat group would be a case in point. He is aware of the princess flicking a glance in his direction, with no interruption of the smiling exchanges with her friends — a woman under a hat slightly less in size than the table parasol, and two chaps who look as though they are not without influence in high places. Gladly would I have shown my knightly adoration right then and there by kneeling to kiss the hem of her skirt, but since she was wearing abbreviated tennis whites the resulting tableau would have got us both chucked out of the club with no question of refund.

I caught scraps of the urbane prattle to which I so hungrily aspired as I strolled back and forth, pretending absorption in the dolphins lolling in the chlorinated deep. "If you're ever in Trieste there's a little restaurant around the corner from . . ." "She's taking Harry's death quite well, as who wouldn't . . ." Oh, how I longed to talk like that, snugly encased in the Smart Set! By chance one of the men in the habitat group said something about upward mobility that made the princess throw her head back and laugh, showing a row of teeth that shredded what was left of my resistance. "Ain't she better'n brand-new," we would have said where I came from, Backbone, Arkansas, and I vowed never to come from there again. Never, ever. You're going to bat in another league, Teeters, I said, so haul up your socks and sintillate. Or however they spell it.

So much is a question of semantics. When I tell people my father was a landscape gardener they nod, wreathed in approving smiles. But say he was a caretaker of the town cemetery, exact same thing, and they give you the mopes. Maybe cast their eyes downward, as though looking for the precise spot in the woodwork I came out of. I can sometimes make a dime by referring to the old man, whom I loved, as concierge of this here boneyard. The right people will laugh, appreciative of the fact that I am subtly playing it both ways *from strength,* secure enough in my own identity to speak affectionately in this way of my kin. How would this particular habitat group take it? Still hovering in the vicinity of what had all the earmarks of a prolonged chat, I had one of those two-minute fantasies that will occupy the impassioned swain, with himself playing opposite the lady of his dreams.

"Tending a cemetery is a grave responsibility," quoth he, and they fell upon him with clubs and knives. They did spit upon him, they did kick and cuff him about something terrible, finally throwing him into a pit, there to be stoned to death, like Joseph and the woman taken in adultery and all that if our Lord hadn't stepped in. Then it came to pass that the maiden on whom he had set his heart happened by, and seeing that the breath of life remained in him, however faintly, bound up his wounds and nursed him back to health. Rocking his head on her breast, speaking of rocks, she did say unto him, "Forgive them for they know not what they do. For which is greater, the words that are spoken, yea even a crummy gag, or the spirit in which they are spoken and the purpose for which they are spoken, namely that of honoring thy father and thy mother? Come, arise and go hence, to meet mine." "You mean — gulp — your *folks?*" "Even those." "Then you must be — gulp — serious about me." "You got it, Jack. Arise then, let us go hence."

Because I wanted the whole ball of wax. A proper introduction if possible, but a graceful pickup if not. An output of lubricating witticisms over a planter's punch, first date, ripening acquaintance. Favor, fervor, fever. The great and sealing rapture, those post-fulfillment languors in which affections grow and mysteries, unveiled, only deepen. The ritual snacks at the icebox and tender bawdy byplay, the restaurant with a string trio forever decreeing both your place and your song. All that. Removal to the city, the return to the suburbs with two children, the girl riding around on a bicycle with a puppy in the handlebar basket calling you an absolute quart of maple walnut, just the berries as a father, the son another story, the inevitable adolescent rebel telling you off at last. The blow falls. "You're plastic. You and your whole society." I'm plastic. Me and my whole society. The epitome of bourgeois false values. Synthetic from tootsies to follicles. Only I had pronounced it epitoam until corrected several months ago, and that on a return to the old home in rural Backbone, tie that. I shook my head like a dazed boxer, still on his knees but trying to get up. To rid myself of the very memory. Like that of once thinking, and not so much longer ago either, that Max Planck's name was pronounced like that of a one-by-six in a lumberyard.

I was a nervous wreck, what with being torn between the wish to have the girl leave the habitat group so I could broach her with some all-or-nothing ploy, and to have her linger on there till I could cook *up* such a zinger. I revolved

7

several on for size. "Pardon me, but observing you just now I couldn't help overhearing myself say, 'Now there's the epitome of something or other.' " No, not good enough. Try another. "Pardon me, but has anyone ever told you your figure has the trim concision of a Congregational church? Architecturally the most chaste in design . . ." This was a line in a novel I'd read on a plane back from Chicago, and it seemed at the time an offbeat but crackerjack piece of description on the author's part. Probably not a good opener out of the blue here though. There was a better, a natural in the circumstances. "Pardon me, but I couldn't help overhearing you talk about a restaurant in Trieste that's not to be missed. I'm dying to know the name of it, if you'd be so kind, as I'm planning to visit Switzerland myself in the fall."

Just then a garbage truck bowled down the driveway fresh from a pickup at the club restaurant, and as it slowed in a momentary traffic clot I recognized the young woman behind the wheel. I had been out with Bertha Colton a few times, enough to realize we weren't each other's speed, all amiable enough. She was a Wellesley literature major who helped defray those brutal college expenses by taking well-paying summer jobs as a swillperson. Fearing I might be socially compromised by returning her wave, I feigned oblivion to it. That was at first. Then when she persisted I returned it by a guarded flip of my hand, concealed from the target female by my intervening body, you see, for I had my back just then to the habitat group.

Slowing to a mere crawl, Bertha leaned out of the cab and shouted something I couldn't make out, and responded to with a sick little smile and a faint nod. Then to my surprise I tumbled that she hadn't been calling to me at all, hadn't even noticed me, but had been shouting her greeting to the object of my vigil, who returned it with a wave of the tennis racquet and some kind of laughing rejoinder. So they were friends or at least acquaintances — possibly classmates. Bertha Colton had asked me in after a date, but only to read me part of a term paper she hoped in graduate school to parlay into a master's thesis, on the interpenetration of social classes in Proust. I fell off the sled about page four, but heartily wishing to be part of that here, of the interpenetration of social classes, and thoroughly in favor of our essential common humanity that is the great leveler, I shouted Bertha's name and waved democratically over toward the sanitation truck, causing her to exclaim with a gasp of pleasant surprise at the unexpected sight of me, and wave one last time as she rumbled on down the driveway. Thus had occurred a three-pronged exchange momentarily linking two people who were so far total strangers — and supplying me with my overture.

"Pardon me, but I see we have a mutual acquaintance. Do you by perchance go to school with Bertha? Perhaps even a classmate? Indeed, roommate? I find that the most delectable of coinkidinkies." No harm in a little light whimsy to get the old balloon off the ground, eh? Show that a chap has a gift for easygoing pleasantries, always great for greasing the sometimes creaky social machinery.

You may have noticed that I'm sometimes more subtle than at others. It comes of a high-school dropout's drive to raise himself up by his own bootstraps, or petard, which I gather is another way of putting it, though I must remember to look that word up soon. I flunked almost everything but nonchalance, sometimes twice. So striving to enlarge my vocabulary is an essential part of my continuing self-education. I also sometimes lift phrases or even entire passages from books I read, storing them up for use at appropriate moments in social intercourse, as per the example already given in mulling over possible gambits with the object of my feasibility study. The lapses are the remaining blanks in my learning, or if you will air pockets dropping us like passengers in a plane who suddenly find their lap lunch at eye level — though now and then they are deliberate, I mean gross usages and corny cracks intended out of sheer vindictive resentment to grate on the very people I strive to measure up to. Social betters like this tight little right little group we see me casing like an outsider looking in, thinking, as I circle them like the philistine lug they no doubt suppose me till they get to know me better, "So you're the upper crust. And the rest of us? The tin plate holding the old apple pie together? You with your numbered Bridgeport bank accounts and your three-car families." What would they think of mine? A tender boyhood memory floats to mind. The time my mother gave my father a muffler for Christmas — a Midas muffler for his battered old Chevy, not the kind you wind around your neck for Christ's sake. And my old man singing with his feet sticking out from under the car as he installed his main present, "It Midas well be spring." Loving relationships. Take it or leave it. I have no way of knowing your particular wavelength. You may be posh for all I know, you out there keeping your own councils. Or is it counsels? I trust you will bear with me when I'm exquisite, and not take it to your own conscience when an elegant turn of phrase or an incisive thought seems a clear heist from some Pulitzer Prize winner imbibed on a plane or curled up with in bed. I try to drink in my share of literature, though at the moment I'm in a fallow period and don't read much.

She had sat down to join her friends, the target female. I edged in correspondingly closer to get a load of the conversation, though gazing idly up at the sky or now and then fondling a tousled child's head as it went by, as though the tight little right little group were the last thing on my mind but listening like a hawk to the smart dialogue, which had its share of what I believe is now fashionably called guerrilla psychoanalysis, ambushing absent or present friends with Freudian shots. Somebody named Cornelia was sniped at along those lines, as a card-carrying narcissist. I was glad to note that of this now quartet my heart's desire wasn't the catty one; it was the woman in the parasol-sized hat who slipped in the stingers. My heart's desire said, "Cornelia's come a long way, but she hasn't forgotten her roots." "No," says the parasol one, "she has them touched up without fail every Friday at Cyril's."

Way to go, I think, and at the same time, knock it off. Showing the two minds I'm of, when it comes to the very stylishness I hope to attain to. Schizoid little old me, what? I have a friend living here in Merrymount who's a master of this type of brittle dialogue, but he's never malicious. Once I heard him say, "Being precocious, I naturally age very fast as well. In fact, at only twenty-five I was already young at heart." It took me three days to figure that one out. Another time the conversation turned to an acquaintance — well, I guess Chirouble can be a little malicious — turned to a local character who had just had a novel published and well received. "He's a writer to be watched," someone said, and Chirouble, "Yes, especially if you have any nubile daughters around." That one's of course easier. In fact I'd probably have said the same thing myself if I'd known the chap in question. You'll meet Chirouble, in, as he would say, jew course.

The habitat group were still vivisecting Cornelia, and seeing this might be a long wait, I parked myself at an unoccupied nearby table which happened to have an abandoned paperback on it. *Existentialist Thought Since Kierkegaard.* Ideal to improve your mind with while trying to impress somebody you've already sized up as the Wellesley or Vassar type, provided your head doesn't nod and you find yourself catching a few Z's in the noonday sun, awakening to find the t.f. gone. I opened it at random.

"Husserl's basic principles, taken in connection with the ongoing dispute as to whether existence precedes essence or vice versa, encourages the assumption that the founder of phenomenology was determined that all considerations of objective reality and of purely subjective response are temporarily left out of account in the study of the totality of human appearances in human experience." Pretty heady stuff. Intellectual mountaintop air so rarefied that as I read it I kept swallowing to pop my ears.

Setting the book open and upside down on the table, I lit a cigarette and gazed idly about as I puffed on it, taking in the clouds, a border of marigolds, the thrashing dolphins. I was sure I had the situation right — blocked out, as we movie people say. She would have to pass my table once she resumed her walk in the direction she had been going when first spotted. When I saw her rise at last to bid her friends goodbye, I stamped the gasper out in an ashtray and snatched the book up again. Peeping over its top gave me a perfect view of the oncoming smasher. A woman always knows when she is being given the old Orphan Annies, and I'm sure she did now, but I was powerless to turn off the gape. She undulated just ever so when she walked, enough but not too much, as though sheer class was operative here as in everything else; as though her gait was instinctively regulated to meet the standards of what we call artistic restraint. I hoped the same might be said of the controlled half-smile with which I awaited her approach, gentlemanly tentative, easily retractable if one person of breeding might think another is going just a tad too far. Everything was *soupçon.* Everything was like smidgen. And so I was glad to see her own lips purse in a faint expression of amusement as she drew near and then swung by, pausing only just long enough — in fact not even breaking her stride — to reach out, take the book from me, and overend it so as to hand it back to me right side up. Like I was some dumb broad!

I rose to watch her undulate off toward the parking lot, where no doubt a Mercedes-Benz awaited our lady. A female must be seen from the back, and walking away, before ratification can be total; without that gander the frontal view is zilch. I had to say the rhythms of those long tawny legs and high tight cusps sealed my approval — or would have if I hadn't just been ticked off. Told to go peddle my papers. To hell with you, I thought. To hell with all of you, and all of this. Smug in your suburban superiority, parasites. You're all plastic. Plastic, do you hear, synthetic from tip to toe and stuffed with kapok. My old man was worth ten of you, my mother maybe twenty. We don't like being upstaged by dames probably cold as their cash in bed. Unbridled chastity, that's you! Rigid with frigid. I like them warm and forthcoming, personally, so perhaps it's all for the best our destinies not merging after all. To hell with the whole lot of you. I don't need you to tell me about dear little places in Trieste that are around the corner from something. I may just damn well go to Switzerland to *live.* How do you know I don't have a numbered bank account there right now?

I was still cooking when I marched off for a hamburger in the coffee shop the club boasted in addition to the restaurant from which food and drinks were served here around the pool, realizing as I opened the screen door that I was still holding the book someone had abandoned, probably out of brain fag on his own part. With it, I could upstage any onlookers myself now, though I noted as I entered the Small Café, as the lesser joint called itself, that you could have done that with *Black Beauty.* I had to shoulder myself in amongst a bunch of lice-bearing motorcyclists crowding the counter where I sat down. This was not my day to cultivate nonchalance. On the backs of their black leather jackets was emblazoned "The Devil's Disciples," and you could hear the roar of their bikes in their stares. I myself was still boiling with anger that could have been turned on *anybody* running afoul of me just then.

"I am aware that what we have here is a counter-culture, but that's hardly a reason not to keep the counter clean, is it?" I said to all and to none in particular as I finally squeezed onto a stool, to face the debris of a predecessor's meal. Most vivid among its details was a cigarette butt floating in the gray dregs of a coffee mug, itself parked in a pool of unidentifiable wet. A waitress wielding a wipecloth with eyes of cerulean blue and cornsilk hair gave me a reproachful smile that positively melted my heart, leaving it akin to the remnants of Welsh rabbit left on a plate she snatched away with testy efficiency. I wanted her more than anything in the world, and not just on the rebound. I was sorry for what I'd said, even though it had been aimed more at the denizens of Slob City than at her. I murmured something to that effect, averting my face so the storm troopers couldn't hear me, and her smile turned a little softer in acceptance of the apology. She had been told to be polite, probably feared for her job. "Yes, sir?" she said when she had swabbed the counter clean, and the faint undercurrent of sarcasm detectable under the customer-is-always-right courtesy only quickened my emotions. As she turned to relay my order for a hamburger to the fry cook, I took her out of all this. I was really smitten, my affections quite switched from Miss Haughty of yestermoment.

She had been waiting for someone to discover her, the scenario now ran, and here at long last she had found him, and vice versa. A movie mogul who would put her name in lights within two years, give or take a few months while we found a distributor for *Coin of the Realm,* a picture already written and soon to be directed by myself. Together we would get rich on a photoplay saying money had nothing to do with happiness. Lots of chaps before me had, why not me? By release date, a December opening in L.A. just in time to get in under the wire for Oscar nominations, of which we would cop eleven, our names would be romantically linked. A wedding would follow, trailed in turn by rumors of *pffft,* the usual trouble mixing marriage with two careers, all unfounded. Two children, both calling us plastic when the time came, for reasons not the least of which was high life in Bel Air and a country club far tonier than this catchall. A second honeymoon, coinciding with a trip to Cannes where my latest was knocking them cold, and some laughingly-gay trouble finding "our little place," it was so obscurely around the corner from something. The same hotel room as the first time, and she was nestling in the crook of my arm at daybreak when I heard a voice on my right. It was one of the verminous brotherhood.

"We been thinking."

"Oh, yeah, what with?" This rejoinder silently thought rather than spoken aloud, in general solicitude for the bones in my jaw and two thousand dollars' worth of bridgework.

"We just dug your crack of a while ago. About the counter-culture?"

Extraordinary. In less than ten minutes comprehension had dawned. Exegesis, if that's the word I'm groping for, had been attained.

"Oh?"

"Yeah. Would you care to step outside and repeat that?"

"Oh, the acoustics are so much better in here, don't you think?"

"Touché," says the sweetheart of the cornfields with pool-chalk eyes, plunking my hamburger down. "Would you like some of Ma's riverbottom coffee to go with that?"

"I think it would be an ideal combination. A true piece of culinary matchmaking," I says, looking at the hockey puck on a bun.

I figured she was being nice to me out of the conviction that this was my last day on earth. Last half-day, to be exact, this being its blazing noontide. But the apes had gone into another huddle, and from their bewildered mumbles they would have their "heads" together for a goodish bit. "Acoustics" would be the stumbling block this time. Yes, it would be a good five minutes or more, by which time the girl's and my acquaintance showed signs of ripening into a lifelong relationship, especially if lifelong was to be measured by her estimate of the factors. Things went so swimmingly, in fact, that my head swam. An opening bit of hostility between the sexes she took to be no impediment at all. A lull in the business bustle leaving her free for a moment's breather, not to say a little civilized discourse, she stood more or less sideways to me, one toothsome haunch pressed against the counter's edge, fondling a toothpick with an aristocratic cool forever beyond the poolside princess and her ilk. By the time the Neanderthals adjourned conference number two, I had secured myself a dinner date for that very evening. Life expectancy permitting, of course. The primate who had invited me to resolve our differences alfresco came over and again acted as mouthpiece.

"My friends and me think your remark was a rap at us, and we demand an apology."

I held a finger aloft to indicate that reply must await my swallowing a fragment of hockey puck currently under mastication, but conveying assurance that it was imminent. The quid of eats disposed of in the conventional manner, I wiped my lips with the shreds of a paper napkin half of which was still tucked under my belt, and with a smile wheeled more fully toward him on my stool.

"Your ultimatum is taken to heart, and under advisement. In loo of an actual apology, which would constitute an admission of guilt to which I remain for the moment averse, let me propose a substitute qualifying it from my point of view, yet from yours implying an admission at least partially fulfilling your requirements. I would have it emphasized that my aspersion, or knock, was *generalized,* to be understood by youse as aimed at no one in particular, but admittedly subject to construeification as otherwise — i.e., directed at you personally or youse collectively. That I regret. You have heard the key word." I smiled again, panning the circle of hearers, who together possessed the equivalent of one human forehead, and all of whose hair looked as though it was combed with their fingers. "I hereby state, declare, insist, aver that no specificity of target was intended, and at the same time I regret — again note my choice of word — regret that I stupidly did not make that clear. Will that satisfy the requirements of honor on both sides?"

These were intelligent men, recognizing that the negotiations in which we were embroiled might keep us in session for days. The huddle they went into was exactly like that of a football eleven before a play, a circle well displaying the "Devil's Disciples" name inscribed in scarlet on the backs of their black jackets. I couldn't say how long they caucused. I was out the door with a full tummy and the assurance of a date with an angel while they were still at it, flicking a wink at the girl as I hurried away. It said, "Thanks for being a counter-irritant, yuck yuck."

Toby Snapper and I followed a good meal at one of Merrymount's best restaurants by going to my place, and after pumping ecstasy for a couple of hours I popped the question. Had she ever thought she might like to be in pictures? Note here that I never offer the Big Chance as an inducement for favors. Only after I have received or at least been guaranteed them. I may be amoral but I'm no heel. In fact I take the old-fashioned chivalrous view of women as sacred vessels. I have never hurt or mistreated one, and detest cads who do. I liked the voluptuous Toby straight off, enough to explore the possibility of a permanent relationship, even marriage, not head-on by bluntly popping the real question, but by cautiously circling the subject, feeling her out under the covers. But there seemed little possibility of the Big Connection just now. She was more or less engaged to a real estate agent named Clifford Bailey, currently out of town. "O tempura, O mores," I thought, in fact cried in my heart of hearts, not entirely approving this degree of flexibility in a girl, but I went through with it anyway. I was committed before I fully ascertained the circumstances. In addition to the long corn-silk hair, which she used for caresses, swinging the tips tantalizingly over your this and your that till you whimpered with pleasure, she had wonderful pinkish skin, that translucent pink that little piglets have? It took me back to the county fairs and stock shows at Backbone. You applied the term "complexion" to her entire *body,* it was so without blemish or flaw. In contrast to my own, which is so covered with moles that Toby abandoned an actual count with "My God, you look like a Toll House cookie."

I said I would remember her joke for possible use as a line in one of my pictures, which frequently featured nudity, often frontal.

"What kind of movies do you make?" she asked as we lay in a lull between our pleasures. "I suppose I should hold it to your credit, Eddie, that you didn't use them as a come-on."

"I hope I'm above that, Toby. Above casting couches."

"What kind are they? Is any running around here?"

"Oh, they run all over. But our big market is videocassettes."

"What are some of the titles?"

"Well, they're educational. Now the cat's out of the bag, and I hope you won't be frightened off by that. Or the word *documentary.*"

"What sort of educational and documentary?"

"Well, they're training films, actually."

"Oh, like the kind salesmen get, or soldiers in the army. My brother went to work for a vacuum cleaner company and had to sit through a film demonstrating door-to-door pitches, and wearing down housewives' sales resistance."

"Well, mine aren't like that exactly."

"What exactly then? You say 'Well' an awful lot, mister."

"Well — There I go again," I laughed. "The best way to put it is this."

I shook a cigarette from a pack on the bedside table and we smoked it together, our heads on the same pillow as we passed it back and forth.

"You know those marriage manuals. Prepare people to lead a fuller, more satisfactory sex life. These are simply the cinematic counterpart of that."

"Oh." She moved back off the pillow a little and lay propped on an elbow to look at me. She took a drag on the cigarette and asked, "Would you say your stuff is hard-core or soft?"

"Hard-core or soft what?"

"Oh, for God's sake. Porn."

Now I sat up to face her, taking the cigarette back. "Come on now. Would you call, say, *The Joy of Sex* porn, just because it's graphic in its details? Interspersed with sketches showing people in various positions and whatnot?"

"You know your oats there all right. Positions. We must

have run through most of them tonight. One or two didn't seem to me to have any redeeming social value."

"They might to a voyeur." I had toyed with calling one of my films *Now, Voyeur.*

"I kept wondering when we were going to get to the normal one." Her expression of curiosity sharpened. "Do you act in your own vehicles?"

"I do the close-ups."

"Aha. The below-the-waist ones I'll bet."

"Why do you say that?"

"From the way you look away. And the general craftsmanship of which I've had a taste."

"I'm not an actor in the conventional sense. I can't — well, act. No, I'm only a writer-producer. And I often do the narration. I have a fairly good voice. Some say it has a nasal musicality reminiscent of Ronald —"

"And I'll supply an affidavit that you're silver-tongued."

"But I don't show my face."

"Especially after they're released. Do you have trouble keeping a step ahead of the sheriff?"

I got up and turned on a light, not here but in an adjoining room, just so we'd have enough illumination in the bedroom, where I began to pace the floor.

"There is ever the Puritan ethic, that hobgoblin itself basically salacious — someone has said, 'Scratch a censor and you'll find a satyr' — hounding with the ever-present threat of punishment any attempt of the pure in heart to celebrate the pagan dignity of mating. Pleading with us to return to Paradise." I gestured to the rumpled bed. "Like we just did."

"That's a set speech if I ever heard one, and I advise you to keep it sharpened up for when you find yourself spouting it through the bars of the slammer, what with the Moral Majority on the march." She dropped the taunting tone the more seriously to answer the question that had started all this. "I can't act either."

"You won't have to. Trust me."

"Not even in a skinflick would I be any good. But thanks for thinking my hips have talent. I'd blush from top to bottom the minute the action started." Now she was genuinely curious. "How can you get it up for the camera?"

"You're bogeying the joint," I said, which is the term used for someone hogging a marijuana cigarette being passed around. I took it from her, drew on it a last time, and stamped the butt out in an ashtray. "I just thought you might enjoy the experience, for the pay if nothing else. Remember I didn't come on as a tycoon offering to make you a Joan Crawford."

I switched out the light, slipped back into bed, and then after a little of what we call tenderizer in the training films — whispered endearments and provocative caresses aimed at rewhetting jaded appetites — we made love once more, before dropping off together.

I awoke from a night of checkered sleep — now I am rounding third pursued by Keystone Kops, now trying to eat pizza through a catcher's mask turning into jail bars — to find Toby up and dressing. One always itches to know how one has performed after a nocturne, doesn't one, and one was no exception. What grade might one expect on one's report card?

"How do you feel, earth angel?" I asked from the bed, trying to sidle crabwise into the subject.

"Great. Battered but great."

"Battered, eh?"

She sat on a chair to draw on stockings and shoes.

"Last night was a memorable one for me."

"Oh?" Uttered in a soft murmur, lazily stretching between the sheets as he smiles.

"A real *número uno.*"

"Well." He can be forgiven for swelling up like a puff adder, in grateful anticipation of the answer expected. "How so, pigeon?"

"It's the first time in my life I ever went to bed without brushing my teeth."

A Quivering Calm

IF YOU'VE ever been humiliated, which obviously you have, on a mortification scale of ten to one where would you put my recent embarrassment? I don't mean Toby Snapper's little unconscious put-down, which only gave me a good-natured laugh at myself. I mean the poolside incident in which the princess as much as called me a dumb broad. I'd have given it a five, or maybe even a six or seven. It still smarted two weeks later, when I returned to the scene of the crime, as victims may no less than perpetrators, unless of course it's a murder. I still hoped not only to see this perpetrator, but even to meet her, helplessly curious to learn whether my fascination revived faster than my irritation festered.

It was mid-July now, and the mercury rose to the occasion. Only one of the three tennis courts was occupied, and neither of the two women lobbing practice shots at each other was my vixen, as naturally I continued to think of her.

Dying to know what she was really like kept alive the insane desire to make her acquaintance, or failing that, to spend a few moments in conversation with her to at least make a quick appraisal. I thought of myself as fairly giving her another shot at a first impression, in favor of which I might eradicate from my rankled bosom the real one. But I seemed to have drawn a blank. She wasn't beside the pool either, or in it. Might she be in the clubhouse, or lunching in the restaurant it contained? Zilch there too. In a disagreeably scrambled mood half frustration and half relief (I myself might flunk a second first impression too) I went for a leisurely ramble about the grounds.

Fenced off in a tiny corner at the edge of the golf links was a sight I'd never noticed before. A small remnant — or maybe all — of a pre-Revolutionary cemetery. Eight or ten graves were marked by cracked, sagging or completely toppled headstones, with names and dates for the most part blurred out of recognition by time and the elements. One or two seemed chipped, as though by golfers with bad hooks. An unintended hazard to the tenth hole. I climbed over an iron fence for a closer look. The only marker I could make out at all seemed to say "Ebenezer Hale, 1711–1788." The unkempt plot offered a sharp contrast to the groomed fairways nearby. Who was responsible for its maintenance? My old man would have kept better care of Ebenezer Hale's and his contemporaries' eternal resting place than this if he'd have had to get down on his hands and knees and run a barber's clipper around the stones. I spotted a golf ball in the thick grass, and picked it up and threw it into a brook running beside the club there, pausing till I heard it splash in the water.

I resumed my walk with a quickened step, suddenly deciding to split and catch the matinee of a movie playing at a local theatre. As I was crossing the pool area toward the lot where my Buick was parked, I was jolted by a scene that stopped me cold in my tracks. She was sitting at a table with, of all people, my friend Jerry Chirouble, of whom I've given you a brief preview. We often wonder what we would do in this kind of emergency or that — a stickup, a fire. Fate decided this stunner for me. I'll never know what I'd have done voluntarily. Slipped away with averted face? Waved casually to Chirouble as I strode on by, leaving the amenities up to him? I mean as to whether a simply returned "Hi" would suffice, or a summons and an introduction were called for. Chirouble spotted me and chirped up in his suavely hearty manner. "Teeters, old horse! Come here. Come on."

Having feigned surprise, I toddled over, thinking, "Hills, fall on me. Mountains, cover me. Ground, open up and swallow me." Lacking these developments, here I stood like a country cousin before the highest tribunal I could have imagined: my hero introducing me to my heroine. "Cynthia, this is Eddie Teeters. He saved my life once, and in the rain mind you. Eddie, Cynthia Pickles."

"Pleased to meet you." Christ, not that! This wasn't the county fair back home in Backbone, this was Merrymount, Connecticut, where paperbacks on existentialism were nonchalantly left on parasoled tables and men in bleeding madras shorts bounced golf balls off pre-Revolutionary gravestones. If she had acknowledged the introduction first, would I have said, "Likewise I'm sure"?

Chirouble waved to a free chair after tipping it back from the table against which it was tilted. "Setzen Sie sich."

"Well, I don't know that . . . Cuz, because I was really . . ." I looked to the young woman, who smilingly echoed, "Do join us." Did she not recognize me, or was she an actress I could have used plenty of? "Well, perhaps just for a . . . Chirouble, old boy, you mustn't go around saying I saved your life. Every time he relates the incident I gain half a hat size."

"I'm bursting with curiosity. Relate away, Jerry."

The reminiscence was soon gotten over with, but throughout it I'm burning in the fires of hell wondering what Miss Pickles is thinking behind those mocha-colored glances.

I'm tooling along the thruway in a Noah's-ark type of downpour when I see a car parked on the shoulder of the road with its hazard lights flashing and, having shot past it, back up again, at some danger to life and limb what with all the maniacs zipping by. Disconsolately slumped behind the wheel, "waiting for the end," is this handsome egg stalled with his second flat of the night, and, of course, no spare. A quick flashlight check having revealed that mine won't fit his wheels, I conjure from my trunk three of those air bombs I always carry with me, roughly the size of a large can of shaving cream, for use in such an emergency. No good in a blowout, but able to seal up a small puncture and inflate your tire enough to get you to a gas station. Both half drenched now, we sat in his car with the dome light on reading the directions. "Warm the can at the car heater if the temperature is less than thirty degrees," which it was on this January night, so we held all three against the dash louvres with the motor going, when not nursing back their vital heat in the palms of our hands. That was how Jerry Chirouble and I not only met but sowed the seed of a lasting friendship. Plenty in common. He a publisher and me a movie producer, thus working in different corners of the artistic vineyard. At last we were ready to try the emergency gizmos I'd never had occasion to before.

"Tire valve should be at the 4 o'clock or 8 o'clock position," ran the instructions on the Fix-a-Flat can. A slight maneuver of the car satisfied the first requirement. "Screw the plastic can nozzle to the tire valve stem as tightly as possible." Squatting in the mud in a trench coat, Chirouble did, while I held the flashlight. Nothing. "Let me try it, " I said, and crouched down in his place. Screwing the nozzle had not been enough, but ramming it into the valve with the heel of my hand as hard as I could did the trick. *Pssst,* in went the air. We emptied a second bomb, and that gave him enough inflation to limp to the nearest gas station for repairs, with me convoying from behind to make sure he wasn't stranded again. We parted after an exchange of names and phone numbers, and a date for the following Saturday, when Chirouble would take me out for the finest dinner obtainable in those parts.

"So you see, a Good Samaritan," he concluded. "I mean how could he know I wasn't a hood planning to stick him up?"

But what was Miss Pickles thinking as she darted those smiling glances my way? Granted she had recognized me and was politely remaining silent, did Chirouble's story do anything more than qualify a firmly solidified first impression? Something along the lines of "He's a klutz, but sweet." Suspense on that score continued while she offered up a story of her own.

"I got myself stalled like that once, with a motor that wetted out. And guess how many men stopped with more on their minds than drying it out for me. At last a married couple drove me to a public telephone where I could call the motor club, and do you know something? I sat in the back seat listening to them resume a fight that stopping for me had momentarily interrupted. I mean God. Not to be able to knock it off in front of a third party."

"Man is by nature contentious," Chirouble said, "and the value of marital arguments is the opportunity it gives two people to air their similarities."

This was Chirouble. Chirouble to a T. Christ, I wished I

could talk like that, everything couched in an epigram and whatnot. I'd give my blond eyebrows to do it for five minutes. Lightly bandying what-do-you-call-it, persiflage, and never hurting anybody. And when Chirouble treated you as an equal there was no danger in treating him as one in return. I mean the element of backlash didn't enter into it. You could be democratic right back to his face and no offense taken. (I guess I'm kind of grooving myself, here, though of course not with his polish.)

But about Cynthia Pickles. She hadn't yet tipped her hand. She was as beautiful close up as from a distance, with the silicon microchip, once known as a beauty spot, on the left forecheek just back of and slightly above a corner of the Cupid's bow mouth. Which you would fain have pressed your own to with moans of joy. Christ, all the wasted, wasted hankering in this our life. She was again in tennis whites, a racquet lying on a fourth chair. She had come to meet a woman friend for a few games but the friend had phoned to call it off, owing to the heat. She had run into Chirouble, who was waiting for his secretary to bring him some manuscripts. He not only rarely went to his office, he never actually published anything either, not wishing to drain away a private inheritance on so foolish a venture as bringing out titles in this day and age. They had both been sipping planter's punches "by way of preamble to a happily extemporaneous lunch" (Jesus, to be able to talk like that), and now he called over to a waitress serving the outside tables to bring two more, for me and the momentarily expected secretary. Who trotted breathlessly up just then, cradling in her arms a stack of manuscripts and some letters for Chirouble to sign.

"Cynthia Pickles you know, I believe, Roxy. This is Eddie Teeters. Eddie, Roxanne Winch, my girl Friday the thirteenth."

Again, this was Chirouble. Ethnically French, as his name shows, but English to his fingertips in point of style. He threw it all away. A lumpier wit would have paused after "Friday," taken a beat on it as we say in the theatrical arts, maybe cleared his throat for just a sec to telegraph that a nifty was en route before actually adding the zinger, but not Chirouble. And your average good-time-Charlie boss, how he would have beat it to death! Probably year after year, especially for out-of-towners being shown around the office, but not Chirouble. Just as — you knew from Roxy's laugh — he had never pulled the joke before, so he would never repeat it. And Roxy, for her part, knew it was a gag the gracious Chirouble didn't literally mean — that hiring her had been bad luck, etc. She was efficient enough to practically run the office across the street while our dilettante did the *la dolce vita* bit around town. And the face and figure that went with that proficiency and good nature? Normally you'd have to commit bigamy to marry it all. When she dropped on the table the stuff she'd been carrying, together with her bag, it was to reveal as scrumptious a pair of mangoes as you could wish short of a Moslem paradise, topping off a figure that just wouldn't quit. How that set of loins sent the streetcar named desire rocketing and clanking through your own. By the time she sat down beside me, on the chair made available by the removal of Cynthia Pickles' racquet, I was so utterly won over as to have worries about what the latter might be secretly thinking completely driven out of my mind. This was It. By the time Cynthia Pickles had propped the racquet against a leg of her own chair, I had fantasized a marriage in which every night of God's world I could devour the mangoes like a starving Eskimo.

The waitress brought the drinks and then we ordered lunch, everybody opting for the fruit plate except Chirouble, who had to avoid berry seeds and such because of a recent nasty case of diverticulitis caused by a tiny pit or something caught "in a bend in the old meandering tripe, you know. I'll have the cold salmon and *sauce verte.*"

It was here that I rather dominated the conversation, I think, keeping the old ball rolling in a manner nothing if not debonair.

"If our intestines were strung inside us straight up and down, like a plumb line, " I observed, "we'd all be thirty feet tall. So perhaps it's all for the best that our bowels are folded and tucked neatly inside us like a fire hose in one of those glass cabinets on a building wall. Like those fire hoses that you break the glass and pull out?"

"I understand," Roxy said. "Once in our building a waste-basket fire —"

"Still it might be nice to be able to look into second-floor windows from the street, you know, like those men on stilts who advertise stuff? Or watch a ball game for free over the top of the fence rather than crawl under it, or pick apples off trees without ladders or those gizmos they use to reach up with. Of course in that case the buildings and parks themselves would be built to scale, wouldn't they, hm, with ceilings forty or fifty feet high and second stories also that much more off the street, and ballparks laid out to accommodate players who would have to, and could, knock home runs into streets two or three miles away. So it's best the old gut is wrapped up as is, nest pa?"

They all looked at each other, smiling and nodding. Till Chirouble, who might have thought even himself a bit out of it with this improvisation, frowned and said, "And conversely, stooping to pick a flower would hardly be worth the trouble."

"Too long a trip. So all in all it's a good thing the Creator packed the old GI tract in like duds in a suitcase. Like if you straightened out a French horn, know how long it would be? Over twenty feet."

Roxy cleared her throat and with a kind of fidgeting movement asked whether she and Chirouble could be excused while they went into a huddle over the letters he had to sign. We two could go on talking while they held a whispered business conversation. I had sensed Cynthia's eyes on me somewhat more sharply than before, and now she said: "Something nags me. Haven't I seen you somewhere before?"

"Alas, I must of made a delible impression on you," I urbanely replied, "but not you on me. I'm the guy who was reading the book you stopped and turned right side up the other—"

"Of course!" She laughed, clapping her hands together. "May I flatter myself by thinking I was right in surmising it to be only a ruse, a cover from behind which to ambush a girl?"

"You may indeed. Held right side up, *Existentialist Thought Since Kierkegaard* would not attract anyone's attention. I was delighted you fell in with my little game. But I was more than playing a game with you."

"What else, pray? Could we have another round?"

Chirouble called over for refills, but even on one, with an empty stomach in the heat of the day, I was beginning to feel a trifle woozy. But what a sense of relief I experienced as I warmed to this little caper.

"I had a hunch, you see, you might be a feminist, and I wanted to show you that we too have our share of dumb broads, we men, as you your share of captains of industry. That's one thing. The other is, you're right. I was giving you the Orphan Annies."

"The what?"

"The old double-O. The peepers."

I was playing a shrewd game here. By dishing out vulgarisms at a rate that could not possibly be characteristic of one lunching with this charming group, I must be doing so *from strength,* secure in the sense of superiority that alone would enable me to enagage in this sort of verbal slumming. The reverse of what I said a while back about deliberately rubbing it in.

"Well, I mustn't pretend to be so surprised, or pretend not to be flattered. A woman knows when she's being —"

"Admired. You are quite beautiful." I drained off the last swig left of my planter's punch. "Your figure, if I may make so bold as to offer the comparison, has the —" How did the metaphor in that novel run again? "The trim concision of a Congregational church. Than which nothing could be more chaste, architecturally speaking."

"Why, what a sweet thing to say. And I might add that you yourself —"

"Please." I waved away the need for reciprocation. "I know what I look like. A girl once told me, and it's engraved on the tabloids of my brain," I said.

Cynthia Pickles, who was on my right, leaned in a little closer, resting an elbow on the table. "What did she say? I'll tell you honestly if I think she was right."

"She said I looked like a dog that wants in."

"Hm." The gaze swinging away. Then back again. "Well . . ."

"You said you'd be honest. Is there something poochlike about me?"

"Oh, come now. You're debasing it to a level not necessarily implied in what you said she said. The two aren't the same thing at all. There *is* about you something endearingly — you won't mind this?"

"Please go on."

"Endearingly wistful in your eyes, which are set in a face, I mean a facial structure that might rightfully be called canine. That's not necessarily said pejoratively." Another word to be looked up. Keeps cropping up everywhere. "Our faces all have animal models. Mine, for example, is anatine."

"What's that?"

"Ducklike. And it's not disparaging. Many beautiful women and attractive men have this shape nose, I've had a sort of compulsion to notice. It's not to imply we have webbed feet. Roxy over there is cervine," she went on, dropping her voice to a whisper. "Doesn't she remind you of a young deer? Bambi? And Jerry's simian. I mean his face is that *type,* and a handsome example it is, with those small monkey eyes set deep in those wonderful cheek planes. There is a type of English beauty which is equine — in plain language horse-faced. I think it's a Celtic strain, but don't hold me to it. So you see, your girl wasn't being derogatory, as I am not in agreeing with her perceptive description. You *have* the look of a hound dog that wants in, an expression of resented alienation, and it's most appealing. So there. Don't boggle at the 'alienation' either. Alienation is big these days. Without it you have no sense of belonging." And she laughed freely at the paradox as though it was, say, Chirouble's. She tapped my wrist with her fingertips and settled back in her chair again with the "so there" expression people wear when they feel they have wrapped something up.

But I *was* in now, wasn't I? I told myself so, there, secretly in the hot sun with the rum working in my veins. For my spirits soared with the most wonderful sense of belonging, what with words coming at me I'd never heard of till now, from the lips of people way over my head. And all beautiful people into the bargain. Ah, we happy few, if you will.

Lunch came, to be sluiced down with a couple bottles of Rhine wine, by which time I lolled back in glutted contentment not unlaced with a keen sense of a vista opened up, sliding down in my chair till I was practically sitting on my spine, half catatonic with excellence. There were times when I wasn't even sure what the hell *I* was talking about. Here again, as with the paperback mislaid I knew not where, the air was so mountain I kept swallowing to pop my ears. Or like ascending in an elevator at dizzying speed. And what a charming little habitat group *we* must have made to an on-looker such as I had been only a few short days before! I was now an integral part of what that other Eddie Teeters, the still uninitiated one, had been so enviously gawking at then. "What a difference a daaaay makes," sang my blood, almost pitying those looking enviously on at we silken types.

I was thus lollybasking (a word I've coined, how do you like it?) in the occasion when I tuned back in again on Chirouble, who was dilating on something or other. Yes, that he was an incurable optimist. So he insisted.

"I don't hold with this 'the gods punish us by granting us our desires' business," he was saying. "I'll string along rather with that Gerontion line, however at odds it is with the rest of the Eliot poem. History guides us by vanities, yes, but — 'what she gives, gives with such supple confusions / That the giving famishes the craving.' With the last of that I'll take issue. I've been given a great deal, but no giving will ever famish my craving. Not for you, my dears."

I smiled dreamily as I nodded agreement, lifting my wine-glass with the rest to toast what we had just heard, and making a mental note to look up this Gerontion bird. He sounded like the goods. I fairly hugged myself with pleasure at integration with this group. And blowing into these re-flections were whiffs of random memories, recollections of long bygone days in Arkansas, of boyhood hours in scenes till now forgotten, in places now transcended. How upredictable these wayward drafts of thoughts, blown across space and time and come when least expected to haunt us, like the wind wheezing through the organ pipes in *Sunset Boulevard* when no one was sitting at the keyboard.

It was then that I got the jolt. The waitress's voice had sounded vaguely familiar, but what with being immersed in the conversation as well as not really looking up because Chirouble insisted on doing the honors and taking full charge of the ordering, I hadn't taken note of her. I did now as she returned and said, "Would you mind settling the check? I go off duty at two o'clock."

I glanced up and it was Toby Snapper.

"For God's sake," I said, popping to my feet. "I had no — Why didn't you —?"

"It's all right. I've been transferred to the restaurant. Promoted they call it. Please sit down."

There is probably no established etiquette for an awkward situation like this. I simply followed the rules of rising for a lady, a reflex in which Chirouble joined me on seeing I did. "So you two know each other," he said. "Do introduce us to this charming creature, Eddie." Which I did, stumbling all over the Pickleses and the Snappers and the Chiroubles and — what was Roxy's name again? She had to resupply it herself. Winch. It was sticky enough without Chirouble saying as he laid some green on Toby's tray, "Keep the rest, and do come join us for a drink. Any friend of Eddie Teeters and all that."

That would have been a fivesome with democracy really rolling up its sleeves and getting to work, a contrast of plebeian versus patrician in both the types of female beauties represented and the male mentalities. Toby, however, answered, "Thank you, you're very kind, but I have some odds and ends to take care of. Nice to meet you all," and hurried back into the restaurant. A substitute problem in human amalgamation swiftly took its place.

35

A motorized roaring up the drive turned out to be the Devil's Disciples peeling in on their Hondas and Suzukis again. Having parked which in a straight line at the side of the driveway, they sent their spokesman over to summon me aside for a renewal of our, as yet, unresolved deliberations. It was the same primate who had served as their representative last time, in negotiations at the Small Café out of which you remember I had snuck undetected while they were huddled in caucus. Sensing resumption in the wind, I excused myself, and before he could draw me aside, strode forward and did it to him, till we stood together under a nearby maple, watched by my contingent and his.

"What's up, amigo?" I said, taking his arm. "Nice to see you again."

What was up was that our difference had not been thoroughly settled, leaving the question of their unsatisfied honor still up in the air. "Air" prompts me to describe his personal fragrance as that of the hot paving tar the brother-hood's black leather jackets put you *visually* in mind of, and like that. They had been "thinking" things over continually since last time, and decided we must have it out before they left town. There was a code to be observed.

"A valid point," I said. "Which moves me to ask what I've wondered since our initial encounter. What brought you birds to these parts anyway? I mean what could you possibly want in, or of, a community so utterly plastic in its values, totally, what shall I say, meretricious in both its aims and the means of their realization."

I had been slowly edging him back toward his fellows, with the purpose of putting them within earshot so that I might once more befuddle them *en masse*. The stratagem appeared to be working again. The same look of collective consternation was my early reward.

"Well, the thing is, we *are* leaving, though we *were* casing it as a place to maybe settle down —"

"Ha!" I guffawed, a horselaugh emitted on their behalf, at the folly of such a quest. A new word recently learned sprang to my aid. "A nest of parvenus like these," with a wave indicating the idlers seated about, "ever meeting youse's standards? *This* a habitation and a home for you with your earthy and more virile criterions? But go on, do."

"That's jist it. We are shoving on, but din't want to leave without settling this score with you."

"Score indeed," I snorted. "Home team nothing, visitors one hundred. Go in peace, and with my blessing."

"But you din't apologize yet."

"We waste time by rehashing old ground. You will recall my, I think valid, distinction between remorse and regret. I did regret, do now regret, that you boys took umbridge at my completely generalized remark, aimed at all within hearing."

They frowned as one, the spokesman still doing the talking. "Took what?"

"Umbridge. U-m-b-r-i-d-g-e." I had to spell it out for these clowns. I sidled even closer to the group, till we melted into one throng. "It means offense, and giving that was the last thing on my mind. Look, how would you boys like to be in a movie?" I spoke out of the side of my mouth and in lowered tones, so as not to inflame eavesdropping aspirants with prospects of a career snapping open like a broken valise on mere acquaintance with me. "I'm a producer, about to start work on a vehicle satirizing precisely what I'm talking about. In it I contrast the genuine versus the synthetic, and there's one scene in particular — Oh, my God, you'd all be perfect for it. A scene showing a group such as yours blazing into town as a means of dramatizing this contrast in values.

A scene quite seminal in purpose. My name is Gerontion, here, let me give you my card." I fished in a pocket known to be devoid of same, coming up empty-handed. "Damn, I seem to be fresh out. But if you chaps can tell me where I can reach you in the next few weeks I'd be most grateful."

A moment's consultation yielded the decision, not to rearrange my features, but to accept my statement of regret as a formal apology, and to give me the name of the motel where they were going to stay in the town they planned to shove along to — Roundtree, a place twenty or so miles south, between here and New York. It was the Soundview Motel, and I must ask for Rock Bascomb, their leader. A round of handshakes and off they roared again. I returned to my habitat group, whose curiosity I satisfied in as few words as possible. Then Roxy and Chirouble went back to the office, which, being air-conditioned, was after all a more comfortable place to glance at the manuscripts and sign the letters.

"Might they be an item?" I asked Cynthia as they made off together, the lean Chirouble and the billowy Roxy, each carrying half of the load of stuff Roxy had brought over. "I mean of the boss-secretary kind so familiar in this day and age?"

"Oh, I doubt it, though he does date her now and again. Why, are you smitten? I thought you were giving her the old Orphan Annies too."

"Any guy with all his red corpuscles would. There's plenty to be smitten by around here," I said, giving her a meaningful look to which she responded with laughing good grace, but conveying nothing specific one way or another as to whether romantic business might be transacted between us two. Then she turned serious on the specific subject of Chirouble himself.

"I keep worrying he's squandering his life in this dilettante way. Even frittering it away. You know what I mean. He's just playing at being a publisher because he thinks he should be doing something, and it's a profession with class. But he's never published anything and never will. It's American, this work ethic, or at least the pretense that you're adhering to it. In Europe they'd say go ahead, use your family textile-fortune inheritance and be a connoisseur. Sit in cafés and sip drinks between trips to the art galleries. He'd be better off collecting pictures rather than playacting as a literary ty-coon. Or — and here I'm going to get a little selfish — investing his money in a worthy venture such as the review I'm starting up. It's to be a newspaper in form, the tabloid for-mat, but a journal of opinion. All shades, all ideas, all opin-ions, pro and con everything. Feminist, antifeminist, liberal, conservative, an organ for anybody who wants to speak up, but intelligently. Articles will be accepted and rejected strictly on the basis of their merit. I have over a hundred thousand dollars raised or promised for *Overview*, which is what I'm calling it. I need that much more, and Chirouble could kick that in himself and not know it." She laughed again. "Have you any friends of means?"

"No, but you seem to have. I might invest a little some-thing myself."

"Really, Eddie? How much?" she asked, her eyes bugging.

I waved a hand in a nonchalant gesture. "Five thousand."

She looked at my empty wineglass. "Are you serious? You hardly know me."

"The fastest way to know somebody is lend them money."

"But this is reckless. I don't know you either. What do you do?"

"It's not Mafia money. Don't worry."

"But it's *something* money. What's your business?"

"I'm a movie producer. Not feature-length films — *yet* — but specialty ones. Educational, if they have to have a category. I'm hoping to get a new short entered at Cannes. Look, before we get too deeply embroiled in boring business talk, you said something about wanting to look at some paintings on display here. Perhaps we could take them in together? Where's the gallery?"

It wasn't quite that. Just a room in the clubhouse exhibiting some stuff by an acquaintance of hers which she had promised she'd look in on.

The after-you etiquette with which we went through the door gave me again a fleeting chance to observe her unobserved. A mere *Augenblick,* as our kraut cousins say, is enough to confirm previous estimates, provided in the course of it you don't blink your *Augen.* I could see what I meant by my architectural metaphor in praise of her a while back, stolen from the novelist whose name escapes me. She was all I'd said. Of course compared with the voluptuous Roxy glimpsed in departure ... But then that's not quite fair. I mean what's the First Congregational Church compared to a banana split?

It was second-wave Abstract Expressionism, or maybe Express Abstractionism, and laid on thick as your Aunt Nellie's pan gravy. Circling the room, we ran into another of Cynthia's friends, a critic for a paper in a nearby city. This chap proved some aid to comprehension, what with pointing out strategically distributed voids in the paint crusts and talking of "bargained space" and "chromatic values." The prices were posted on the wall beside the entries, and at eight hundred and a thousand berries apiece they didn't strike me as much of a bargain any way, spatial or otherwise, or anything to write home about in the way of values. But again I had the exhilarating sense of belonging, what with pictures I didn't understand and people talking over my head nineteen to the dozen. Again, I found myself even talking over my own head. For, emboldened to speak out by my suspicion that these blobs weren't really making a dime with Cynthia Pickles either, I said, "I too believe in every kind of experimentation, freedom for the artist to shovel on reds and greens and oranges and purples in any quantity and as higgledy-piggledy as he wishes. But somewhere he's got to draw a line."

They both threw back their heads and laughed heartily. But I didn't get it. I still don't.

∽

THREE

The Winning of Mrs. Pickles

I SOON wished I hadn't so impulsively offered the five thousand fish to our pretty entrepreneur. Not because I regretted
the investment as such, but because I couldn't now know
how much of Cynthia's presently agreeing to dinner was a
reciprocation of the shine I'd taken to her, and how much
was a hustling businesswoman's gratitude for a stockholder
acting like the last of the heavy spenders. Not getting an ac-
curate reading of her motives graveled me. All that vanished
on our second date — in the light of the ardor with which
she went to bed with me. She tore her clothes off like a nun
forsaking her vows, and some of mine. A chap instinctively
likes this sort of thing, to which I can add that it sent my
doubts flying like her garments around the room. Making
nice-nice with a few dinner engagements might be construed
as buttering up an investor. Not this. For the acrobatics that
ensued between the old percales, think of a load of wash in
the tumble-rinse stage of the cycle. Hard-core prudery I had
once thought, when stiffed with the paperback prank. Was

that a wrongo! Then the ritual raid on the icebox, tucking in flaps of salami and chunks of cheddar, washing all down with jug wine as we sprawled naked in living-room arm-chairs.

She spoke of her hopes for *Overview*. The first issue would be devoted to the new sexual mores. One thinker friend had promised an article about the prenuptial contracts being increasingly drawn up by couples about to marry.

"Did you know that some of them specify what each will get in case of divorce? *Before* they say 'I do'? And either party can dissolve the marriage on the basis of the contract signed. That is to say, walk out on the other and no questions asked. What do you think of that?"

I walked over to pour her some more white wine. "Any woman walks out on me gets a lump settlement." I tapped the old coco to indicate goose eggs on the location intimated.

"My mother will like you."

"Oh? How so?" Casually, but thrilled to his very bones with the "will" rather than a "would." The girl was serious about him. No maybe stuff here. He was to be trotted in and shown off to the family. There's a quantum leap.

"Because she's so very straitlaced and old-fashioned. She said her first husband got out of line on their wedding night. Can you believe it?"

" 'First'?"

"Yes. She's just my stepmother, I suppose that's why I can talk this freely about her. She would be horrified at this scene. I mean quite disinherit me — which she'll probably do anyway. There's no real bond between Amanda and me. I never call her Mother. I adored my mother, but this one. Daddy was her second husband, and I'm the only semblance of a child she's ever had or, of course, will have. My parents are both dead."

"So are mine."

The exchange cast a sad spell over us, broken only when Cynthia, after a thoughtful sip of her wine, said, "She's crazy. She talks about adopting a grandchild. I mean seriously. Can you imagine? She's crazy."

I shook my head in sympathy, not that I didn't secretly take some perverse satisfaction in this evidence of a tarnished family. It would make it radically harder for anybody in that domestic shambles to high-hat a Teeters! Not that I didn't feel sorry for Mrs. Pickles, sight unseen. She hadn't been in evidence either of the two times I'd called to pick up Cynthia. But adopt a grandchild! How crackers can you get in your sunset years?

"Isn't there a more likely way of coming by one of those?" I said, gingerly, not venturing out onto thin ice myself, but sending a dog out to test it, as one read people sometimes did in Holland to see whether the canals were frozen over enough for the local citizens to follow on the old Hans Brinkers. Cynthia didn't pick up on this feeler, which I instantly knew had been too premature.

"I really should go," she said, heaving herself to her feet. She knelt on my chair with her knees between mine, and after a few moments of kissing in this posture stood up again and began to dress. Some of her clothes were here in the living room, some in the bedroom. A stocking was draped over the shade of a floor lamp. "I won't dress with the same wild abandon. It's been nice."

"More than nice for me. I feel as though I've been pulled through a hedge backwards. Always a sign of true fulfillment. When am I going to meet what there is of your family?"

"Sunday afternoon. What could be more conventional than that? May I introduce you as my steady?" Her hearty laughter identified this as principally a joke, but she did seriously add, "It will get you off on the right foot with

44

Amanda. That's still her language. A girl's 'steady,' or her 'intended.'"

"Steady Eddie. That's what they call me back home."

"Several girls at once, I've no doubt." She sat down again to pull her stockings on. "Don't come expecting a lark, in fact you're being sucked into something you'll probably find a bore. There'll be a crowd celebrating the tenth anniversary of HASH. Homeless Animal Shelter Hospital. Mother's pet charity. No pun intended. It's to be a tea, with a group singing madrigals. Want out?"

"What are those again?"

"Unaccompanied vocal compositions for two or three voices in simple harmony, following a strict poetic form — scream if you're bored already, but I remember this from a music course at Vassar — developed in Italy in the late thirteenth and early fourteenth century. Two centuries or so later it developed into, let's see, don't help me —"

"I won't."

"— into a polyphonic part-song for up to six voices, sometimes accompanied by strings that either double or replace one or more of the vocal parts. Since this group of men call themselves the Lyric Trio they obviously sing the simpler versions. It's a parlor tea set for two-thirty, but you come a little earlier so you can meet Amanda and have a dear little chat with her."

This looked to be It. I could really see myself with the quality now, listening to madrigals whilst sipping tea with my pinky in a permament state of erection. The old member hadn't had a workout like that in years, ever since my own mom "poured" for a church bazaar. I would get it up and keep it up while the warbling went on, the singers' tongues, teeth and even soft palates visible from where you sat in the very front row as an honored friend-of-the-family guest on a folding chair borrowed from the local undertaker. *Both* pin-

45

kies up if it came to that, what with the butter cookies and dainty canapés to nibble on as the tea was sipped.

I wore a blue suit, white shirt and necktie with well-behaved polka dots, and new black shoes that meowed. Speaking of HASH, were my dogs killing me. Driving to what I knew would be a convocation of ardent animal lovers, I realized how little experience I'd had with our fellow creatures. I had a childhood memory of a collie pushing a neighbor boy into a pond, for others to fish out again, spluttering and half drowned. I wouldn't tell that story, of course, but if called on to contribute I could relate to my credit the time a birdbrained sparrow fell out of a tree and broke a wing, and I nursed it back to health in a carton made into a nest by lining it with an old shirt and kept on an upper garage shelf out of reach of rapacious cats. I was polishing that up for narration as I parked my car on the street and walked up to the half-timbered manse where dwelt my Cynthia and her stepmother, Amanda.

I liked Mrs. Pickles, though I wished she didn't look so much like William Powell. There is nothing wrong with these transsexual resemblances (my own father looked like Marie Dressler) but William Powell! Because the thing was, you expected any such person to be suave and debonair, you know. Which she was anything but. So it was a good job that Cynthia wasn't her daughter, which eliminated the threat of a family likeness skipping a generation only to reappear under your very eyes in a passel of little Powells, some of which might be girls. I came early, as suggested, and so had a chat with Mrs. Pickles who "received" me on a chaise in an alcove adjoining her upstairs bedroom, everything papered so pink I felt I was inside a watermelon. She was so obviously hypochrondriac that without realizing it I fell into the humoring "we" dear to nurses. Cynthia's briefing had emphasized that she liked to be treated with sympathy, as an invalid. So it was "How are we today?" Not too well, we feared. Our hands were that much stiffer than yesterday, our ankles were swollen, and we were getting Gregorian chants on our bridgework. A phenomenon sometimes accompanying the hazard of a radio broadcasting station in the vicinity.

"It's a funny thing about musical tastes," I said. "We once had a neighbor who played nothing on his phonograph but Hawaiian music, and you know that few things can make you more seasick than the twanging of those woozy guitars. Talk about mal de mare. In summer when all the windows were open I thought my poor dear mother was going to have to hang over the back porch rail, like a ship's passenger, and woof her cookies. There was a story that the man next door had to take Dramamine, though it may have been apocalyptic."

"What does that mean again?"

"Maybe not true. Do you regularly pick up broadcasts on your teeth, Mother Pickles?"

"In addition to the radio station, there's a man nearby with a shortwave set, and will you believe this? It can render inaccurate Breathalyzer tests at the police station, for drunken drivers? The testimony can be thrown out of court on that ground."

"I'll be doggoned."

Cynthia had stepped out of the room for a moment, the better to let us two get acquainted, and by the time she returned I was deep in my story about the birdbrained sparrow.

"It was an advanced fledgling, in bird adolescence you might say, that had fallen out of its nest, and there it lay on the ground, aw, fluttering about pitifully in the grass. I quickly rescued it from marauding kitty cats, of course

47

they're only behaving true to their kind by chewing up bird-ies. One must like them both for God made us all, and there you have it."

"It's nature," Mrs. Pickles agreed.

"That's what it is exactly. So what did I do, I got a box, and after making a nest for the birdykins by lining it with one of my old shirts, aw, and having my heart melted into Welsh rabbit by its pathetic little cheeping —"

"Aw."

"— its heartrendering little cries, I thought to myself, 'How can I feed it? What can I put into its little beak, so open and looking up all the time with its mouth open?' "

Cynthia stood at the window looking out with folded arms, sighing from time to time, but, braced by the unmis-takable ambience here, the aura of polished quality, I plowed ahead with my story — quite actually a true one, however tailored in tone to Mrs. Pickles' quickly divined temperament.

"And what did you do?" she asked, straightening a little in the chaise lounge as she hung on my every word. "What did you feed it?"

"Worms."

"You dug up some worms for it. Aw."

I shook my head, closing my eyes for a moment of sus-pense. "I made my own worms."

"How?"

"You'll never guess."

"How!"

"Out of peanut butter."

Mrs. Pickles clapped her hands in delight as with a glance she invited her stepdaughter to share in her appreciation. "He twirled peanut butter in his fingers into little worms."

Cynthia wheeled around at the window and watched me levelly, her arms still stiffly folded.

"I dropped those peanut butter worms into the birdykins' little beak, and do you know, she ate them. Of course it may have been a he for all I knew, that's not the point. I nursed my little friend back to health, aw, and seeing it had begun to flutter about in the box — which I kept high up on a garage shelf to safeguard it from the kitty cats — seeing that its wing was apparently healing, I took it up, held it in my palm in the spring sunlight, and said, 'Fly, little sparrow. Fly away.' And away it flew. Fell. Tried again. Fell again. But finally sailed off into the nearby woodlot, free again. A free one of God's creatures."

Mrs. Pickles again clapped with delight. "How old were you at the time?"

"Ten."

"Character will tell already then."

"Well, thank you."

Heaving another sigh, Cynthia rolled her eyes to that heaven whose creatures we all are, and said, "I believe that's the doorbell. Come, Amanda, our guests are beginning to arrive. Or it may be the singers."

It could only hasten my consolidation with, maybe integration into, this family to be seen at the door with them greeting the newcomers, and as we neared it, Mrs. Pickles a step or two behind, Cynthia whispered, "I'm going to need Dramamine myself if you keep this up. Aw."

The Lyric Trio turned out to be triplet brothers nearly seven feet tall, as though the Almighty had had several yards of leftover innards to cope with, and being unable to tuck them all into your normal body cavity, had had to give the recipients near-circus height, as per our intellectual poolside conversation which you may remember. Becoming round-shouldered being the only means of accommodation to the real world available to them, unless they tooled around on their knees, they tended to hover over you in a stoop, and

49

even at that one soon developed a crick in one's neck looking up at them from one's paltry five eleven in stocking feet.

But could they sing! All of us approximately seventy-five of the local cream could testify to that. They sounded like angels as they harmonized away of shepherds and maidens, the middle one strumming a lute. That made the thud with which I came down to earth the more sickening.

That this was a "benefit" for HASH hadn't sufficiently penetrated, or I had let the world slide off the top of my head without taking in its full implications. Not being charged an admission, say ten or even twenty-five clams, had puzzled me a little, then been forgotten. The explanation struck with full force as we were having our tea, at which Mrs. Pickles presided in royal style at an ancestral silver urn the sale of which alone could have kept the shelter stocked with mongrels for a full year. Checks for the cause were to be collected now, or pledges in the case of those who had forgotten to bring their checkbooks. That was when the old pinkie suffered severe malfunction. I couldn't get it up again for the life of me, after it detumesced on receipt of this bleak info. How much would be expected of me by the family into whose good graces I was trying to worm my way, if I may allude to worms one last time. I stole glances at the women on either side of me, busily scribbling out checks heavily infested with zeros. Did one say a thousand dollars? Surely not. Must be a hundred. The other one seemed to be in that amount. On the pledge card passed me I scrawled two hundred and fifty, which should satisfactorily meet, if not top, the general average, for some of the ladies appeared rather less than wealthy, wearing hats that looked reduced from nine ninety-five. I could uneasily imagine Cynthia and her mother curiously hurrying to read my card before I was down the front steps. Of course there would be no worry about the check itself if I made it out sometime toward the end of the week. Written today, it would have bounced, but I had a plump amount in Treasury bills coming due Tuesday. By the time the last guests had dribbled out the door I had charged it off to the high cost of romance these days — no more than two dinners at Lutèce.

It is now time for answers to two questions that have probably also been nagging you. Had the madrigals been interfered with by the music coming in on Mrs. Pickles' bridgework? And why if we were such animal lovers were there no cats, dogs, parakeets or even canaries in the house?

1. Since radio waves weren't picked up anywhere in the house except the bedroom alcove, the problem was limited to that area. Which was a mercy, because the station's recorded broadcasts included every conceivable kind of music including hard rock, and were interspersed with comments of a disc jockey cracking jokes in highly questionable taste. This was gone into while the housekeeper, Mrs. Rampart, tidied up the parlor where we sat after the guests had gone. Much of the vast cookie overrun disappeared into her own mouth, I noticed in a vigil as furtive as the disposals. With justification I thought, on hearing that she had arisen at dawn to bake them all herself.

2. Mrs. Pickles was allergic to all animals conceivable as house pets, so the premises must remain devoid of them; regrettably, since she would have liked nothing better than a tabby or two around to play with her balls of yarn and catch the mice that would soon enough be coming into the house again with cooler weather. She had gone through nearly a year of graduated injections from an allergist, with no effect. She still broke out in hives and respiratory distress in the mere presence of a cat or dog. "That's why I do my best for HASH," she said.

"It's a way of showing your affection," I said. Tales of my own sterlingness in this area continued to rain unabated, but one will suffice to illustrate again the kind of human worth we are talking about here.

"I have a special fondness for the nocturnal creatures," I said. "The wee beasties that slip out of their little abodes at night to forage for food. Like raccoons — how endearing those little faces are — possums and skunks. Skunks are really quite good-looking. I get them all in my backyard, and so far from considering them pests to shoo away I throw table scraps out to them. By morning the tidbits are all gone, sometimes by midnight. One thing I'm careful about is that 'toothpick' bone in a chicken drumstick? Right alongside the tibia or whatever? That they can chew up all right, but the toothpick bone is like a needle and could get stuck in their little throats. So I always carefully remove it. Nor would I toss out the breast ribs, which are also small and sharp. I edit my garbage, so to speak."

"You hear that, Cynthia? He edits his garbage for the stray animals. Isn't that sweet."

"I heard," she said, adding sotto voce to me who was on her right on the sofa, "I'm beginning to get diabetes."

"Couldn't sleep well if I didn't," I said.

"Aw."

"I think that much affection for dumb creatures shows a warm nature throughout," said Mrs. Pickles, who addressed many such remarks directly to Cynthia, who might even as an interested young lady have overlooked certain virtues in her steady. "Someone who'd come through in a pinch every time."

"I think I'd like a drink," Cynthia said.

"I keep telling her it's not a good habit to get into. Do you drink, Edward?"

"I drink to be sociable."

"Not that I'm a sourpuss temperance person. Far from it.

Just stating a medically proven fact. Mrs. Rampart will fix me a Presbyterian, but you young people have what you want. It's all over there."

"What on earth is a Presbyterian, Mother Pickles? Sounds intriguing."

"A cocktail made of ginger ale and grape juice, though some people prefer another kind of fruit juice. I like grape. But have what you wish."

"I quite agree that a relaxing cocktail is a blessing that can become a curse if you up your consumption. The trouble is — well, heck, I'll have a sherry with Cynthia long as she's fixing one for herself. Make mine on the rocks too, would you, Cynthia?"

So it was that over sherry and Presbyterians the talk turned to the departed guests, a type of conversation that can quickly curdle into gossip be we ever so Christian. Cynthia whispered to me at one point in it, "Sorry you can't rack up any Brownie points on this type of talk." Well, we would see.

She was herself a gread aid in satisfying her stepmother's curiosity, particularly about a couple named Hanley. Was their marriage really threatened by some sexual misconduct on the part of Mr. Hanley, lately revealed to be rotten? An affair with his secretary had recently come to light. Cynthia couldn't speak with full authority, but she knew that Mrs. Hanley, as well as the three children, had been rocked by the revelation. She had to add that Mrs. Hanley was rather a dull prune, and good for only ten dollars. She had clearly peeked at the pledge cards.

"I didn't think that people who subscribed to the *National Geographic* ever had affairs," Mrs. Pickles said.

"Well, you never know," I said. "We had a neighbor lady once who saved all her *Reader's Digest*s — people save them, you know, as they do their *National Geographic*s — and the next thing we knew she had run off with a haberdasher. At least the haberdasher's wife got the store."

"Still in all, it seems disgraceful, all this permissiveness."

"I couldn't agree with you more, so help me Hannah."

"It's time we brought back the ducking stool."

"And the pillory."

The old pinkie had recovered its potency, really coming up as I sipped my sherry. We might note just in passing that lifting the little finger is no more prevalent among genteel tea drinkers than it is among beer swiggers. That's a fact. I mean among guys drinking out of a glass, even sometimes a bottle. Grasping stein handles of course doesn't count. Anyway, we discussed the new sexual freedom, and here I engaged in a practice of which you've already had an inkling, in fact a fair sampling. Throwing into the conversation remembered passages verbatim. When I was trying to be a real actor, I was known as a quick study, and still am. I can take in quite a long speech at one reading, and reel it off letter-perfect. I can't act my way out of a box of Kleenex, but the memorizing habit remains with me in full force. And here I threw in a measured observation made by a character in a novel I'd recently read.

"Most men who have jealously preserved what — Might I have just another wee drop of sherry? Thank you — who have jealously preserved what they regard as their freedom are more habituated than they realize. Not marrying one woman, at least not loyally, they live in snatched moments of mock domesticity with a succession. A mistress in addition to a wife, or two mistresses at once, or three, or whatever degree of anarchy their independence requires, all this exacts a commensurate toll in loyalties and attentions. Footloose, they plow familiar furrows on the prowl for company, and if they don't find it suffer the worst boredom of all, single boredom."

"I think we should —" Cynthia began.

"There are no doubt free spirits worthy of the name, rolling stones who roll without indignity or apparent loneliness, even though downhill as the circumstances inexorably ordain, but the average male pursuing such a life will usually be found on closer scrutiny to be not a free spirit at all, but just another man in more than one rut."

Cynthia rose, as though driven mad with the momentary delusion that she didn't live here at all, but was a guest who must toddle along. As a consequence, she took the rest of this standing up.

"And as for the administrative strain of arranging that one hour of careless rapture! Huh!" Mrs. Pickles kept briskly nodding her head, in total corroboration of what I was saying. "No, really, it is hardly worth it, as the pathetic Mr. Hanley must have discovered arranging his quickies or nooners or matinees, or whatever they call them in the vulgar parlance of the day, with this secretary of his." I crossed my legs and looked at my sherry glass, held aloft at arm's length. "Eating lotus is one of the most wearing occupations on earth."

Mrs. Pickles looked at her daughter and pointed at me. He's the one, she was as much as saying. This is Mr. Right if ever I saw him. Then we were talking about money, in a lightning switch engineered by Cynthia, in connection with whether Hanley was going to divorce his wife or vice versa, and how much it would cost him. A disaffected squaw can really scalp a man, I was on the point of observing, but feared that either the language or the observation or both might liquidate my credit with Mrs. Pickles, who might herself had come by much of her money by shedding the mate who had preceded Cynthia's father, and the rest of it when he died. Instead I made a reference to some reverses I had recently suffered in the stock market, in the manner of one quite able to weather such setbacks. I followed this with some gingerly prying to get a "feel" about Mrs. Pickles' own financial picture. Cynthia obliged here, from the cellarette where she was pouring herself another stiff sherry.

"Amanda has investments she doesn't even understand. Her broker has put her into some hot electronic and computer stocks, and now she wants to know what the devil semiconductors are."

"Oh, that's easy," I said. "Think of Leonard Bernstein sawing himself in two with his own baton, or better yet — better yet," I went on through the laughter Mrs. Pickles was doubled over with, "a trainman vertically sliced in two by those automatic double doors. Cut neatly in twain, don't you know."

Mrs. Pickles put down her second Presbyterian to hold her sides, or rather one side as with her free hand she again pointed to me, recommending me to Cynthia. This was the one. She need no longer look. He had not only intellectual depth and moral integrity, but the sense of humor with which to leaven them both. This was Mr. Right.

Whether Mrs. Pickles' bliss-out over me cut any ice with Cynthia's own judgment was hard to say. Three attempts to ring her up resulted only in Mrs. Rampart's voice telling me she was out. Nor did she call me back, though I left my number each time, to Mrs. Rampart's growing boredom. Each time, Mrs. Pickles was resting. Cynthia, who had seemed so openly responsive, had turned inscrutable. Had I come to seem equally changeable to her? Likable when met over drinks and lunch at the country club, palatable enough to go to bed with, then dubious in the way I had curried favor with her stepmother? Shameless, even a fortune hunter? I could have countered that charge with the doubts a man might have about after all wanting for a wife a woman that accessible, even in this day of short-order sex. Would a woman who wanted you for a first husband let you get that lucky that quick? And vice versa for the man's thinking. The problem that gray week, then, seemed to be this: we had trouble reading each other's character.

You can imagine the stew of emotions in which I kept wandering back to the country club, half hoping to find her there so I could saunter over and, showing a little indifference of my own, say, "Oh, hello, Cynthia nice party and the madrigals were something else," yet more intensely hoping she'd be nowhere about, which might mean she was out of town and couldn't have gotten my calls to return. I was spared the sight of her on the tennis court or dawdling at a table with her social equals, but one midday I spotted a hardly less spearing sight — the two runners-up for my heart, still pounding neck-and-neck up the homestretch of my emotions. Roxy Winch was at a poolside table giving a drink order to Toby Snapper, each more lusciously *zaftig* than the other.

"Well, if it isn't the two most ravishing creatures in Christendom," I said. "May I sit down?"

"Please do," they said together, Toby with her satirical little smirk emphasizing the fat lot of say she had in the matter. "What's your pleasure?" she went on in the same vein. "Miss Winch has ordered two planter's punches."

"Chirouble will be here any sec," said Roxy.

"I'll have the same, please, Toby." I sat down. "Well, Roxy, you're looking more radiant every day. And I like that blouse. Red, green, orange and blue are my favorite colors. Oh, and yellow. I see some of that there."

"Your favorite colors, then, are those in the spectrum."

57

"I always feel they're the best."

"So it's no wonder they call this a rainbow shirt."

"It matches your eyes."

"What part?"

"The iris. Which incidentally means rainbow, my dear." (A bit of info recently acquired while flatboating through the dictionary.)

"No, I mean of the shirt."

"That streak, sort of dominant near your throat. Picks up the blue."

This rapid-fire exchange of wit again instantly picked me up as a principal to it, an exhilaration only heightened by the present arrival of Chirouble himself. That wiped out any opportunity to explore my chances with Roxy, but at the same time brought with it the prospect of conversation even more sparkling than hitherto. Chirouble always topped you, yet always raising your own level.

"We were just engaged in a sprightly exchange of repartee, Jerry," I said.

"Better than anything in here." Roxy laid a hand on a pile of manuscript she had brought along for him to dictate a letter of rejection for. "And it *preens* itself on its dialogue."

"Good dialogue should give the reader a sense of eavesdropping on a scene," Chirouble said.

"You're right," I said, again lolling back with the wonderful sense of belonging. "Ideally, the reader is a fly on the wall."

"And in most novels these days that means the bedroom wall," Roxy chipped in, apparently well able to stay the course with accomplished conversationalists.

That deflected my mind to thoughts of pillow talk with her, as it would those of any red-blooded youth, and so for a few minutes my mind was only half on what was being said, even by myself. Hopes of a rebound with either Roxy or

Toby continued to soften what disappointment remained over Cynthia's silence. I might even be big about it and go ahead with the promised investment in *Overview*. What was five thou to a successful producer? It was as such that my wandering interest in the discussion returned with a jerk when it appeared we were deep in the distinction between pornography and erotica. When did a literary or cinematic work deserve the one name, when the other?

"It's very simple. Thank you, my dear," I said, pausing to smile upward at Toby, who had set our drinks down. "It's very simple. Erotica makes you feel good, pornography makes you feel lousy. Cheap even. Precisely the same as when you make love, actually. Who with, and why. A quick lay, or a deep emotional attachment. Love always has lust in it, sure. But not the other way around."

"Exactly the way I feel," Roxy said, an expression of agreement that filled me with the warmest sense of compatibility between us, quickening my fantasy of mating with her. "This novel here is just filth. *Feel Free* it's called. Gawd."

"Gawd," I echoed, and took a long pull on my drink. It was a title I had been thinking of for one of the training films. Now washed out. Forget it.

"Why would the Loring agency send it to you? They have such good taste, normally, and this is degrading. The kind that inspires flap copy like 'A sexplicit exploration of modern marriage between two people determined to live totally liberated blah blah blah in an atmosphere of personally fulfilled blah blah blah.' You don't have to bother reading it, Jerry."

"Apparently not, seeing how thoroughly you've cased it, Roxy."

She took a drink from her glass, licking her lips provocatively.

"No, Eddie's right about the real-life parallel. What taste

does it leave in your mouth. That's all the criterion you need for either. There's some rubbish going around for TV cassettes. But you have to give the producers credit for a kind of low cunning. They call them training films — like preparations for marriage? Isn't that a howl."

I had thirstily gulped off nearly half my planter's punch, and was basking almost voluptuously again in the sheer sense of belonging, almost comatose with contentment. Now I slid up erect in my chair.

"Oh, I don't know about that," I said. "I've seen some of those, and whatever other names you might want to give them, they must be judged as falling in the category of erotica. Oh, definitely. They are tastefully done. Done with impeccable, oh frank, sure, utterly frank in their depictions, but done with impeccable taste. And a fastidious sense of the emotional and romantic values. I happen to know the chap who makes them, and a more sensitive —"

"Well, I haven't actually seen any. A friend of mine just told me about them."

"Ah!" Ecstatic relief. "There we are. As I say, I happen to know this chap, and a more scrupulous sense of artistic integrity —"

"Maybe you should rent a couple and show them at your party next Saturday, Jerry. Jerry likes to show naughty things at his bashes. After eleven, that is."

"Well, maybe. But getting back to the subject," Chirouble said, "the most beautiful bit of erotica in our time was written by — wait for it — Edith Wharton. The elegant depicter of genteel turn-of-the-century mores, product of the most sheltered and proper home imaginable. The manuscript was discovered among her effects after her death, a mere fragment of what had evidently been intended as a full-length novel. And do you know what it portrays? With the most exquisite literary beauty? Incestuous oral sex. Mutual oral sex between father and daughter."

"There, you see?" I spread my hands. "Anything can be done provided it's done tastefully. As I say, I know this producer fellow, and a more perceptive —"

"But how do you like 'training films' produced by something called Sexucational Films? How does that grab you?" I shrugged tolerantly. She turned to Chirouble again. "How about the party? I mean *after* you've had a look at them yourself. Not that everybody there won't have seen *Deep Throat* and *The Devil in Miss Jones*. They won't care."

"I'll see. Why don't we order some lunch? Where is that lovely friend of yours, Eddie? Training films put out by something called Sexucational Pictures did you say?" Chirouble laughed. "That's rather neat, that subterfuge. Clever bastard who thought up that gimmick."

"Now maybe this entrepreneur is perfectly sincere," I cut in. "Acting out of the most unimpeachable —"

"Cynthia! Hey! Come over!"

Chirouble had spotted her crossing the lawn, again in tennis whites, towards the courts. He rose and waved her over. She veered in our direction, waving back with her racquet.

A jug of cider mulled by a succession of sizzling pokers would have been a good metaphor for the mixture of emotions that was your correspondent. I felt my guts churning as Cynthia advanced smiling on our little group, to join it by taking the chair Chirouble and I simultaneously rose to draw for her. She undid the sleeves of a sweater knotted around her throat, swung it off her shoulders, and set it on the back of her chair.

"Eddie, I'm so glad to see you. I tried to call you last Tuesday just before I lit out for New York, to tell you I'd be gone for several days. Sudden appointments I'd been fishing for with three, well, tycoons I'd been trying to hit up for money — and guess what. Two of them look to come through, giving us almost enough to start issue number one. I'm meeting someone for a game in ten minutes, but may I have one of those you're all drinking? On me, as a celebration. Eddie, I'm sorry I didn't call you from New York, but I got so caught up." She stroked my head as though she was soothing a child, which was just what I felt like in my rapturous relief.

"I'm so glad for you, Cynthia," Chirouble said. "We'll call my party Saturday night the official celebration. You can come, can't you? And Eddie?"

"If I can have dibs on Cynthia," said I from my seventh heaven.

"You can indeed," said Cynthia, with a pretty little pout converted into a blown kiss.

"When we're all properly snockered we're going to show some porno Roxy here says she's onto."

"Erotica," I said. Toby had come down from the clubhouse stairs to get Cynthia's order, and out of the tail of my eye I saw her stop in her tracks to eavesdrop, the impish little grin on her face as she pretended absorption in her order book. "I was just saying, I happen to know the producer, Monty Carlo," I continued, using the pseudonym behind which in any case I could remain safely concealed till I saw which way the wind blew, "and a more finely grained — Ah, here's Toby. Another round of these, and then since Cynthia has to run let's order. And this lunch is on me."

F O U R

Easy Doesn't Either It

YOU CAN imagine the thrill it was to walk into Chirouble's bash with the beautiful Cynthia Pickles on my arm. We were the intellectual cream of Merrymount, besides being a rather decadent little group, a not unusual, or unfashionable, combination. An obsession with sex is often characteristic of your creative element. At the same time I was worried about what the discovery that I was the creative element behind Sexucational Films would do to my rising status in the Smart Set. Early inquiries revealed that our host indeed intended to entertain his guests with one of the cassettes when everyone was brandy-squiffy. I had every safeguard against exposure but one. As writer-producer I used a pseudonym, and though I acted in most of my films it was only, as I had explained to Toby Snapper, in the lower close-ups. The actor playing the male leads is a little on the small side where it counts, so I was his stuntman in the scenes of explicit sex. Not that I'm prodigious, no intention to imply that; just average. That was what we wanted. We didn't want to show a virgin being gored by ten inches. That would have thrown our entire purpose out of perspective. We wanted to show ordinary people enjoying to the full the most beautiful of human relationships.

That was particularly true of *Come as You Are*, the cassette it turned out Chirouble had bought or rented. In it — and here my window of vulnerability — I did the narration. Anonymously in voice-over, true — but might someone recognize the voice and thereby spill all the beans? There were those who might find it amusing to know a porn king, as in another era members of the upper crust took a kind of inverted delight in knowing a gangster. But what would Cynthia think? Would she drop me like a hot potato? If so, had she, or anybody else, a right to? Could you justifiably patronize somebody whose works you enjoy as social entertainment? In that case I would be the victim, not of my own occupation, but of somebody else's hypocrisy.

Having set all these factors in their proper focus, I tried to put them out of my mind and enjoy myself. Here I was, part of the bohemian bourgeoisie that showed my stuff, so get a little oiled and mingle with them on their own terms. Easy does it.

I had turned from the bar with a champagne cocktail, and was sizing up the crowd of about forty in various stages of revelry, when a tray of hors d'oeuvres materialized under my nose and a familiar voice said, "Have a cocktail tidbit, sir?"

It was Toby Snapper, in a black dress and white maid's apron.

"My God," I said, "are you everywhere?"

"I'm often seen at these catered affairs. Mrs. Dalton's is good to moonlight for and the pay is excellent. Have one of those with the fish paste," she said, pointing out a specific dainty. "Oi 'elps make them at Mrs. Dalton's shop before we trucks them over," she went on in some kind of mock-cockney servant-girl chatter, "and then Oi has the added pleasure of passing them around to the quality, downcha know. Oi'll be servin' you your *coq au vin* at table, sir, it'll be moi pleasure."

"Come on, knock it off, Toby," I said as with an excruciating little curtsy she lowered the tray even as I reached for the recommended delicacy.

"Then after dinner, when Oi'm done passin' the coffee in the teeny cups and the liqueurs in the even teenier glasses — wot looks like eyecups downcha know, sir — then maybe us from below stairs can stand in the back and watch the movie wot's to be shown for the hedification of all. Oi understand hit won a prize at the Ash-Cannes Festival. In the documentary category Oi believes they calls it."

"Look, cut this foolishness, O.K., Toby? Like stow it," I insisted through a mouthful of fish paste.

"Anything you siy, sir," she said, and with another mock curtsy twitched off through the crowd.

I was trying to fit this new development in among my proliferating hazards when I spotted Roxy Winch making her way toward me. I swallowed what remained of the fish-paste appetizer in time to say, "Roxy, darling," and try to plant a kiss on those ripe-plum lips, managing only to graze the corner of her mouth as she turned her cheek to take it. Probably didn't want her lipstick smudged. Yes, that must be it, as her greeting couldn't have been warmer. "You're more ravishing every time I see you," I said. "What are you doing after the orgy?"

"I might ask you that." She gave me a quizzical look as she jerked her head in the direction Toby had taken. "That little piece who keeps cropping up everywhere. The way you and she, well, *are* together. Half gemütlich and half furtive. Are you, or have you ever been, an item? Don't take the Fifth."

"Well —"

"That's what I thought."

"But I only said 'Well.' "

"That says everything. So. The boulevardier who's ruined the little seamstress. Or the little flower girl. Or the little nut vendor."

"She's a nut cracker."

"Ah, the reverse then. She's ruined you, but emotionally Left you a psychic cripple."

"She only made a cameo appearance in my life."

"Enough to leave you unfit for future human relations." Roxy seemed Toby's match in starting up a few shenanigans of her own. "After bleeding you white of all your money she tosses you aside like an old shoe."

"That's right. And now, Roxy, I want you to do the same. I've made a second fortune, which is all yours to milk me of, me who I realize am your helpless victim as our affair winds to its inevitable close." I realized something else as I jabbered away at my flirtation. I saw that, under all the kidding, I was mending my romantic fences everywhere, always cooking up a substitute here in case a relationship there washed out. Knocking back my champagne cocktail, I snatched another from the passing tray on which I set the glass. I took a healthy swig of that, the better to lubricate myself for the pitch that, however shamelessly, I was determined to make right here and now. Roxy and Chirouble, I had learned, were *not* really an item. There was a long moment of silence between us, and then, gazing at her with my dog's eyes, I said, "You know damn well I could run a fever over you. You must notice the way I look at you. And I flatter myself there's some response, from this lingering eye contact at our lunches. And just now, across a crowded room, you spotted me right off and came straight over."

"Who couldn't in that jacket," she laughed. Then sensing she might have made a gaffe she quickly added, "It's quite — beautiful. I've always liked checks anyway." Her face softened, and she laid a hand on my arm. "Did I wound him? No, of course not, colors are back in for men, we know that. Look at him over there." She pointed to a human Christmas tree, already sloshing his drink.

I seemed suddenly to have got a fix on Roxy, a clue to her makeup. Or to give her the benefit of the doubt, seemed to be asking a question about her. Did she, where men were concerned, like to inflict wounds for the pleasure of healing them? I'd had this experience with her before. Apologizing for something she'd said and in so doing creating a kind of emotional voluptuousness between the two of you. A subtler, but therefore trickier, mystique to handle than Toby's more openly satirical japes and didoes. "Women!" my father used to say, summing it all up as he blew my mother a kiss after some difference or other, and then shuffled off to his peaceful cemetery.

But every case is different, and here I had the beguiling Roxy to cope with, and the second of two cocktails with which to do it on an empty stomach, except for Toby's circulating appetizers.

"We Teeterses have always liked bright colors," I said. "We were poor, and many's the time I remember my mother staying up after midnight mending prunes. We children often went around ragged and half starved. Our great treat was to have Shredded Wheat for dessert. Once my father gathered up spilled produce from an overturned trailer truck full of meat and refrigerated vegetables like other people, and running home with a frozen pork roast and some cabbages he was mistaken for a thief, and pursued for twelve blocks by an off-duty upholsterer, whom he finally gave the slip in an alleyway. At last he got a job as a landscape gardener in a cemetery, which he held till the day he died. Being caretaker of a cemetery is a grave responsibility."

Again Roxy laid a hand on my arm, this time giving it a squeeze. "Lamb. He's been hurt. Terribly, sometime, somewhere. I've hurt him too. His wounds need licking."

Anytime, baby, I thought. And vice versa. Wait till you see me in action tonight and never dream it!

The host was making his way toward us, slowly, like a swimmer through a sea of persons, now the overhand, now the Australian crawl, now and then flicking a finger aloft to indicate that arrival was imminent. None other than Chirouble himself, unaware that I had his secretary's left breast stuffed deep into my mouth, spiritually speaking, and was feeding like no tomorrow, or maybe all too aware of it, having picked it up on his antenna, a message corroborating previous intimations received at club lunches. I had to have this girl, despite the number she was doing on me.

"I never found out whether my father stole to support me while I wrote the study the Guggenheim people refused to give me a grant-in-aid for, *The Changing Role of Corn Pone*," I was ladling out when at last he reached us, puffing a little after his choppy Channel crossing. He looked at Roxy's hand still gently laid on my wrist, withdrawn as he glanced down.

"You two look pretty knit-up here. I came over as soon as I could."

"Eddie's just been giving me a hard-luck story about his life," Roxy said. "Quite checkered, to hear him tell it, in a surrealist sort of way."

"You'll find me vastly more intriguing in that area, doll," says Chirouble, taking in both his own the lost ministering hand, "with more than a touch of the darkling. There's a legend in my family that dogs howled when I was born, as they do when other people die, and my first word was 'Rose-bud.' "

"This is a great party, Jerry," I said. "The greatest. You're the Gatsby *de nos jours.*" I hoped I'd got the phrase right. I'd picked it up from another book I'd read in the ongoing effort at self-improvement, rather than from the course in high-school French which I'd flunked twice. Also that Chirouble hadn't read the novel in question, or Roxy either for that matter, because I fancied they exchanged glances not easily deciphered, unless it meant they had simultaneously discovered a thief in the house. I bristled a little, with a flicker of resentment all too familiar to me as the new kid on the block from the other side of town — the wrong side. Hell, we're all pickpockets in a minor sort of way, no harm in that. What is personal development but a long process of learning by example? In other words, plagiarism.

With a happy sigh Roxy said, "What more could a girl want than dialogue from the likes of you two guys. If I was stranded on a desert island with one of you and the other showed up it would be trouble in Paradise. Who'll get me a refill?" She rattled the cubes in her empty glass. "It's vermouth and soda. Dry vermouth." I took it and left them for the bar. What else? By the time I wormed my way back with her refill and another champers for myself, Chirouble was regaling her at a great clip with his own personal brand of amusing foolishness. "So I said to her, 'My dear,' I said, 'I'm going to get you out of this whorehouse if it's the last thing I do. It's much too sheltered a life.' " How would you like to be able to talk like that, eh? Subtle, throwaway, offbeat, everything. I sure would.

Circulating our way again, Toby stopped to have a word, encouraged by Chirouble. Some chitchat about the new chef who was to take over the club restaurant. There being only one appetizer left on her tray, which nobody wanted, Toby popped it into her own sassy little mouth before continuing on to the kitchen. It amused the others, but I wasn't so sure. I had my doubts — to be soon enough justified.

We were next joined by a local doctor then in the news for having developed a method of vacuuming excess fat out through your navel, and a current wife and showpiece with a stomach as flat as the pizza she could now again tuck into it, for a while. A real testimonial to his breakthrough. I had read a story about him in the local paper, and his face had seemed familiar. Seeing him now in the flesh, with or without any flab edited out of himself by his method, I recognized him. He was the chap in the habitat group at the club where I had first glimpsed Cynthia, who had so jet-set-knowingly talked about the little restaurant around the corner from somewhere in Trieste. Now here was another habitat group and me in it. Definitely part of the scene. I reveled in the thought. But with the burst of elation accompanying it came again the stab of fear, the question of whether my membership in the *crème de la crème* would survive the evening's entertainment. So "Revel a little harder, Teeters," I told myself, "bask a little faster. The clock's ticking, and may soon strike."

Dinner was buffet from which we scattered to seven small tables set without place cards, so it was on a pick-your-own-company free-for-all basis. Cynthia and I, like most couples, sat together, though not of course side by side, at a table including also the doctor who vacuumed unwanted pounds out through your belly button, and a kindred pioneer in the scientific disciplines, a dental expert who had recently discovered that chocolate prevented tooth decay. His research conducted on monkeys had ended when some foundation failed to renew his grant, but he was now happily financed by the candy industry itself, which hailed his revelation as the dawn of a new era. Their wives vied with each other in releasing data certifying their husbands as geniuses, on the strength of their behaving with a luminous childlikeness around the house (cf. Albert Einstein) and, presumably, in the laboratory.

"Franklin is so out of this world," said the slenderizer's wife, "that he'll sometimes come home and I'll ask him what he had for lunch and he can't remember."

"Julius can never get the new slang expressions right until they've gone out of style," said the other spouse. "He said only today that something was driving him bunkers, thereby usurping the female's right to malapropisms, don't you think?" she finished, with a glance at me.

"You're absolutely right," I said. "Classic Greece gave us men as large as gods and gods as petty as people." This was another snitch, I think from the same book as a few minutes before. The others looked at me as Roxy and Chirouble had then, no doubt appreciating the epigram but struggling to fit it into the conversation — negotiating my way through which was like trying to go through a revolving door on skis. But I swifly came on with a contribution in re the subject of talent and impracticality by recalling a girl acquaintance of my teen years who wrote poetry of lasting value but couldn't boil an egg, remember what time it was, name either of her two senators, or manage to put on shoes that matched without maternal assistance. "She was so ethereal," I said, "she didn't know how many ounces there were to a pound. She has since married a real estate agent or something and had a child or two, but I doubt she ever got to the bottom of it."

"How many are there?"

This from a voice behind and above my right shoulder. It

was Toby Snapper with a bottle of red wine in one hand and white in the other, offering the guests their choice for the *coq au vin* we were hunched over.

"How many what?" I said, craning democratically around.

"How many ounces are there to a pound?"

"Thirty-two."

"I thought it was sixteen. Not that I may not be just another dumb broad."

"You're right, Toby. I feel that it's sixteen too," said Cynthia, laughing helplessly at something, no doubt the audacity. I tended to take a sterner view. This was what Chirouble's permissiveness led to. Equality was fine, liberalism was admirable, but you had to draw the line or all was chaos. Here was a chick who had slept with me acting like she was one of us. I figured out later that what may have got her goat was the reference to the real estate agent, which if memory served was what she was engaged to, or at least had been the night of our little fling between the old percales. Maybe it was my "or something" that had struck the note of condescension setting her off. One of those microscopic nuances you apparently get in Proust, to hear Bertha Colton the swillperson tell it. Maybe in Toby's case guilt was being discharged in the form of animosity toward her seducer, a reversal of the male's classic reaction as first embodied in Adam's "the woman though gavest me" beef at the Almighty. Both show how illogically we can behave when our emotions muddle our reason, how we can respond in a spirit of pique under totally irrelevant situations.

It was hardly in the spirit of pique that I said, "Yes, it is sixteen. Of course, my dear. I was probably thinking of two pounds. It's so easy to get sixteen and thirty-two confused since one is exactly twice the other. Miss, would you mind fetching another bottle of the red? I see all that's left in the bottle you have is dregs and sediment." And lo and behold if she doesn't dribble said residue into my glass before sashaying off for replenishments with a "Certainly, sir." About as obsequious as your next-door-neighbor's mastiff sinking his teeth into your shins.

By the time she got back I had managed to shift the subject to Cynthia's journalistic venture, without actually listening to the talk I had prompted. Toby's unexpected presence and precarious humor inspired a fresh anxiety about the movie, second only to, or even maybe exceeding, my fear of being recognized as the narrator from his voice, which I'm told is distinctive for its pleasantly nasal resonance. Would the noted permissiveness about servants in this house have her watching the short from the back of the room and, after more of some obivous tippling in the kitchen, letting the cat out of the bag, either directly or when overheard twitting me about it? After what I'd told her by way of pillow talk that night, she would certainly put two and two together and realize who Monty Carlo was — possibly even assume everyone else knew and start chattering accordingly. In my rattled state I turned these reflections around again. What was I jittery about if I wasn't ashamed of the documentaries? Who the hell were any of these people to upstage a guy who produced guides to lovemaking that if they were books nobody would think twice about, might even look up to him as a respected author? If they thought the footage rolled for their pleasure smut, so much the worse for them. I had nothing to regret. Well, yes, I might: if embarrassment on Cynthia's part soured her on me. That was the crux of the whole problem. Leaving with Monty Carlo might not be the same as arriving with Eddie Teeters.

I finished off two glasses of red wine and was grateful when the dental research scientist's wife, I think sensing I was in some kind of stew, offered me her largely untouched white. That and a brandy had me fairly well cushioned against whatever fate had in store when, toward midnight, the lights went out and Chirouble's twenty-four-inch television screen came on.

Cynthia and I sat together on a love seat near the rear of a long living room in which the furniture had all been shoved around to more or less simulate a projection room. Snugly settled, there in the dark, soon holding hands, we waited for the film to start.

Monty Carlo wasn't the only assumed name on the credit crawl. The female principal elected to call herself Mea Culpa, not to hide behind but as her permanent acting pseudonym. Never doubting that she would become a star in more conventional enterprises, she insisted on being addressed by the crew as Miss Culpa. You practically had to sleep with her to call her Mea. The adoption of the moniker was not unbeset with difficulties. First, somebody had to tell her how it was spelled. Where she had picked the expression up or what she originally thought it meant is known to God alone, but she thought her first name was Mia, as in Mia Farrow. She even wrote her new signature that way until somebody who'd made his way past the third grade straightened her out, and that only on the basis of vaguely remembering reading it somewhere himself. The next stage was an acquaintance a little higher up on the educational ladder telling her what it meant, at least according to *his* lights. "It means 'Me guilty,' or 'Me to blame,' something like that," he explained. "You know — like in 'Me Tarzan, you Jane.' "

"I know it's from the Bible," she said. "It means 'Don't touch me.' "

"No, that's something else," said the educated type.

74

"That's 'Nole me tangerine' or something like that. That's a whole nother can of succotash."

"Are you sure you don't have it confused with a legal term?"

The tutor screwed up his face in puzzled thought, then tumbled. "Oh, I think I know what you mean. That's 'Nolo contendere.' I do not contend." And with a sigh rested his case there.

I don't know what made her hit on that name. What strikes our fancy is often mysterious, even to ourselves. But it no doubt had the right exotic ring to a rather affected young woman bent on being just too too.

She was pretty steamy in the opening scenes over which could be heard my voice in anonymous narration.

"This is not a 'how to' demonstration, or an offered set of rules about making love," we heard me begin, as I steeled myself there in the half-gloom. "Everyone knows how to make love on a crude animal level. 'Slam bam thank you ma'am' is all too woefully often the case. The problem is how to do it in a manner providing maximum satisfaction to both parties, the fullest, richest emotional realization for two people. Or three, or more, if you're so inclined, for we make no moral judgments here." (Laughter and some murmurs of "I'll bet!") "First, some don'ts. Here's a scene showing how *not* to, one of the crudest and least rewarding ways of debasing that relationship which is among the most beautiful in human experience, though it often understandably occurs thanks to the unavoidable pressures of time and place. Here we have Alice and Tom taking a quickie, or nooner, at a nearby motel on their lunch hour."

I'm damned if the scene being condemned wasn't an exact duplicate of Cynthia's and my first time together; to wit, the pair tearing the clothes off each other's back in their haste to get naked and into bed.

I felt Cynthia tighten her grip on my hand as she whispered into my ear: "Notice anything familiar about this?"

"Yes," I laughed gently back, returning her squeeze. "Couple of eager beavers all right, eh, sweets?"

"No, I mean the voice. It sounds exactly like you."

"Really? I hadn't noticed. Of course recordings of us never sound like we think we sound. Often never recognize ourselves. I think he sounds a little like Ronald Colman."

"Shhh!" came from somewhere up front.

Narration in any case was soon suspended for a prolonged scene showing how it *should* be done. Having participated in it I knew what was coming. There was Jack Sweeper caressing Mea Culpa as a tremulous, still undeflowered bride, in a sequence of what we generally know as foreplay, though on the set we call it, as I say, the tenderizer. I doubled for him actually from the neck down, which included the hands. Jack has big rather lumpy lunch hooks, with heavy knuckles, and we decided my more tapered ones would be better for the caressing close-ups. Not that I preen myself on being exquisitely put together or anything; in fact my hands are somewhat disproportionate for my broad shoulders. But it gave me an eerie start to realize that Cynthia was in fact pressing in real life what she was watching graze over a naked body on the screen. She responded very amorously to what was going on, indeed, nuzzling in closer to me as she reached for my other hand, only to let it go a moment later and steal up my leg and settle on something else. Which was of course rising to the occasion. My God, I thought to myself, here I am getting off on myself. Nor was there any doubt about the effect of the scene on Cynthia, whose breathing quickened, and who, after a hurried glance to make sure there was nobody behind us to see, began to bite my neck. I seemed to sense a little heavy breathing everywhere in the hush which, equally significant, had fallen over the room.

76

"He is plucking that flower which blooms but once," my voice was saying as my hands parted the virginal thighs. "She is giving that gift which is hers but once to give." This was in the subsection entitled "The Defloration: How to Handle It." Now we see me gently, reverently mounting the bride and entering that flower whose petals open to receive me, while with Cynthia's hand actually prying its way under my clothes until she's grasping my spike, I'm not at all sure I'm not going to "geyser," as we called the climactic scenes on the set. It was touch and go. As the screen me began writhing and heaving aboard the bride, herself bucking under me like a bronco trying to throw a rider, I'm damned if I didn't really feel a paroxysm gathering in my vitals. "For God's sake," I whispered, plucking Cynthia's hand away — too late.

When we shot the scene, the synchronized consummations being fictionally filmed had been far from faked, as it happened. Here was something else crazily in sync. My own convulsion coincided with the cinematic ones, so that having removed Cynthia's hand I snatched it back again for the last few pulsations, which had me likewise blending smothered pantings of my own with the fortunately louder cries and moans of the newlyweds on-screen. My God, it was wild, madly wild. Someone started a round of applause for the beautifully accomplished mating, probably as a nervous relief from the spell to which everyone had rather guilty succumbed.

"Well!" said Cynthia when the short was over and the lights went on. "Now I think we should have a good old Laurel and Hardy." We all laughed at that, and as the group broke up she whispered to me, "Sorry. It did sort of turn me on. Are you all right?" I nodded and dismissed the subject with a covert wave. "But that actor is a great little old technician. I wouldn't mind going to bed with him myself."

"I'll fix it up," I said.

When the party showed signs of disbanding, a quarter of an hour or so later, I made a quick dash into the kitchen with the excuse of going for a glass of water, but actually to look for Toby, of whom I had seen no sign after dinner. She had left the instant her cleanup chores were over, I learned to my vast relief.

A threat more serious than any posed by our comely little vixen came to my attention as we prepared to leave. A lawyer named Avery Socker was telling a habitat group at the door about a double threat to the producers of the little diversion we had seen tonight.

"You know Frisch was elected governor on this Moral Majority ground swell. Reaction to all this X-rated stuff available on TV and cassettes like this one. Kids getting exposed to it at home, even teenagers showing it at slumber parties when their parents are away and no chaperones around and so on. Time to crack down is the idea. So I've caught wind of a civil class action that's going to be brought by this irate group *if* the federal or state government doesn't prosecute criminally," he was saying. "As they did in the case of *Deep Throat*. They're sore because that got stalled. Really up in arms."

"How much do they expect to sue for, Avery?" I asked, through what seemed a mouthful of peanut butter mixed with epoxy.

"Five mill is the gossip I hear. Really want to sue the pants off what's his name, Monty Carlo. Not that he can have much use for them if he spends his own time in shenanigans like these," Socker added with a laugh. He had a ruddy face well stocked with features, including two noses for the price of one and jowls a pair of which would make one paunch such as he had tucked away under his tattersall jacket. It was he whose coat, alone of the assembled revelers', outshouted my own. He had the bluff good nature of a man who if he smashed your car up would be a good sport about it. Nuisance of exchanging license numbers? Forget it. Having to dish out a dime for you to call for a tow truck to haul your demolished heap away? No problem. No end of insurance company red tape? Piece of cake.

"But training films like these — " I began.

"*What?*" He liked to bust a gut over that one, and plenty he had to do it with. "That ruse is really a lulu."

I wanted to tell him to go have Dr. Arnold vacuum some of the blubber out through his belly button by way of eliminating what must be a hazard to his own lovemaking, but checked myself enough to continue the argument with a civil tongue.

"What's the difference between sex-counseling films and books offering the same thing?"

"Oh, that's just a subterfuge, a ruse to show hard-core porn. Not that it isn't clever, I give them credit, but nobody's taken in by it. No parent is likely to give his growing children one of these cassettes the way our parents gave us a copy of *What a Young Man Ought to Know*. And even supposing them on a par, movies are by their nature more graphic, more easily pandering to prurient tastes. Which none of ours here are," he added with another jolly laugh. "Well, it's been fun. And thanks again, Jerry."

I continued the dispute outside on the sidewalk, despite Cynthia's attempt to shush me.

"Do you agree with the mental attitude behind that kind of censorship?"

"Oh, not necessarily. Hell, I'm broad-minded on the subject. But I'd been expecting it was time for the bluenoses to surface again. Puritan ethic striking back after a period of increasing permissiveness. Backlash, the old pendulum principle, you know. Well, good night, all. Beautiful night, isn't

79

it. Makes you glad you're alive. Monty Carlo, Mea Culpa. Oh, that's rich. I wouldn't have missed it for the world." His laughter boomed out across the night just given the seal of approval, like an empty oil drum rolling down a flight of stairs.

I thought to myself, pearls cast before swine. Now here was a man nasty as the first two weeks in February. What was the use of trying to educate or improve the likes of him? What was the sense waging this eternal war against ignorance and philistinism? Why strive to mold into something just a little finer the unredeemable clods of this world? I often wonder

.

Happy Families
Are All Different

IN JEW COURSE (as Chirouble pronounced it, having lived
some years in England, where he also got to saying "medsin"
for medicine, harmless little affectations all), in jew course I
would propose to Cynthia Pickles (a classy British enough
name in itself). Sooner than I had planned. Because in jewer
course it looked as though the law might indeed come down
on Eddie Teeters via Sexucational Films. There were other
unexpected portents of it. My eye was caught for example by
a headline in *Variety.* "Frisch Flails Fresh Flesh Flicks."
Meaning apparently that our newly elected Moral Majority
governor was tuning up for his promised crusade on the
adult cassettes, promising "criminal action in the courts of
this state if the federal don't take it soon." That we had here
yet another bluenose unable to distinguish between high-
purpose erotica and goons playing hide the salami on camera would do Teeters little good if in fact he found himself
heading for the tall timber with the judiciary snapping at his
heels. It behooved me therefore to make all haste in present-

ing to the world as irreproachable an image as I could: to wit, that of a respectably married man of property with a lovely wife from one of our finest families. So here we see my two aims converge: I would show the world I was a solid citizen, and the love of my bosom that I wanted to put down roots with her right here in Merrymount. Obviously I wouldn't buy a house without consulting her in that event, but house hunting as such would show I meant business, and presumably strengthen my cause when I popped the question.

So I kept my ear peeled for a piece of real estate that would melt a maiden's heart at the sheer prospect of being carried over its threshold, and sure enough, I presently heard tell of a manse type of place on a wooded hill on the outskirts of town, that was up for hardship sale. Its location and some other facts supplied by my informant seemed to match an entry I found in a classified ad in the real estate section of the local paper: "13 rms. 3-½ bths. swm. pool, ballroom (convertible into gym for children). Secl. in 7 wooded acrs bordered by stream. Owners in dire hardshp, must sacrifice. A steal." I called the phone number supplied and made an appt.

The ad didn't say what it was a steal *at,* but there seemed little doubt I had the broccoli for it, what with money rolling into Sexucational Films, of which I now owned a tidy chunk thanks to stock options allowed me as the creative spirit behind the enterprise. "Hell, *you're* the Gatsby *de nos jours,*" I told myself euphorically as I tooled on out to Greentop, as it turned out the estate was called. You couldn't see it from the road, that much was to be said for the bosky haven it claimed to be nestled in. Or maybe somebody already stole it, I thought as I twisted slowly up a winding dirt driveway, its ruts so full of rocks I said to myself, "Forget the damage to the front wheel alignment, old boy, the gold fillings falling out of your teeth will more than pay for it." Trees obviously let go came so close to the driveway that it was worth your fenders to neglect your navigation one second, and their density made for a gloom so heavy you expected at every turn to come upon the dank tarn of Auburn. Then with a sudden swerve sharper than most I came in sight of a clearing — itself in need of clearing. An obviously long-neglected garden was overrun with waist-high weeds. Then bang, there was the house, three stories and about as broad as it was high, a little the worse for eczema I thought, till I realized it was red brick covered with white paint now flaking in a way that I remembered discriminating types swooning over as "that weathered look money can't buy." In point of fact I like that scaly appearance too, and recalled my preference for it once I was over the shock of the entire property's dilapidation. I sat in the car a moment after I turned the engine off to give it a critical gander.

Between tall white pillars themselves in need of a paint job, I glimpsed innumerable leaded windowpanes to which were pasted decals that on closer consideration, and with a little deduction, turned out to be human faces returning my curiosity. What did we have here, a dozen crazy uncles and aunts who had escaped dunking in Auburn? And would I myself be pitched into same if I tried to leave, say, without ponying up a binder?

I climbed out of the car and started toward the house, the weeds going *whoosh-whoosh* around my legs, making my way along an overwrought iron fence running around the defunct garden, sagging picturesquely here and there, its gate hanging by one hinge. "This place has possibilities," I said to myself, as in fancy I saw and heard guests streaming through the blazing doorway to the first of my Gatsby bashes, the women saying as they pecked my cheek, "My dear, where did you ever find it?"

The knocker came off in my hand when I rapped it, which is always nice. You want charm, you got it. Ripeness is all, as I think someone said. There were sounds behind the door like someone rhythmically scraping burnt toast, and then it was opened by an eighty-year-old man in a shawl given to his grandfather by Abraham Lincoln because Lincoln very much wanted him to have it, and a pair of slippers improvised out of leftover pancakes. "You're the one who called," he said.

"How much do you want for this place?" I asked, handing him the brass knocker as I entered, or trying to.

"Keep it, keep it," he said, "as a memento of Greentop."

"Thank you so much," I said, pocketing it. "It'll come in handy as a paperweight, when I die."

"A what?"

"Paperweight. You know, like in *Citizen Kane*? Snowstorms in glass balls are terribly *démodé* now. Brass knockers are the thing. And instead of saying, 'Rosebud' when I drop it I'll say 'Greentop.' "

"You will?"

"Honest Injun. Did you know that my *first* word as a baby was 'Rosebud'? Fact. And that dogs howled when I was *born*. You've no doubt had them baying for a fare-thee-well around here on occasion." I heaved a jolly sigh and gazed about the capacious vestibule into which I had been progressively making my way throughout this colloquy. "Well!"

"We like it."

The plural was suddenly appropriate, and on a wholesale scale. For the decals had all come unglued from the windowpanes and their owners now shuffled in one by one, for a total of about ten or eleven, but that's a ballpark figure you understand. Ranging in years from middle-aged to elderly, they gave the impression of being not a family as such, but kinfolk once dependent on a fortune now, for some reason,

84

lost, so that they had collectively fallen on evil days and were making the best of communal life in a sort of white elephant that alone remained of that fortune, and it no doubt heavily burdened with taxes. Someone had blown the wealth on an unwise investment or taken a bath in the market. The man who admitted me was clearly their patriarch, and as he started the grand tour he intermingled his spiel about the house with another about himself, obviously a set piece.

Central to it was a metaphor he had hit on for himself, which started out interestingly enough but drug in the middle, I rather thought, and finally got to be what you could fairly call labored. He was a stricken oak, was the basic theme, riven by lightning, denuded of half his limbs by the buffeting winds of Fate — often taking the form of imbecile stockbrokers — what remained of his trunk disfigured by the cement patchwork alone holding it together, most of his root system upheaved and withering above ground, but himself standing yet, the sap still running inside him. But surely the metaphor itself was by now pumped dry? Wrong. There was more as we wandered from room to room, variations having to do with blistering suns borne and ravaging insects laying waste dwindling remainders, half his bark sacrificed to needless financial losses . . . That's it, I said to myself. You guessed right. Someone sank the wad in a beefsteak mine, and here we are.

The oak tree motif sounded like the fragments of some long epic poem he had once tried to write, but then he suddenly became more literal and switched to accounts of specific medical trials he had been through (and for which the bills had probably not been paid) such as the removal of his gallbladder without his being entirely convinced it was necessary. All this time the entourage was in our wake, itching to get into the act, and seizing on the cue now given them, judging by the torrent of competitive hypochondria to which

I was now treated. They had all had their insides edited by knife-happy croakers to hear them tell it. To a visitor it was like a voyage through the gastrointestinal tract.

"They took out a third of my duodenum," said a man in a jacket of oatmeat tweed, who for some reason I took to be a slightly younger brother of the oaken cicerone.

"They can do wonders," I said. "Ulcers I guess, eh?" Before he could answer an elderly woman in a Paisley caftan cut in.

"I've had seven polyps removed. I won't say where."

"In a hospital I hope," I said, determined to preserve the light note as well as respect her tone of delicacy.

She lowered her soft brown eyes with an expression of maidenly modesty, which I returned with a kind of acknowledgment of same, intending to communicate gentlemanly respect, knightly you might almost say, somehow also to subtly convey — what? Say an assurance that I knew she had once been a beauty. Suitors at the door whose knocker no longer worked, in fact a piece of which I now had in my pocket. Flowers and chocolates being delivered no end. All that. There was, say, a three-second amorous spell between us, such as youth and age can sometimes share across the chasm of years otherwise cruelly separating them, which I will have to see whether it can actually be reversed with a maiden when my time comes to be a hoary old puss. All this was going on when the spell was broken by an uncle or cousin or something in a ragged red sweater who piped up long enough to say that he'd had six inches taken out of a blood vessel and replaced with nylon tubing. This at least got us out of the GI tract, but not for long. A man in a trench coat chimed in with a tale about something called a dilatation, advised by doctors for his esophagus, for which he hadn't the money. A question was nagging me.

"But aren't you all on Medicare?" I asked.

They shook their heads as one. "That's a form of health insurance, like any other," the guide said. "We can't even afford the premiums, and the meagre Social Security we get barely pays for the barest necessities we have to scratch along on. That's why Greentop must go, so we can huddle out the rest of our days in something smaller. Where we'd get the fee for Melvin's dilatation I don't know, but he should have it. He's always getting things wedged in his crop, so setting down to table with him is very nervous-making."

"What is this dilatation?" I asked.

"A procedure for expanding the esophagus, which in his case has a constriction."

"Right here," said Melvin, who clutched his throat with both hands in a gesture of strangulation dismal to behold, so don't look. But I had experienced a shock of recognition.

"You mean you have trouble swallowing, have to be extra careful, always have a glass of water handy when you eat because things get stuck in there and you have to wait for them to go down, and often give them a little assist?" I said.

"Right."

"Masticate your food thoroughly —"

"Chew it well —"

"Fletcherize it, another generation called it. Why, I have the exact same trouble. Twice I've gone so far as head for a hospital, but each time it went down in the emergency room. Always does, of course, nothing to worry about, but awful scary — Well I'll be damned!"

There is nothing like a common physical complaint to establish a bond between two strangers, and Melvin and I were now blood brothers, each both exaggerating his version of the trouble while assuring the other that it was nothing to worry about — its very persistence bred the caution necessary to safeguard against critical harm.

"You might look into this dilatation thing yourself," Melvin said as we made down a corridor arm-in-arm. "Nothing much to it, do it in the doctor's office. Swallow a tube of some kind or other that spreads the old hatch. Give you a local, Valium and something else, I think, that just makes you feel you've had three martinis."

"Well, I'll certainly look into it."

The stricken oak was visibly annoyed at this diversion as taking my mind off the main business at hand, as were the others, both for that reason and as hypochondriacs from whom the show was being stolen by an interloper. We had been coursing systematically through rooms possessing the large scale expected from the sight of the house itself. Now we reached what was obviously the *pièce de résistance.*

He flung wide both halves of a double door and there was the ballroom, and in fancy your correspondent sweeping across the parquet floor with Cynthia Pickles Teeters in his arms, heedless of the fact that he had two left feet, if not three, and was known to have been known as the Fred Astaire of wallflowers. In this swell hallucination the draperies at the soaring windows had been changed to brocades of another color and richer texture by the new mistress of Greentop, but the great teardrop chandelier I believe they call them remained the same, only its crystals taken down one by one by servants on a ladder and polished till they glittered like diamonds. Our guests would be the *crème de la crème* of Merrymount society, people who when they weren't returning similar hospitality at home were dining at little European restaurants around the corner from something, Chirouble dropping epigrams like trees their autumn leaves, Roxy or another steaming number in *his* arms, all whirling till dawn to the music of a rented five-piece band. Or sometimes an after-dinner movie shown . . .

"Or, if there are children in the family, it can be used as a gymnasium," the guide broke in on my fantasy. Another took its place. In good time two or three lovely children, fruit of this union, tumbling on mats, performing feats on parallel bars, possibly a rowing machine in one corner for their father to remove a middle-age tire not susceptible to being vacuumed out by Dr. what was his name again? "A basket erected at either end."

"How could you play basketball with that chandelier there?"

"That's the only thing you'd have to sacrifice to make the room *double as both*. Now you'll want a tour of the bedrooms, but first let me show you the full basement. You'll want to see for yourself how dry it is."

"But we're in the middle of the worst drouth in ten years."

"That's just it. How dry it is now is exactly how you'll find it after forty days and forty nights of torrential downpour. Let's just look at it now and then go upstairs to the bedrooms."

I tiptoed downstairs after him to the full basement, where I thought that along with showing me how full and dry it was he might be going to dig up a few lepers to clinch the clan's claim to medical destitution, and the reason why a purchaser would know he was getting a steal. But the trip was without further incident in that area, at least for the moment, and then up we trooped to the second floor where, again, the bedrooms were all you'd been led to expect from the outside. Two of the five had fireplaces, and the rest were of decent enough size, and cheerfully chintzed and calicoed up, though one bed seemed to contain an old lady with a bag of frozen parsnips on one shoulder.

"My sister," explained the oaken cicerone as we backed off. "She has osteoarthritis, and has been treating it with moist heat, a Hydrocollator pad we boil in a kettle for her. But it's done no good, so we've been told to try the reverse — cold. We searched high and low for an ice bag, in vain, so somebody got the bright idea we take a bag of something frozen out of the fridge, and it does seem to help, a little. Of course the parsnips will eventually thaw out, and then we'll eat them."

"I love parsnips," I said, gagging. "I sometimes fix them myself the way my mother did. You parboil them and then finish them off by sautéing them in a little butter. A highly underrated vegetable, so rich and sweet. How much are you asking?"

By now I felt so guilty over having taken up this much of their time and energy that I figured the least I owed them was a show of interest I no longer, in fact, genuinely had.

"Three hundred and twenty thousand," he said, "but the price is negotiable."

"Of course it needs a lot of work."

"Still, it's not a barn you'd be converting. That's a great fad around here. Wouldn't take that much doing."

"No. It just needs an editor."

"That what you are? Lots of them around here too, God knows."

"No, I was just..." I was just borrowing another of Chirouble's nifties. He often used it, like on a girl. "She's attractive but she needs an editor," he would say, of someone overdressed, or overcoiffed. Or as a crack about some bloke who talked too much. "I was just using it metaphorically," I told my host. "The grounds have of course been let go to pot. Need a good barbering."

"God knows. But you see that's another thing. We can't afford a gardener. How high would you be prepared to go?"

"Well, actually, I'm a little tight myself these days. I had set a hundred and seventy-five thousand as my top."

"Sold."

That rather set me back on my heels. I had named the figure mostly to discourage him, and now the guilt over wasting these people's time was compounded by the implication that I was a deadbeat welshing on a deal if I didn't go through with it. I met the embarrassment by stammering out something about the folly of putting a binder on something till you've had an architect or at least a builder go over it for you.

"We'd take a very small binder."

"I've only got about thirty dollars on me," I said, hoping to laugh this thing out of court.

"I'll take it."

Stark, staring mad, I shelled out three tens, more as a way of compensating the occupants for their time, besides facilitating a quick exit. After all, they didn't know my name, as far as I remembered from the phone conversation, and this would at least buy the arthritic patient an ice bag with enough left over to keep them in parsnips for a few days. Mumbling some fake name when asked for one, and declining a receipt, I scuttled down the stairs and out of the house, trailing assurances that if I wished to pursue the matter further they would hear from me about an appointment with an architect. The door having closed behind me, I managed to slip the knocker back into its hinge and hightail it toward my car.

Halfway down the driveway, I stopped, shut off the ignition, and, out of some curiosity I only half understood myself, doubled back on foot among the trees to the rear of the property. I guess it was my Gatsby dream dying hard. I wanted to see at least more of the acreage, which presumably ran to the stream itemized in the heartbreaking ad. Sure enough there was a brook, down to a trickle in the drouth. And there was a pool, with a few rubber animals bobbing faintly in it, and ringed by garden chairs. Had it slipped the host's mind, or had he decided it was unnecessary to show it? There were a few fruit trees and another withered garden. A patio with some more summer chairs on it. Looking past it, I could see through a French window into a "morning room" I had been shown on the tour. Something about the figures moving around in it made me steal up for a closer look.

The transformation was remarkable. Everybody had perked up, no doubt buoyed by news of a buyer. It being the cocktail hour, they all lounged or sauntered about with drinks in their hands, chatting and gesturing with great animation. The woman in the Paisley caftan made a remark that had them all laughing. The man in the jacket of oatmeal tweed leaned against the wall, smoking a pipe. Nor had their health gone unrestored. Not a sign of infirmity. Jesus of Nazareth had been through, and all was well. I could make out no one to indicate that the old woman with arthritis had taken up her bed and walked, though she may have been the figure in an armchair with her back to the windows — or she may have been their one legitimate claim to pity.

Healed too was my sense of guilt. Slipping past the side of the house and climbing back into my car, I decided I would now have no compunctions about bringing Cynthia along for a look after all, both to get her opinion and to fortify my position as a suitor seriously searching for property. I telephoned right off to ask her to dinner — to learn from Mrs. Rampart that she was again "away for a few days." Where the hell was she now, what were these mysterious trips? Fired up, I asked whether in that case I might drop in and pay my respects to Mrs. Pickles. It was all part of my cause, Mother's good opinion of me being important to nurse along.

Mrs. Rampart set the phone down to convey my request to her mistress, returning a moment later. "Yes, Mrs. Pickles would be delighted if you could come and have a Presbyterian with her. About six."

I arrived with a miniature bottle of vodka secreted in my pocket, from which to furtively pour a dollop into my Presbyterian, which resultant concoction, quite good actually, I called a backslider. "You might make it brief," Mrs. Rampart suggested when she let me in. "We aren't too well this afternoon."

That was true enough. We weren't. Indeed, we verged on the dismal. Our digestion was upset, our eyes were troubling us, and we were getting punk rock on our bridgework. I had a flash of short-term *déjà vu* on this; I mean it was like a continuation of the very scene I had just been through, except that in this case I knew the complaints to be legitimate. I suggested we go downstairs into the parlor, where I knew there was no reception of the local radio programs on Mrs. Pickles' teeth, but she preferred to remain in the bedroom alcove into which I had been shown, where a shaft of afternoon sunlight slanting through a window brightened the scene up, and where everything was so pinkly cozy. Mrs. Rampart fetched us our Presbyterians and withdrew, leaving me free to wander into a corner and surreptitiously unscrew the cap from my vodka miniature and empty its contents into my glass.

"I don't know where Cynthia is myself," she said. "Young people don't regard themselves as accountable to their parents anymore, as we did when we were young, I can tell you."

"And that's a loss, from a moral point of view," I said, after a healthy slug from my backslider. "The home is breaking up, values going to pot, no sense of — cohesion."

We went on in this vein for quite some time.

"It's the parents themselves' fault," she said. "We shouldn't have relaxed our grip. Of course Cynthia is only my stepdaughter, but even so. The principle is the same. Young people are running wild. Stay out all hours, no explanation. In my day, a girl was in bed by ten-thirty."

"They're in bed a lot earlier than that today," I wanted to

say, but checked myself. I would have had to say it with a delicately shaded sense of ironic disapproval that I didn't trust myself to bring off. The strain of hypocrisy was already beginning to tell. "Nowadays the children raise the parents," I said.

"You put things so well. What college did you go to, Edward?"

"Knox," I said, meaning to justify the deception by thinking of it as a contraction of the school of hard knocks. Something like that. In any case, I didn't want to let on that I hadn't gone to college at all, for fear of downgrading myself as matrimonial timber around here. I may already have mentioned that I didn't even finish high school. I dropped out in the eleventh grade when a psychopathic English teacher tried to make me memorize a poem called "The Hound of Heaven" in its entirety. I never stayed with it long enough to find out who was chasing who, or why. And I mean lines like, "Up vistaed hopes I sped; / And shot, precipitated, Adown Titanic glooms of chasmèd fears." If that isn't a mouthful of marbles I don't know poetry. I told the demented teacher as much. (He was eventually put away.)

"Where is it?"

"Where is what?"

"Knox."

"I think it's in Massachusetts," I said, picking a state bursting with the right kind of ivy-clad educational institutions. "But getting back to the integrity of the home, or lack of it today, I've been looking around for a home myself — that is, a house in which to *make* a home. I'd like to settle down around here. Put down some roots. I've just examined a really capital property that only needs a little fixing up. I might have to throw in another thirty or forty thousand, but we'll see. Well, this has been most jolly. I don't want to tire you by overstaying my welcome. I just wanted to pop in and pay my respects. You must tell Cynthia I called."

"Perhaps you'll go to church with me sometime."

"That would be nice. I don't think it's too much to ask a man to worship his Maker one day a week."

"That's another cause for the general breakdown. No sense of a Divine Being. One who, having created us, knows our nature and our needs."

"That we're dual creatures. Physical on the one hand, spiritual on the other. And so He has given us the means of administering to both elements. He gives us — how shall I put it? He gives us ham hocks for our bodies and hollyhocks for our souls."

"That's very well expressed. You must come from a nice family."

"Thank you. I like to think so. And a happy one."

Happy families are all different, no two alike, I thought to myself as I drove away. I believe someone has said that, or something like it, and it's the truth. Each is happy in its own individual way, while domestic misery tends to have about it a certain gray uniformity. You've certainly never seen any like mine. Don't worry, I'm not going into a flashback here, but I was moved to a little reminiscence by the contrasting history of unhappiness associated with the house I had just left. There could hardly have been much warmth and joy in it, as there had been in mine. And *color.* Yes, lots of color. Take for example my father.

The first thing he did on arising was draw on a pair of pajamas. Having slept in the raw all night, what else would you do if you fancied lounging around in deshabble, as he called it, through breakfast, before dressing for work? Movies and television commercials showing entire families chattering fully clothed at the breakfast table always make me laugh, they're so grotesquely unlike the facts. My old man slumped in deshabble, and looking more than ever like Marie Dressler after a good night's sleep, is certainly closer to the domestic truth. One of my earliest memories is of Pop slouched in deshabble with his legs stretched under the kitchen table of a Saturday morning, closer to noon, drinking a cup of Mom's sump-pump coffee à la maison, which, the spoon dish being empty just then, he stirred with a ballpoint pen with which he happened to be doing some budget figuring. I remember to this day his overturning the pen so as to muddle in the sugar and cream with the butt end rather than the writing tip, which seemed to me to strike a nice balance between indifference and discrimination. He was nothing if not fastidious.

Had there been under Mrs. Pickles' childhood roof, or Cynthia's for that matter, half the fun there was under mine? Pop had a little shtick about eyeballs, with which he amused first us and then the neighborhood kids. He would start with some factual remarks about how they were prized as a delicacy among Orientals like the Arabs, who found sheep's eyes a particularly luscious tidbit, and then proceed to pantomime eating one of his own. He would "pluck it out" with his fingertips, close the lid to signify its removal and permanent loss, and pop it into his mouth. A long rigmarole of gourmet pleasure would ensue. He would thrust his tongue first into one cheek and then into the other to produce suggestive bulges telling you where the dainty was, roll his remaining eye in an ecstatic display of savoring it, enact some chewing motions, and swallow. "Mmm, delicious," he would say, and walk away, leaving us or the neighborhood urchins entertained, except for some of the younger tots whom the vivid routine scared half out of their wits.

96

And Mom! She sometimes wore around her neck a locket which she said was a talisman that warded off superstition. She claimed its magical properties — the ability to make you a skeptic immune to all the occult foolishness going around — could be transmitted from her to others when the moon was full, provided a certain ritual was enacted. On such occasions she would swing it back and forth in front of your nose, intoning, "Abracadabra chicken gumbo, now you're safe from mumbo jumbo."

She referred to Pop as "my horny-handed mate" when he openly pawed her after coming home from a day's work, a designation even more earned behind the closed bedroom door through which my kid sister, Petal, and I often heard unmistakable sounds of dalliance. "As though there aren't enough of us already," Petal would say, and once or twice she even went so far as to shout through the door, "Hey, there's enough of us already!" That was when she came to years of discretion. With the door open there was sport for more general consumption. They shared a certainly spacious enough dresser, but Mom filled her half and even crowded over into Pop's with things like blouses and sweaters that could easily enough be hung in a closet. "This is bureaucratic waste!" he would shout, flinging garments in all directions like an F.B.I. agent searching a suspect's room, and once he shoved Mom against the highboy in question with such a burst of affectionate good spirits that she sustained a dislocated shoulder that semi-crippled her arm for some time. Their life together was hilarious.

But the one I truly adored was Petal. She was well named, if you think of the flakes of the rose. How had my parents stumbled on it? They said it just came to them at the sight of the pink cherub to whom my mother had given birth. With each passing year it more sweetly fit her, as the pinkly glowing skin seemed ever more tightly to encase a slim young body that itself appeared about to burst into flower. Most of all in the nubile years about which we are now talking.

We were crazy about each other. Neither had a more cherished playmate than the other. I would read to Petal in the bed we often shared in innocent childhood years, until my adolescence and then hers began to make our intimacy a rather ticklish business. We are now past playing doctor and all that. One critical night, there in the dark beneath covers we had once used merely to conceal a flashlight with which to read a book after hours, we wriggled out of the pajamas our parents insisted we wear while they reached a decision about how long this could go on. The delicious peril of gathering Petal naked into my arms still burns in my memory, along with the struggle to purge from my instincts every intention I knew was wrong. The desire and the guilt together fused in a flame called shame. I was fourteen to Petal's twelve, old enough to understand and sense and, now at last, wickedly savor the girl on the brink of bursting into maturity. I fancied I could feel the unarrived breasts swelling under the hard buds. My hot hands grazed downward over slopes and hollows I knew forbidden, maidenly sculpture that was at once the last of baby fat and the first of womanhood. "We shouldn't, Eddie," she whispered in my ear, and I gulped out a strangled "No." "Oh, my God, your . . . your . . . Is this the way it gets then when . . . ?" And so I may as well confess that this was my inaugural swoon. What an initiation! Even now I relive the pride and satisfaction of not having deflowered my pet. Now I can cherish to the end of my days an affection forever untarnished by defilement.

Obviously sensing what turn our childhood romps might be taking, our parents banned any further nesting together. "All right," Pop said, sticking his head in the door later that very night, luckily to find us once more back in our pajamas, "we're not Egyptians, and you're no Pharaoh that has to keep the royal lineage pure by mating with his sister. Back to your room, Buster. Amscray."

Not that our sport together was entirely over. It only assumed a more acceptable form. With a camera I got for my next birthday I took endless pictures of Petal. Petal posing in an apple tree, stretched out languorously in the tall grass chewing a blade of it, sitting in a rowboat trailing a hand in the water. It was only a so-so camera, which, together with my own lack of skill, may have made for a few shots possessing the "poetic" quality we celebrate in scenes shot a hundred or more years ago when the camera was in its infancy. This poetic quality arises more than half from the rudimentariness of the instrument; the cab horses steaming under streetlamps and storefronts in snowstorms naturally have the mystic feeling that results from poor definition, obtaining for the photographers having no better equipment to work with a vagueness and indistinctness like that of impressionistic paintings. As I say, I sometimes got it myself when I shot from too great a distance on a cloudy day, or used the wrong exposure. There is a haunting shot of my parents where they look like ectoplasm. Perhaps that was going too far. But anyway, this vagueness and lack of clarity does have its charm for that very reason, no doubt like some of the poetry being turned out at the time when shutterbugs were clicking away at their "nocturnes." The glory departs when you can make things out in too great detail. The poetry turns to prose. This baloney about photography being an art form isn't heard so much anymore except when you get another of those musum "retrospectives" showing old barns and bobtail nags and farm wives churning butter, shot with equipment contemporary with the bobtail nags and butter churns themselves. With the perfection of the camera, photography ceased to be an art form.

Next I went on to a movie camera — whereby hangs our tale (and maybe, ultimately, me). My fascination with *that* led on to my getting into the line of work I did, and a subject matter that is part and parcel of my attitude toward women and sex. One of total piety. The former are sacred vessels of the latter. It's what has made me a feminist. I see now that I have indeed slipped into a brief flashback, and also why. It comes to me even as I bring it to a close. It was obviously from my adoration of Petal that my chivalrous view of women arose. And that knightly deference is summoned and reflected once more in regards to the woman on whom it is just now particularly focused. When after a week Cynthia still hadn't returned my call, I gave her one more chance. I buzzed her again.

SIX

❧

How to Sink or Swim

SHE WAS still away, but this time it developed that her step-mother had learned she was in Wilmington, Delaware, which I knew to contain an uncle more than comfortably well off, whom she was probably hitting up for the last of the capital needed to start *Overview* rolling. Expected back in a few days. I was dying to see her, but not dead to the possibility, even feasibility, of other pastures pending her return. I narrowed them down to Roxy and Toby, in that order of preference, if possible for a bed date. All the more so because of my impatience to see Cynthia and solidify my position in that quarter. My reasoning was as follows.

If you're eager to marry someone, it's important that that eagerness be not dictated solely by mere physical attraction, which is notorious for clouding the judgment and setting people on the road to Reno via the middle aisle. I must make certain that I wanted Cynthia as a spiritual companion and lifelong helpmeet, for whatever length of time, a factor to be intelligently sorted out from the simple hots. That objective is best realized by a young blade not simply chafing under two or three weeks of sexual starvation.

The most desirable lover pro tem on the local scene was undoubtedly Roxy, but that would entail a major seduction from scratch, which if realized might muddle the very emotions I was trying to clear here by separating them from plain animal instincts. It could introduce into the picture a bona fide infatuation rivaling that for Cynthia herself — which, remember, I was trying to parlay into matrimony, an honorable estate (whoever happens to have it — the estate). Besides, I wasn't sure, despite my latest information, but what Roxy *was* Chirouble's current squeeze, which might, if I got lucky, muck up a friendship as well as a romance. Or two romances. Ergo, it must not be Roxy simply because I wanted her. No, infinitely the saner one-night choice would be Toby, already a memorable precedent in that department, while leaving no serious injuries. Her being, like me, also half of a meaningful relationship put us on a similar footing. (Assuming her rather rickety engagement to the real estate broker was still on.) And lo and behold if Providence itself didn't lend a hand in these matters by arranging that I run into Toby exactly at this time.

I bought at one of the new gourmet take-out places springing up everywhere a quart of their minestrone, which I especially liked, to make a lunch of. "You must like this, you buy it so often," said the pretty Japanese girl who worked there. I found when I got it back to my apartment that it needed salt, but the saltcellar was empty, so I filled it from the Morton's box. Just as I was about to screw the cap back on the shaker the phone rang, and when I finished the call I had forgotten the cap was still loose, and so when I went to season the soup the entire contents of the shaker cascaded into it, ruining it of course. But perhaps not totally. It was a small shaker, and maybe doubling the soup might make it edible. So I dashed around the corner to where the food shop was and bought another quart. "You must *really* like this, to be putting it away at that rate," the girl said. "I'm expecting guests," I said, paid for the second lot, and hurried back home. Still too salty — but one more quart should do the trick. So back I trotted. "Some unexpected friends called, and I'm having more people than I figured on," I hurriedly got in before the girl could get in her refrain. It was when I steamed out the door that I bumped into Toby Snapper.

"Well, if it isn't Monty Carlo," says the little wasp.

"I don't know what you're talking about."

"Oh, come on, who do you think you're fooling?"

"*Whom* do I think I'm fooling. In what regard?" Playing dead on my part was the quickest way to get all this out in the open.

"I saw part of that movie, from the back of the room of course, when I could pop up from me proper chores below stairs, downcha know," she said, threatening to wing off into that awful little cockney shtick of hers. "Oi remembered your offering to put the little match girl into the moom pitchas, that night you 'auled 'er off to your lair, and then when Oi saw the bloke in the nude scenes had a strawberry mark on 'is 'ip exactly where you have yours, why, Oi put more than two and two together. 'E acts in the below-the-waist arf of the films as well as produces them, just like I guessed that time we was one flesh." She turned that smile on. "Must be fun being the stuntman for the pretty boy playing the part. You still haven't answered the question I asked that time. How do you get it up for the camera?"

"You are a brat, aren't you? But I like your flapping shirt, and those no doubt designer jeans. I thought I'd tuck my shirttails in today, in keeping with the new formality."

Annoyance had grown into resentment, which now showed signs of billowing into the hostility that often as not turns into a rage for sexual conquest. But I was still short of again wanting the date her snide chatter had begun to cool me on. I suddenly had to know the worst of what I could be up against (other than what might be dished up by the law).

"I suppose you go blabbing this all over town?"

" 'Oo, me? Naow. Your secret's safe wif me. Oi wouldn't go queerin' 'is chances wif the quality 'e's bent on gettin' in wif. Especially the princess." Here she patted her back hair and settled over on one hip, in a gesture intended to mock elegance but misfiring hilariously as an unintentional spoof of Mae West. I laughed with relief and said, "How about dinner tomorrow? Tonight then."

The unfailing thrill of watching a woman undress, Toby enhanced by making a striptease of it, thus throwing in a little more out-of-pocket entertainment. She made me wriggle into garments she shucked off, thus getting in return a little transvestite amusement for herself. This she even escalated by insisting I let her make me up, and I felt a bit of a fool as she knelt in front of my chair and applied mascara, rouge, and even lipstick. "From lowly origins, 'e sank to utter degeneracy," she said. She even made me press my mouth over a tissue as women do, for reasons I've never understood. To even off the paint job I suppose. When we kissed, the result made us look like children who had been at the jam pot. "There, don't you get a secret charge out of this?" she said, leading me to the bureau mirror. "Psychologists tell me we've all got both sexes in us." I shuddered at the spectre of myself in the glass and turned away, wondering what people would think if I died and was found this way. As I pulled her dress off over my head I asked whether she still had "this open engagement" with the real estate agent, which allowed such latitude in the pursuit of happiness. She didn't answer, her own cat curiosity having been roused by a script lying on the dresser.

"*Coin of the Realm.* What does that mean?"

"It's the term for a nation's currency. That's a screenplay I've been working on for two years, and that I'll produce myself if I can't get one of the major studios to do it."

"Your serious work, for which the other is your bread and butter while you plug away at it," she mused, riffling the pages, pausing here and there to read a line. A naked girl flipping through your opus in a standing position, while you itch to get her into bed, is not the idealest test of literary merit. She read a few of the lines aloud while I drew the covers back. " 'Tom: I want to marry you the worst way, Lila, and that would be in my present impecunious state, I'm afraid. Lila: But I'll never marry you if you quit your painting and take that job your uncle's offering you, even at that salary. *Boy Not Shooting Pheasant* is the best thing you've done.' "

She let the script fall closed and turned around.

"Would the theme be that money has nothing to do with happiness?"

"Something like that."

"Well, lots of writers have got rich saying it," she said, and popped between the sheets. What an uncanny echo of my own observation!

Any irritation with that shrew's tongue vanished in the other uses to which she could put it. She was a delicious tactician, whose tantalizing preliminaries brought out your own best virtuosity. Only one unfortunate coincidence marred our bliss. I was expecting an important call, and that came as we were going into orbit. There was nothing to do but reach for the phone without disengaging myself. It was, as anticipated, Jack Krumholz, who directed all my stuff.

"Eddie? Everything is set. I've got the studio for three weeks, but we *have to start Monday.*"

"I'll call you back."

"No. I'm leaving for the Coast in an hour and can't be reached. I've got them all lined up. Mea Culpa, Jack Sweeper again, and a new find, a girl who bills herself as Miss Fore and Aft. You'll see hee-hee why."

"I — I'll guh guh — Oh, my God."

"What the hell's the matter with you, Teeters? You sound like you're aboard a bucking bronco."

Indeed my partner, in what were now mid-throes, was heaving and thrashing beneath me, arching herself in paroxysms that might in the end very well have thrown her rider but meanwhile must have made her oblivious to the distraction in which I was trying desperately to suspend my own. That in fact was one of the male arts in which viewers were schooled in an early Sexucational short — "keeping yourself on hold for the lady." A business discussion with someone giving you a buzz might be considered an ideal retardant, but it is no circumstance under which to execute an orgasm already under way. There seemed no way of putting a stop to either it or the phone call. That much was becoming apparent. I tried to end the conversation and hang up, but Krumholz went on.

"By the way I love your title for the new one. *Toot Suite.* They get drunk in this hotel, and you know what slays me?"

"What?" I panted.

"What's the hell's the matter with you, you got asthma or something? You sound like you're hyperventilating."

"No. Well, maybe a little."

"The scene where she opens the telegram while he's barking up the canyon."

"Oh, my God," I moaned, in a combination of now irreversible convulsions and sheer disgust with Krumholz's vulgarisms, which on the set had always, for me, degraded the depiction of life's greatest joy. Toby, for instance, thrashing naked under me while she rocked her head from side to side in wild abandon typified, in that sense, pure spirit. The sacred spirit of man purged, rather than consumed, by his very animal flame.

"What's that noise in the background?"

"Jack, I suh — suh — simply must — Oh, my glug glug . . . You'll have to ex —" The phone, which I tried to drop into its cradle, missed, and the whole works fell off the bedside table to the floor, where it landed with a hideous clatter. The last of my rapture was pierced by the sound of Krumholz faintly yelling from what seemed a thousand miles away. Then Toby and I were lying, spent, beside each other.

When our hearts had stopped hammering and we had quite recovered our breath, she said, "What in the hell was that all about?"

I leaned down and picked up the phone, from which instead of Krumholz's baffled jabbering now came a recorded woman's voice saying something about hanging up and trying again. I settled everything to rights on the nightstand and swung back to Toby.

"It's a new short we're going to start shooting. That was my director and sort of advance man. I had to take the call. I'm sorry."

"That's O.K. I was only half conscious anyway. As we all are when shooting the rapids. The French have a term for it which I can't remember. *La mort* something. Do you know it?"

"No. I flunked the course in high school. Hey, wait, I think I do know the phrase. I've heard or read it somewhere. *La mort douche.* Could that be it?"

"I don't think so, but it means something like sweet death. We really are out like a light then, oblivious to everything. What's this new movie?"

I explained that *Toot Suite* referred to a drunken revel some groupies have in a hotel. "A total round robin debauch."

"And this is a training film on the art of love?"

"Well, that's just the point, you see. The moral of the scene. This is *not* the way to go about it. Sex should be *intensive*, not extensive. Its aim is to show how libertines abuse the new freedom. A cautionary tale we say."

"And the audience gets its hacks while being preached to."

She sat up, and after giving me a cynical grin, reached over to the table on her side and dug a couple of cigarettes from her bag. She lit both and gave me one. "I once served at a catered party here where Bette Davis was a guest, and she said that Paul Henreid improvised that famous bit. Made it up right there on the set."

"We do that a lot. Wing things. Don't let everything get too fixed and rigid. Give the actors a certain amount of free play — in fact *demand* it of them. Helps get spontanuity into it, as Krumholz says. They're amusing, those mistakes of his. But what gravels me is all those expressions for sexual acts that I swear I've never heard of. He used one just now. For instance, for oral sex with a woman, have you ever heard the term —? Never mind. I hate it so it grates on me every time I hear it, so why should I inflict it on you?"

"What is it?"

"No. It would be degrading to you, as a woman. As, yes, a lady."

"Tell me about some of your other virtues. Like you justify the por — the erotica as a source of money to do your serious work. Like that script. The end justifies the means, is that it?"

"Not at all. My erotica needs no defense. It's justifiable in its own right. Are you and the realtor still an item?"

"No. Are you and I?"

When I didn't answer immediately, being thoroughly occupied with dragging on my cigarette, wadding the pillow under my head and other business, as we call it in the dramatic arts, she undertook to reply for me.

"You want the princess. Well, I'll tell you something. We're a pair, you and I. You're just about exactly as much over your head with her as I am with you. We're both trying to step out of our class, bat out of our own league."

"Didn't you regard yourself as doing so with the realtor? Dealing, no doubt, as they all like to call it, in 'selected properties.' "

"We've at least got that in common," she went on, ignoring my interruption. "I think it's a lot, don't you?"

"Right. Makes us compatible," I babbled on.

"If you plan to ask her to marry you, will you tell her before or after? What you do I mean. I gather she hasn't tumbled yet."

"You make it sound like I own a string of brothels or something."

"It's what Oi 'ears below stairs. 'E's not only a porn king 'e's a vice lord wif a string o' brothels from 'ere to Buenos Haires, is wot Oi 'ears."

"Look, if you're going on with this bit, I'll stake you to a diction coach. You ought to get it right. You are a little vixen, as you must know, but on you it looks good. Seems to fit, somehow. You'd be incomplete without the bitch facet. I'm beginning to rather like it. It's what Oi says when Oi 'ears talk about you as a toff above stairs. She'd be incomplete wiffout it."

She was a great little ordainer of silences, one of the best in a profession at which woman are notoriously tops, and she ordained one now. Not that silence is exactly the word for a pause in which she smoked a cigarette. Again as lots of women will, she would suck back a deep mouthful of smoke, inhaling it with a popping separation of her lips. Watching Toby smoke made me more mindful of the surgeon general's warning than when I lit up myself. She spoke at last.

"When are you going to ask her? The princess."

"You make it sound like I've got some kind of timetable."

What would she think if she knew my dating her was part of the preparation? Lying here beside her now, it seemed kind of farfetched, in an almost idiotically grotesque sort of way. Yet I had made my plans soberly. The silence of which we were now joint proprietors threatened the prospect of "seconds," as Krumholz crudely put it. I should get another director. He cheapened everything, bellowing those seamy instructions through his megaphone. "All right, let's go for the tapioca." His slang for the male delivery. "Let's go for a take now as he pops his tallow." My God, he was low.

There must have been some ESP in the bend Toby now gave the conversation. After turning away long enough to stamp out her cigarette in an ashtray on the table there, she turned back and with that mischievous grin on which she had a patent said: "You remember you asked me the first time if I'd like to get in pictures? What if I said yes now? Not showing my face, or being named in the cast or anything, but like you. Maybe a scene with us together. We are pretty good together you'll admit. We could dish them up a fine little old sequence or two. Even those positions of yours that have no redeeming social value, as even the Supreme Court would admit."

This took me by surprise, while also sparking my interest. It might be a special experience doing a scene with someone you had some genuine feeling for, as I suddenly realized I had for Toby, despite all attempts to put a brake on my emotions. But the very recognition of these emotions simultaneously dampened any enthusiasm for the idea. Of publicly putting on a two-backed-beast display with her. (Is that from Shakespeare?) There were more serious bugs in the notion, which had not been there when I had proposed it myself. Namely that any participation of Toby's in the projects at hand might in some way cause her to really betray my connection with them. That worry was part and parcel of the question on which Toby had cunningly put her finger just now. How long could I postpone the inevitable with Cynthia? I worked out a scenario as Toby, her query unanswered, slept beside me. It seemed ethically waterproof. See what you think.

I would propose to Cynthia and then soon afterward reveal that I was Monty Carlo. If she had turned me down, there would be nothing lost. If she'd said yes, she'd be free to break the engagement as having been contracted in bad faith by a suitor who had not laid all his cards on the table and who must have known in his heart of hearts, just because he had failed to do so, that a woman in her social and professional position could not without embarrassment be the wife of a man in mine. But aha! Hold it. That would expose her to the same charge of hypocrisy, as one who freely enjoyed herself as long as the stuff objected to was shown for the amusement of the social set of which she was a part. Was the suitor "unsavory"? Not so unsavory as to keep his secret until he married her; only until after he had been accepted. And his justification lay in eliminating from her consideration everything except the man himself, irrespective of what he might be doing. A case could have been made out for actually marrying before spilling the beans, on the ground that now I had made a bundle sufficient to support me as I put the past behind me and turned to my serious work. But that far I wouldn't go.

Having solidified my plan of action, I turned out the last of the lights and slipped back in beside the gently breathing Toby.

Sleep was elusive. The night was hot, and through a number of open windows I could hear at intervals Mr. Hammock's motorboat snore next door. Toby showed fewer qualms about staying out all night than the first time. Had her parents relaxed their discipline? She put her own foot down? She kicked back the single sheet I had drawn up, leaving us both naked again. She had her back to me, and I wanted to put an arm around her and take a breast in my hand, while pressing my loins against the even more voluptuous twin hillocks there. What a sumptuous bundle she was. What a wife for the right man. And she wouldn't *turn* waspish, she was already all she would ever be of that, and as part of her nature it was mostly unmalicious teasing. She was tart-sweet, like a — what? Macoon apple? No, like a damson plum. Maybe she just needled to keep me off guard, to show her advantage over me without exercising it. Keep the whip in view and you won't have to crack it, etc. It was sweet of her to consider me above her station. Couldn't marriage to a more superior person raise the level of the inferior? It was known to have done so, despite a sour epigram I read somewhere that such a life is always lived on the level of the lower of the two parties to a marriage. Wouldn't the reverse, to improve the lesser, be Cynthia's task with me? One already commenced that first day around the pool?

I wished I hadn't branched off into that line of thought, because I seemed to have carried the problem into my sleep, which was restless. There was my recurring dream of trying to eat pizza through a catcher's mask, along with the standard "frustration" ones everybody's familiar with — frantic inability to find a street, to get through to someone on the telephone. I kept waking up, but there were no "seconds" until daybreak brought with it the customary signs of male revival. "Dawn," Toby mumbled, maneuvering submissively into position under me. "The crowing of the cock."

I made a mental note to work that in somewhere, with taste. On the back burner was a training film that would show the uses of bawdy humor in lending zest to a relationship possibly in need of some such stimulant. An entire short giving instructive examples, with helpful illustrations. Mea Culpa wasn't too good at either the literary *or* comedic side of things, but Toby here — she might be just the ticket. Though of course that would entail the head shots which were mainly what she wanted to stay out of. I must avoid unwisely entangling Toby in the series. I might regret it. No, best not to take her up on the suggestion.

"Have you always wanted to be a hunk?" she said, climbing out of bed.

Just what was that supposed to mean? I lay there brooding on it till she came back out of the shower.

"No," I said. "I just want to be a knight in shiny armor."

"It was quite a bash."

Cynthia was back and she and I were dining at Hercule's, and, everything there was to tell about her profitable descent on the Wilmington uncle having been told on the drive over, she wanted to reminisce about Chirouble's party. She smiled as she cut into her duck *à l'orange* and said, "This Monty Carlo character, the producer. I seem to remember your saying at lunch by the pool that day that you knew him, and that he was — I think it was your word — sensitive?"

"None sensitiver."

She laughed openly. "But some other things as well. That name — rather cleverly cooked up to suggest the idea that he was taking a gamble with this stuff, I must say — and the whole ruse of their being training films. Sheer porno under the guise of sex education. What a way to pull everyone's leg, while telegraphing a word to the wise that we all know it's a subterfuge."

"Oh, not to him, I wouldn't say. Monty?"

I doubt that she even heard my protest for the amusement with which she went on, "Even the name of the production company. Sexucational Films, Inc. Was that masterstroke his idea too?"

"That's right — I think."

"What's his real name?"

"That's it, as far as I know. Oh, it could be like Montgomery Carlton or something, and he just condensed it into something catchy."

"As he telescoped 'sex education.'" She shook her head in appreciation. "I'd like to meet him."

"You may."

"He's the world's biggest four-flusher or he's one smart apple."

"He's no four-flusher, that I assure you. So how's your duck? Is the rice wild enough for you?"

This was not as lamebrained as it may sound. The rice in question looked a little two-toned, lots of white in among the brown, meaning that backstage at Hercule's they were not above mixing Uncle Ben's long-grain in with whatever was flown in from the Minnesota lake districts. Cynthia agreed with my criticisms. I was having the chicken *Véronique*, despite my history of having poultry tend to lodge in my gullet, like that Greentop tenant with whom you may remember I compared notes on the tribulation. There was precious little *Véronique* on mine to help lubricate the breast meat on its downward journey, and I was experiencing the nervousness I must avoid when tucking in dindin, for fear of eating too fast and winding up in Chokesville. For I was in a tizzy of indecision. Was I being handed the God-given moment to unmask myself, to she whom my heart desired? She who would be damn well stuck with the praise she had just been showering on me? Or should I stay with the timetable meticulously worked out while lying in bed with Toby? It was a nasty tough dilemma, and for a second or two the mental wheels spun in vain. Then I opted for the latter, while totally unsure that I hadn't let the psychological moment slip by. Cynthia at least delayed its ultimate departure.

"I suppose you know him as a movie man yourself."

"Right. And, oh, as to that, I finished *Coin of the Realm*. At least the third draft. I'm anxious to have you read it."

"Oh, by all means, Eddie. I wish you'd brought it along tonight."

"Tonight we're celebrating your getting the last coin of the realm you need to start rolling with *Overview*. Here's to an early first issue and hundreds more."

"Cheers." When we put our wineglasses down again I found we had by no means changed the subject. "Where does he live? Your friend. The porn genius."

"Nowhere in particular and everywhere in general. Itchy foot, like me in many ways." It was like walking a high wire with thin ice for a net. Her flick of a glance revived a feeling that this was a cat-and-mouse, with no certainty as to who was what. "But now I want to settle down."

All right. I was "playing fair" with Cynthia the way murder mystery writers are honor-bound to do with the reader, by planting all the clues necessary to the solution. It was a perilously ticklish moment as I paid out just a little bit more in the form of a sly grin of the kind she might have expected from cunningly prankish good old Monty Carlo as conceived by herself. But she didn't seem to tumble. She returned to the surgery ever entailed by Long Island duck. My secret was safe — for the time being. Mine would be the moral advantage of revealing my identity at the time of my choosing according to the scenario, with all that soul-searching beside the slumbering Toby, not the chagrin of having it discovered and thus being caught out. And I would have played it square, like an Agatha Christie pro. I forged stealthily ahead, on a cue picked up from a few moments before.

"Cynthia, speaking of settling down, I mean it. I've been looking at properties while you were away."

"You have?" More surgery, tricky especially around the shoulder joint. "Whatever for?"

"I'm weary of being a wanderer on the face of the earth. I want to put down roots right here in Merrymount. To that end, now that I have the financial means, I feel I want to buy a house. Have you ever heard of an estate called Greentop? Just off Two Ledge Road, there at the edge of town. I'd like you to come look at it with me." Here my heart began to pound, yet the question shot out easily as a melon pip from between your fingers. "See if it's something you might like to be carried over the threshold of."

I felt my cheeks burn as my eyes fell. When I looked up I saw that she had raised her own eyes from the inoperable duck. She dropped her knife and fork and became all melted woman as she smilingly gazed at me, cocking her head now to one side now the other in tender evaluation. There was absolutely nobody like her. She was Toby to the life in being your hard-surface-soft-center Christmas candy. Or another comparison springing to mind was Pepperidge Farm's claims for its line of croissants as extolled by the hick currently doing their television plugs: crisp and crunchy on the outside, soft and pully on the inside. It was to that steaming pith, her woman's heart of hearts, that I appealed by gently humming, "You'd be so nice to come home to ... Dum de dum da da da dum ... Well, is it yes or no?"

I counted two or three expressions on her face, for surprise, fluster, delight, even the maidenly confusion for which it was technically a little late. I experienced again the pang of regret that she for whom my heart yearned had given herself to me that fast; I might have appreciated having been a little stalled, even repulsed. But then you can't have everything. Not the way things are these days.

"There's no question of yes or no, Eddie. I want you to understand that I'm not replying to a proposal — and believe me I'm flattered to the soles of my feet — when I say it's not a question of not wanting to marry you. I don't want to get married period. Marriage and a family just aren't in the cards for me — much to Amanda's disappointment."

I was left to ponder this while the waiter with perfect bad timing toddled over and refilled our wineglasses, from a bottle of white Burgundy the name of which I had forgotten since pointing at its number in the cellar book, and which I thought I should catch now in case it became "our" wine. At last he left, having turned the empty bottle upside down in the ice bucket preparatory to carting it all away. I would never know what "our" Burgundy was — not much loss considering the headway my proposal was making.

With Daffy Duck given up as a goner on the operating table, Cynthia scooped up a forkful of the semi-wild rice and tucked it into that cherry mouth. "And Eddie, I'm frankly worried. Now that I've flatly laid it on the line to her that she'll have no grandchildren from me, she's reopened this crazy business about adopting one, *seriously*. My refusal to even pursue such a nonsensical thing with her has made her more angry with me, so it's a kind of vicious circle. Not only wouldn't she put a nickel of her considerable money into *Overview,* which she foresees as just another heathen modern publication, she may even disinherit me."

Hey, how about me, here? How about me in rejection? I refused to accept it.

"You're all a man could ask for in a woman," I persisted. "Certainly all I've ever dreamt."

"She heard a panel discussion on TV in which one of the participants was a 'single adoptive parent.' So if the agencies are loosening up that much, in recognition of what divorces themselves have done to parenting, why not give someone a grandchild to love and care for? What did you say? Look, Eddie, it's not, not, *not* a turndown. I swear, Eddie. We can still be, well, 'us.' Still go on seeing each other."

"Name the day."

"Maybe oftener than ever now that I won't have to make so many business trips."

"And now that I've promised your poor dear mother that I'll come visit her often," I answered dryly. "Like will you be on the scene next week? I intend to call and pay my respects again then. At least as much as promised the poor woman I would."

"You're going to what?"

"Pay my respects."

"May I watch? I've often wondered how that's done."

"I think something has gone out of life with the passing of so many of those old-fashioned . . ."

"Amenities."

Her supplying the word for which I had been groping hardly went very far to relieving my sour mood.

"Lots of them. Gentlemen extending their compliments, even leaving their cards. Tipping their hats, not of course that anybody wears them anymore, that's not the point. Going up to ladies traveling alone and asking whether they may be of service. Now what have you got instead of style? A lot of decadent sophisticates bandying filthy language around tables beside a swimming pool, no respect for the other sex at all, really, nobody ever rising to offer a lady his seat on a public conveyance — in fact even running the risk of a *glare* at this outworn notion that women are the weaker sex, deserving of chivalrous treatment. Why, the other day a woman did just that to me in an elevator when I made an 'after you' gesture. Wouldn't budge till I was out of there first. How do you like them apples? No, siree, put me down as one who prefers the old amenities. *Let* a woman beat you at squash. Maybe not tennis, which of course I don't play, so that in our case is . . . That's . . ."

"Academic."

"Academic as all hell, my dear. But let's not wind up thinking testicles and ovaries are the same, though I believe they're both medically classified as gonads, leave us not go for that homogenization," I said, luckily remembering a word I came across in a magazine article at my dentist's, and thinking to myself, well, this is it, baby, a sample of keeping the old conversational ball rolling at breakfast, lunch *and* dinner. "No, testicles, ovaries, each offers its own particular hormonal balance. . . . Harmonal balance . . ."

To hell with it, I suddenly thought to myself. Even being a rejected suitor has a solid old-fashioned ring to it, so take with a smile the load of ice cubes this broad is handing you. To hell with it all. Forget the house and go buy yourself something else with the money. Something that'll really make their eyes pop, these people with their status symbols here in statustown itself. I'll show them status. You want status, you got it.

I went to New York and bought myself a secondhand stretch limousine twenty-eight feet long, calculated to reduce the most blasé country-club sophisticates to bug-eyed yokels. She had radio, TV, and a tape deck. She had a wet bar, refrigerator, and a cabinet for a picnic hamper. She had a shortwave telephone. The back passenger section was so roomy you had to sit on your shoulder blades to park your heels on the facing sofa. I refer to her as "she" because I thought of her the way boat people think of their craft. In fact I had "Land Yacht" painted on her gunnels, you might say, in discreet shades of purple and gold, over her own lilac color. All very tasteful. The painter I hired had to first obliterate "Esmerelda" on her port side, that being presumably the name of the previous owner's sweetie pie, said by the dealer from whom I made the purchase to have left him for a rock singer named Dink Ormsby. I had the hunch that Esmerelda might have obtained the vehicle as part of a divorce settlement and then sold it to suppert her Dink, who never hit the charts with any release anybody ever heard of. The limo had bulletproof windows that, of course, slid up and down at the touch of a button, which made me suspect Mafia or Administration connections on the part of the previous owner, a likewise slidable partition pane separating the front from the rear, and an intercom mouthpiece communicating with the chauffeur. Which gave me my first pause.

"I clearly can't ride around in you like this, baby," I said aloud to my pride and joy as I purred up the thruway toward home. "My own driver." That hadn't occurred to me in the first flushed ecstasy of purchase. Not that I couldn't afford a chauffeur, at least intermittently obtained from Temporary Employees, what with Greentop so abruptly abandoned as a practical investment. I had mainly gone into the city to huddle with Krumholz on plans to shoot *Toot Suite*, and to interview and audition Fore and Aft and some other hopefuls. "Reading" Fore and Aft consisted mainly in watching her walk naked a few times across a hotel room floor. Talk about human Jell-O. In the course of all that I'd had a reunion with Mea Culpa, who on learning that I had bought a stretch limo offered to chauffeur for me for a modest wage. She could do that in conventional livery getup or give the thing some real class by driving me around in a string bikini, at least for the summer months. I thanked her and said I'd keep the proposition in mind. So having taken the train in, and being thus unencumbered by the old Buick, I was free to pilot myself home in grand style up the old thruway.

Flying like a lavender cloud past the rabble gawking from their humbler heaps, I amusedly turned Mea Culpa's offer over in my mind. Why not? Didn't one hear tell about some literary lights who had secretaries work in bathing suits in their Hollywood office? Another idea of Mea's had been, for the winter months, stretch pants trimmed with a string of multicolored lights that would go on at the touch of a pocket switch when she opened the door for me to get out or in. That might be carrying style a little too far; simple jealousy would be enough in the onlookers, one wouldn't want them to absolutely eat their hearts out as one glided up to a restaurant door. One had evidence of that even now as one zoomed up the road. It goes without saying that the Land Yacht had air-conditioning, but I lowered my window in order to hear some of the witticisms shouted at me on the evening breeze. "You don't *look* Arabian," and "How many gallons to the mile, Mac?" were a couple. I smiled urbanely at these sour-grape wisecracks.

There was one worry, popping to mind as I swung into my driveway. Would she fit into the garage. The answer was no, by several feet. I learned that soon after I backed my old car out, to park it overnight under a maple. Preferring to shelter my new acquisition in the garage meant I couldn't now shut the overhead door, thanks to the protruding surplus. My digs were one of three small apartments into which an enormous old rambling Victorian structure had been cut up. An original two-car garage was shared by the other tenants and I used a small single-car stall the owners had built to supplement that. I was climbing the also-newly-added flight of outside stairs when I suddenly realized how famished I was after such a checkered day. I quickened my pace as I promised myself a wafflewich — a generous mixture of cream cheese and strawberry preserves on a toasted Aunt Jemima waffle, or in cases of extreme need such as this, between two of them. I was pigging out on same when the phone rang. It was Cynthia.

I was still smarting under what I persisted in seeing as a rejection. However you sliced it, it seemed to me to mean: "You're beneath my station." It came to me now on hearing her voice how dying I was to have her get a load of the Land Yacht. We would see about stations now!

"Where the hell have you been, Eddie?" Popping out of town for a week without telling the other was not a game two could play? "I just got Alice Dankworth's article for the first issue. It's called 'Stamp Out Smut.' "

"Stamp out smut."

"To balance off the 'Stamp Out Censorship' one I told you about. It'll dramatize *Overview*'s policy as a journal of opinion for all sides, provided only the articles meet certain literary standards."

"Smut as distinguished from legitimate erotica you mean, or Alice Dankworth means. I don't like her name. It smacks of clammy Puritanism."

"She makes a valid case for what many people are coming to think — Are you eating something? You sound as though you're talking through a pound of glue. Or a horse pulling his foot out of the mud."

"I was just having a bite after an exhausting day, nay week, my dear. In New York. How would you like to come —" I checked what would have been a regretted invitation to join me. I didn't want her first glimpse of the Land Yacht to be of her derrière protruding from a skimpy garage, prior to partaking of a spot of tea and wafflewiches. I wanted to spring it as a surprise when next I called to pick her up for dinner. Following that hastily assembled agenda, I made a date then and there for the following Saturday. That gave me two days to locate and hire something actually quite easily found in Merrymount. A cop who moonlighted as a chauffeur, sometimes for a fancy livery service with limousines of its own for hire, sometimes driving private parties in their own cars hither and yon. Meredith, whom I knew slightly from a traffic ticket he had given me, agreed to work the evening freelance for me for thirty bucks. All he had to do was chauffeur my lady friend and me to the Coq d'Or and back, and between times hang around and upstage the huddled masses, even those themselves hurrying into the Coq, as we regulars called the restaurant.

I chuckled to myself that eventful Saturday night as Meredith held the door open for me on our arrival at the Pickles residence. Climbing out, I thought I caught a glimpse of someone watching from the drawing room draperies, which would have to be Mrs. Rampart, as Mrs. Pickles would be up in her little pink snuggery, and it would not be like Cynthia to be waiting in a tizzy like a debutante for her date. My ring brought Mrs. Rampart to the door fast enough to confirm the guess. Cynthia herself was ravishing in a sleeveless dress of raspberry linen and a pink bolero, a kind of monochrome accented with off-white slippers and a brocaded clutch bag. Down the stairs we tripped and toward the waiting car — which turned out to be only half the surprise intended.

"Oh, you've rented a limousine. With Meredith. Nice to see you again, Meredith."

"Evening Miss — Pickles, isn't it? I remember you from the Havertons' theatre party last spring."

Well, hell, maybe this misunderstanding will turn out to be all to the good, I thought as we sank into the upholstery.

It divides the treat into two parts, the second to be relished by me as I anticipate it for a few minutes.

"How thoughtful of you to think of this as a special occasion," Cynthia said, giving me a second peck on the cheek. "How will you top yourself when the first issue really comes off the press?"

I'm going to top myself now I thought, smiling secretly to myself as Meredith got in behind the wheel and off we purred toward the Coq. That was about ten miles away, and I figured about halfway there would be a good time to spring section two, the major half. Cynthia was amusing herself with some of the appointments, such as the shortwave telephone, and commenting on how plush the local livery service was getting to be in what it had available, when I broke in and said, "I didn't rent this, my dear. I bought it. It's mine. Picked it up when I was in New York."

She turned to me openmouthed. When she had recovered she said, "Bought it. Whatever for?"

"As a means of transportation." I lifted my lapel to smell a carnation in it, but it had fallen out somewheres. "I believe this is the use to which automotive vehicles are customarily put."

"But I mean —" The news so stunned her that it drained the delight out of her original response, leaving a vacuum of dazed curiosity. "All this for — one person?"

"There seem to be two of us in it now. Three counting Meredith." I pressed a button to slide up the glass panel isolating him, afraid he might be eavesdropping. "One can never have too much room, or privacy, don't you agree. In fact I was thinking of adding onto it."

"Putting it in two sections, like a fire engine? For turning corners?"

She saw herself that her tone had turned ironic to a degree unbefitting a festive occasion, because she emitted something like her original laugh of delight and added, "I'm only kidding."

However, her fire-engine crack seemed to be well-taken, because Meredith just then looped away around to the left in order to make a right turn without riding over the curb. But our spirits were bubbling as we glided to a stop in front of the Coq and both a doorman of five-star-general rank and Meredith vied for the honor of opening the car door to leave us out. Meredith defended his prerogative against a military takeover by reason of superior agility and because the doorman must after all hop to his task of opening the *restaurant* door. At which Cynthia paused while Meredith and I exchanged a few words in discreet murmurs.

"How long do you think you'll be, sir?"

"Oh, tennish. Ten-thirty maybe. Depending on how many brandies we dawdle over. You know how it is."

"Of course, sir. And do you wish me to stay with the car in the parking lot, or am I free to depend on the attendant there?"

"No, no, feel free to nosey around the town. Just lock the car and make sure the burglar alarm is on."

"Thank you, sir." He looked critically around. "I don't know what a guy would do in a burg like this."

"Stamp out some smut," I said, and went to join Cynthia.

It turned out we never got to the brandies. I had the *poulet Montmorency* to Cynthia's lamb *à la grecque,* and there being no more *Montmorency* on this particular second joint than there had been *Véronique* on the drumstick at Hercule's, to lubricate its downward passage, a chunk of it got stuck in my throat, this time for good. No amount of water or wine would sluice it away. Not that the obstruction drastically interfered with conversation, so for a time I held up my end of it without Cynthia's realizing that a medical crisis was in the making.

125

"I mean I wonder, and again ask, Eddie dear, where do you get all your money?" Cynthia said, still at it about a vehicle that with a better understanding might have borne her name on its rear doors in, like I say, letters of purple and gold. "I mean where?"

Here I did some fancy literary stealing that in a cumulative way probably added up to grand larceny.

"Well, my dear, you remember the woman in Proust who, asked where she got all those astonishing hats of hers, replied, 'I don't get them at all. I just have them.' Similarly with my money. I don't get it at all. I just have it. How is your lamb? Enough *à la grecque?* We could ask for a smidgen more."

For all my memory, oddly enough, I couldn't remember whether I had read this somewhere or got it from one of those high-flown (and one-sided) discussions with Bertha Colton the swillperson, who you will recall my saying was deep in scholarly work on Proust. I was certainly talking over my own head again, that unmistakable sign of belonging.

"Speaking of money and Proust both, did you know that he liked to invest a lot of his dough in American stocks?"

"No, I didn't," Cynthia said, looking at me rather peculiarly now, with suspicion I thought first, until I realized that she had sensed my distress. She broke off in mid-quiz and rose, preparatory to coming around behind and applying the Heimlich maneuver. I waved her away.

"Nothing like that," I said. "This is a different genre. And for God's sake don't call the waiter. I don't want any bear hugs from behind. Just sit still till it goes down."

But it didn't. And there was nothing to do but head for the nearest hospital and sit around in the emergency ward till the trouble cleared up. It always had the other three times I had reached that stage. "It's like a toothache stopping the minute you make an appointment with the dentist. Where the hell is Meredith?"

For we were now outside, after my dropping a fifty on the table, looking in every direction for the chauffeur. At last he appeared, strolling into view around the corner.

"Take us to the hospital," Cynthia said. "It's halfway home just off the Parkway. There's a sign. Nothing serious."

But Meredith floored it, so that we were in the emergency ward ten minutes later, Cynthia wringing her hands and me trying to calm her. The nurses and interns on duty were far better able to do so than I, what with the unruffled composure with which they went about routinely attending to a crisis no doubt familiar enough to them, and nothing to get excited about. A doctor on duty told me to sit down quietly with a glass of water from which to take very *small sips, not bulldozing gulps, while he got preparations under way for an X-ray. And w*hat he sat me down to was a desk at which somebody registered me in for an overnight stay, and surgery if that turned out to be necessary.

That's the way it went. With the situation unresolved an hour later, I told Meredith to take Miss Pickles home and then drop the car at my address, giving him full instructions about which garage to pull into, or pull partly into, and to retain the keys for safekeeping until I phoned to pick them up. That, according to what the doctor led me to believe, would be the day after tomorrow. Waving cheerfully from the doorway in the nightie and slippers for which they had already had me exchange my civvies, I noticed that Cynthia was riding in the front seat beside Meredith, presumably so they could commiserate about me. I ran out to protest, losing a slipper, so that one foot spanked the asphalt while the other scuffed along it. I pattered along on Cynthia's side, gesticulating to her to let the window down.

"This is crazy," I said. "Get in back. It looks funny, and embarrasses Meredith. Doesn't it, Meredith?"

He shrugged noncommittally while Cynthia objected in return. Half choking herself, and threatening the water-works, she said it just wouldn't feel right, would seem, well, frivolous, to ride in luxury in the back seat while I had a piece of chicken stuck in my throat.

"But it's chicken *Montmorency*," I protested, still trotting along, *spank-scuff, spank-scuff.*

Meredith stopped while we concluded this exercise in casuistry, as I believe the Catholics call such ethical hairsplitting. By now he had also reached across to help her get the window down so we didn't have to shout through bullet-proof glass, have I told you that's what it had?

"Which reminds me, it's something you might mention to the doctor." Cynthia was now quite moist-eyed, handkerchief at the ready to tweak her nose in case there was real precipitation. "You say it's always and only chicken that does it to you. Why is that do you suppose?"

"I guess they're laying for me."

She burst full into tears, nodding that she got the gag, as the window slid up again and the Land Yacht swept away on the last leg of her maiden voyage, and, retrieving my slipper, I went guiltily back into the hospital for my esophago-scopy they call it.

⚬⚬⚬

Deliriously in Love

THIS CONSISTS in shoving the handle end of a golf club down your hatch until the bit of recalcitrant victual is pushed into your stomach where it belongs. The surgeon will use some other name for the instrument in question, a tubular contrivance equipped with lights so he can see into your craw and with brushes to collect scrapings for biopsy, etc., etc., and having a fine French name, but the achieved result is the same, and likewise the sensation to yourself. Since of course the procedure (that surgeons' euphemism for everything including total evisceration) is done under complete anesthetic, the sensation doesn't begin until you've regained consciousness in the recovery room, where your throat feels like you've spent the intervening period gargling with carpet tacks.

But all that was on the morrow. For tonight, you were trundled on a gurney, as they call those stretchers on wheels, along a corridor to an elevator which took you to the third floor, and then down another few corridors to private room 317, where you began your stay by deploring the low-comedy gowns all hospitals get you into. "It's defamatory to the human form and degrading to the human spirit," I told the redheaded nurse I was happy enough to be eased into bed by, regretting only that it was solo. She laughed. "It ain't Eve St. Laurents," she agreed. I assumed her to be one of the fashion designers, an area I know little about what with spending most of my time with naked people, on and off camera. I had by now mentally peeled the nurse herself right down to the russet fleece (O centrally located auburn locks!) while, having told me her name was Madeline, she bustled about on some other chores relative to me. (O divine divot!)

"You're here for an esophagoscopy."

"That's easy for you to say." (O cunningly placed little goatee!)

"By Dr. Drdla. That's not so easy."

This looked to be more fun than hailstones when we were kids. Bandied pleasantries, verbal byplay, who could ask for more, short of unzipping Madeline in actual fact.

"I shouldn't be joking at a time like this," she said. "You going into surgery in the morning and all."

"Don't get all choked up. That's my department. You get many cases like this?"

"We get many cases like everything. There's really nothing to the procedure as such. On a seriousness scale of ten, I'd give it a two."

"That's very nice, coming from a ten."

"You seem to have no trouble talking. Whereabouts is it?"

"Right here. About halfway down. That's where Chicken Little stopped."

"Well, Dr. Drdla will persuade it to finish the trip. Now

I'm going to start an I.V. on you. The usual glucose solution. Because you're to have nothing on your stomach come anesthetic time. Nothing by mouth. Usual practice. So. You can look at television if you want." She pointed to a contraption the size of a toaster affixed to a bracket over the bed, and close enough to ruin your eyesight. "And if you'd like a painkiller there's a Demerol-permitted instruction on your chart. If you think you'd like a shot, for pain or merely to get to sleep, just ring and one of us will come in and bayonet you in the tush."

"Oh, I think I'll just lie here and have spiritual thoughts about you."

She paused in her exit long enough to smile with a pretty little toss of her cinnamon head, after which I lay there humming "You Ought to Be in Pictures." This could be the real thing. I started a long fantasy about her.

Madeline was everything you could want of a woman, and something to boot. Quick ignition, yet a long lingering cruise down the highway of pleasure to the hundred-mile-an-hour destination burst. The inflammability popularly associated with redheads (high sulphur content or something) ultimately expressed in a flame of compliments likewise gratifying to a chap. "Oh, you're so . . . Oh, my God, how can anybody, I mean you pneumatic drill you, let's rest awhile while you recite some poetry. A girl likes that, she misses it from so many guys these days."

All I could remember was scraps from that "Hound of Heaven" poem the demented high-school teacher expected me to memorize without having a nervous breakdown myself. Some lines from the second or so stanza which was as far as I got, before he was institutionalized and I nearly was. I brushed a lock of the Titian hair aside as I panted into her ear:

"Across the margent of the world I fled,
   And troubled the gold gateways of the stars,
   Smiting for shelter on their clangèd bars;
       Fretted to dulcet jars
   And silvern chatter the pale ports o' the moon."

Between the daydream (at this hour?) and faint footsteps in the hall which I always took to be hers passing my closed door (breaking into a trot when someone yelled "Nurse!") I thought I'd never get to sleep. It's interesting how the horn gets up in danger situations — life reasserting itself I suppose whenever death looms as an environmental possibility. So in my distraction I swung the toaster-sized TV over on its bracket and got some late-news wrap-up. It wrapped it up all right.

"— was how the President interpreted the recent drop in consumer spending. In other news, the organization known as Citizens Against Pornography has stepped up its drive on obscenity in videocassettes. Said Charles Leland, president of CAP and longtime Moral Majority activist, and I quote, 'If the federal courts don't take criminal action soon, we ourselves shall sue into bankruptcy these nuditymongers bringing into the American home —' "

"Nurse!"

I realized as I simultaneously called out and shut the TV off that there was a button on the same general bedside panel for summoning one, which I duly pressed. Madeline shortly appeared, none the worse for our thrash in the straw. Not a hair out of place testified to our orgy, not a ripple in her outward composure betrayed our passionate dishevelment of a few minutes ago.

"What is it, dear?"

"How about that shot of Demerol you said I was permitted?"

"Sure. Feeling some pain, are we?"

We nodded, though in fact that was by no means the case. Indeed it seemed that the pressure was diminishing, as though Chicken Little was preparing to ease on down where she belonged. We wanted it for sleep, was the thing, after being so riled by the latest blast from the bluenoses which sorely threatened the sleep we so sorely needed for the morrow's ordeal. Too, there was an element of curiosity about the drug we had heard so much about. Here was the chance to try it legitimately. And all in all, it quite lived up to its billing as a downer. The delicious passivity that set in ten minutes after the shot, the sense of being lapped in physical peace, made me understand its addictiveness. But just as I was about to slip into slumberland my phone rang.

"Eddie, darling, I hope I didn't wake you up," Cynthia said. "But I've been calling around in my worry and all, you know, and got my own doctor on the phone to see what was going on, and he just phoned back to say he learned a Dr. Drdla was going to do the — you know, whatever it is. I can't say it."

"Esophagoscopy."

"Well, you can, so you can't be too bad." There was a laughing-through-her-tears note in her voice that I tried my best to offset. It touched me to the quick, but at the same time I fought against leaving her in that state. "He said Dr. Drdla is the best ear, nose and throat man in the country. So you'll be in good hands."

"Piece of cake."

"I'll find out more about the exact time tomorrow, but I hope to be there in your room when they bring you back."

"Back to bed and ready for love. Did you know that hospitals frown on that sort of thing? Why, even prisons permit intercourse between inmates and visiting wives."

"Did you get X-rated again ?" This time she laughed openly. "Odd slip, that. I meant X-rayed."

"No, but let it stand. I'm X-rated. Good night. Thanks for calling. You're an angel, and remember where you heard it."

It was with a sense of having sportingly offered *another* clue that, peacefully enough, given the circumstances, I drifted off to sleep.

Anyone who has ever been in a hospital knows that that's the last place to get any rest. No matter how many times you may have been interrupted in the night by nurses taking your temperature or blood pressure, giving you medicine or checking your I.V., reveille is at first light. An aide comes in to tidy up whether the room needs it or not, collecting debris you didn't know existed and overturning a wastebasket into a bigger one of her own, setting it down again with a merry clatter before retiring to make room for somebody who offers to bathe you whether you want it or not. All is now abuzz in the corridor, where the shuffle and scuffle of feet are no annoyance only because obliterated by the rattle of wheels, possibly including those of a tumbrel on which somebody is being trundled off to surgery, at which you refrain from glancing out your door to look for fear it may be you. Now comes the tinkle of the chuck wagon, followed by a nurse pushing a cartful of scheduled medicines to be delivered and administered. The major sound in this swelling symphony of renewal, as every wretch who has been in dry dock knows, is the rumble of some kind of boxcar propelled up and down the corridor by a janitorial sadist, empty at first, for maximum tympanic effect, slightly less deafening on its return trip, thanks to whatever contents it has acquired. If after all that racket your head still doesn't feel like a terminally ill squash, someone will slip in long enough to move a piece of furniture, like a chair, with a hideous scraping sound, and that should do it.

Around nine o'clock Dr. Drdla strolled in, and he was quite nice to meet. He was probably the nattiest man I've ever seen, with a crease in his pinstripe trousers he could have used to make an incision with. The suit was medium gray, set off by a red figured tie knotted over a white shirt collar nipped in with a gold pin. He wasn't wearing over all this the white tunic favored by medical people. He shook hands cheerfully.

"So we've got a piece of chicken in there."

"Actually it's pheasant."

I don't know why I said that except out of a sudden hunch that he was a snob. A deep-seated underdog's urge to impress a man I instinctively took to be so high-toned there was almost no hope of otherwise meeting his discriminating standards. Which it turned out I was right about, so some radar beamed from somewhere made me pick the correct moment to prove I had risen from my humble origins. And as a matter of fact it might very well have been what I said, the *faisan Bombois* under glass having been one of the items on the menu I'd been torn between, opting for the chicken no doubt for fear of winding up with a piece of glass in my crop, given my medical history.

I'm damned if it didn't seem to give Drdla himself a little more sense of class to be asked as a surgeon to go in and win over pheasant instead of chicken. Because he raised his eyebrows in an impressed way as he gave his tie and collar pin a little adjusting fidget. Maybe his own family were strictly from hunger, immigrants from Bohemia or wherever the name originated, and now he could dine out on having had a patient stymied by something really tony.

"Pheasant, eh?"

135

I nodded, eyes momentarily shuttered. "Under glass. *Bombois.*"

Every evidence I heard later bore out my guess he was something of a snob. Member of the Century Club (nonresident, of course, but then), clothes from Savile Row, skiing at Kitzbühel. (Stowe? Forget it. Utah? People, please.) Now I had a sudden fear that they might be able to tell I had been lying, that it was plain old chicken and not pheaasnt at all, from some kind of spectroscopic examination or something. Then I would be exposed as a fraud as well as a pornmonger. A social climber, and a flunkenstein even at that, to be driven from Merrymount by hoots of derision, saved from shame only if it turned out that the facts had been brought to light by an autopsy. But crafty querying confirmed that the object was to nudge it down, not fish it out.

Drdla strolled to the window, which gave out on a fine vista of the town, including, in the foreground, a shopfront with a sign reading "J. Wilkerson. Heating Appliances and Handwriting Analysis."

"Bombois was a painter, as you no doubt know, though you may not know he'd once been a wrestler in a traveling circus," he said.

"That I hadn't realized."

"I wonder if the name of the dish has anything to do with him or his family."

"I wondered about that too, at the time. Perusing the menu at the Coq, wondering what to order."

"A very charming painter. A sort of naïf. Primitive." Drdla turned back. "I'm glad to see you're not feeling such discomfort that you can't talk. This procedure shouldn't be such a big deal."

"One hears of the most fantastic things surgeons have to get out of people's throats. What are some of the more interesting things you've had to fish out, Dr. Drdla?"

"Would you believe a fish*hook*? Child, of course. Always swallowing coins, children. But my God, the things I've had to remove from adults. Half a lamb chop bone, bridgework of every size and description, and once, believe it or not, a gold toothpick that had been in the family for generations. Well, you're scheduled for one o'clock. I'll want a series of X-rays first — Ah, here comes an aide for you now." A strapping blond bruiser you could see moonlighting as a tavern bouncer pushed a wheelchair into the room. "So I'll see you at one, Mr. Teeters. Tout allure."

"Tout allure."

I've flunked French twice and still don't know what that damned expression means, let alone how to spell it. But no matter. I go merrily on saying it like everyone else. I suppose it's one of those all-purpose departure things, like "Toodle-oo" and "Take care." I was musing over it as I was wheeled down corridors and in and out of elevators into the X-ray department below, trundling before me my I.V. pole.

I never did learn what the visiting hours were, but Cynthia clearly violated them by being in my room when I returned around eleven. She had brought me a toothbrush, toothpaste, and other toilet articles, as well as a seersucker bathrobe obtained from God knew where. Probably a closet at home, because this was Sunday, and while there were drugstores open, hardly a haberdasher's. She also left Xeroxes of the two main articles for the opening issue of *Overview*, "Stamp Out Censorship" and "Stamp Out Smut," so I would have something to read when I "got back." For reasons that will emerge soon enough, I never got much of a chance to curl up with them, but I knew that between them they would exhaust the pros and cons of the subject, so much so that they would cancel each other out. To state as much, I weighed them suggestively in my hands, one in each, like Spencer Tracy hefting the Bible and Darwin's *Origin of Spe-*

cies off against one another, before stowing both into his briefcase and shambling on out of the courtroom in the last fade-out of *Inherit the Wind.*

She stayed to chat in the self-conscious manner of two people one of whom is about to head for the chop shop. Conversation was so strained that I was actually glad to see the tumbrel come for me around twelve-thirty. I was by then somewhat dopey from a pre-op shot, but alert enough to milk a little histrionics from my departure. Stretched out on the gurney again, I waved with a brave little smile as I disappeared from view around a bend in the corridor that led to the elevators. For all that I realized I was laying on the drama, I was a bit alarmed at the way everyone kept wishing me good luck. Wasn't this supposed to be a piece of cake?

I don't know how long I was under, but when I came to in the recovery room my throat felt indeed as already described — as though I had been gargling with small nails — and my voice sounded like Donald Duck's. Everything had run smoothly, I was told, the pheasant was gone, and Cynthia was waiting for me in my room. She stayed for an hour or so, doing most of the talking of course, with the barest minimum of quacks in return. I was still groggy when she left, and slipped gratefully off to sleep after another shot of Demerol, this time certainly for pain.

I awoke in the dead of night on what seemed a bed dancing to the rhythm of castanets. The castanets were my chattering teeth, and the illusion of a shimmying bed was my own shivering frame. I rang for a nurse, who turned out happily to be Madeline back on her night shift.

"I feel like I'm freezing to death," I quacked in my Donald Duck voice, forced from a furiously aching throat through clicking teeth.

"You're shooting a temp," she said even before poking a

thermometer into my mouth. I was afraid of biting it unintentionally in two and thus leaving the good Drdla something else to deal with, by way of an encore. "Lickety-split," she said of my pulse while taking it. She read the thermometer. "Hundred and two and a half. Could be worse." And it was, and soon. It went up to a hundred and four and still climbing. "Some infection you've got going," Madeline said.

"How so?"

"Well, you know, here's the thing." She addressed me from the foot of the bed. "Your GI tract — *our* GI tract — is a sewer pipe. O.K.? Teaming with germs nature sees to it are confined inside it, right? Until there's a tear in it and the bacteria pour out into the system. Are you sure there wasn't a piece of bone on that thing? Either that or a bit of sharp gristle tore a hole in your gullet and has let the bad guys out. You've got a doozy going, but not to worry. The good guys here" — she indicated the bottle of antibiotics now also hanging from the I.V. pole — "will rout them. Let me get a washcloth and wipe that dewy brow."

A more blessed ministration I cannot recall receiving from a woman's hand. But the fever went up to a hundred and five — and I was turned over to the poetry of delirium.

I am going naked on all fours through a car wash. The lathered rotary brushes bruise my flanks, already tender from the fever. Then there are those hanging strips slap-slapping my hide in that weird ballet so much fun to watch through the window separating the motorist from his machine, but not to have executed on you in the buff. The suds like mad dog saliva are rinsed off me, and then I am blow-dried and, finally, given a coat of wax, if I remember the sequence I wonder even in my dream whether I have got correct. Some possibility that I may have to start all over again from the beginning if I have it wrong. The boys administering a final cloth wipe-off watch me sharply as I get up, wondering how much I'll put in the tip box at the end of the run. I explain I have no money to pay for what was not my idea in the first place, but that of some unidentified tormentors who never personally appear on the scene. They set upon me angrily, now using their drying cloths to snap my legs, the way horseplaying boys in a high-school shower will snap their towels at one another. Both Cynthia and Madeline fight them off, and having done so, battle between them over me. The winner is unclear, merging into one as characters will in dreams, but then Toby appears and unmistakably as herself marches off with me. But soon I turn a street corner without her, and proceed to slip between parked cars and around hedges to hide my nakedness, which, again characteristically for dreams, nobody is paying any attention to. I either read somewhere or was told by one of my female intellectual superiors what Freud's explanation of this is, but cannot remember it, rack my brain though I do. The tavern for which I successfully make, in a last sprint, as though for "sanctuary," is empty at first, but soon a second customer turns up and joins me at the bar, where to my relief I find myself fully clothed. A bartender with a nose like an exit bulb, like W. C. Fields', draws us steins of beer whose foam is reminiscent of the mad dog saliva the car wash suds in turn resembled. The man has the blues. "I'm a brother-in-law," he says. "You don't look like a brother-in-law," I say, to comfort him.

Twenty-seven people were baptized by total immersion in the ocean and nobody did a thing about it. Not a bystander wanted to get involved. They swam or sunbathed or strolled along the beach, ignoring the converts as they staggered, dripping but redeemed, out of the hydrophobic surf. Waves like the tongues of rabid seabeasts lapped the shore. My mother was baptized by total immersion in the church where that was still the custom, but I was merely sprinkled. My father declined the sacrament altogether, while occasionally attending the divine worship to please my mother. Yet it was she who laughingly left me the amulet with powers to ward off superstition. Odd, the paradoxes and inconsistencies in human beings. Madeline bends over me to take my temp and blood pressure again, then once more to soothe my forehead with a cool wet cloth before vanishing like a ghost into the twilit corridor, murmuring a sweet word I fail to catch. Something about half a degree. To the west, then, and toward what latitude? Oh, no, not that voyage yet, no moaning at the bar, just always the laughter of buoyant youth around a beach campfire. Girls, girls, girls. Sweet ministering nymphs let me have still my share of you, let me bag my quota, dining and motoring and abed. Capsizing our bottles of wine, taking picnic hampers into the woods, picking wildflowers to twine in your hair. Do you remember how I plucked a daisy from amid the meadow grass and set it *there* with the stem inside your own fringed flower? You clenched your legs and laughed into the maple boughs beneath which we had spread our blanket and hauled the sweetmeats from the wicker hamper. We were caught in a downpour and had to drive through such mudholes we stopped at a car wash on the drive home when the skies had cleared. We watched through the window like children as she went through the tunnel, half drowned under the splashing suds. The girl at the cashier counter had a radio going. *She wore bullue velvet . . . Blue was the color of her eyes.* Was that our song? We never formally elected one. In a little Mexican restaurant around the corner from something we had chili con carne originally spouted as lava from a volcano thought to be extinct. Oh, my mouth. The brimstone. Your body is the work of an ice sculptor molding his figures with a blowtorch.

Now I remember my mother reporting in the dear dead

days beyond recall to a telephone caller on my father's blazing influenza. "How is he? Not so hot. He's burning up with fever." Same here. Turning over in the sweated sheets my skin feels raw, or rather that I have been flayed and my flesh is flaming tender. I slip back into the saloon, where we make an enormous pop art wafflewich out of a strawberry blonde who has or has not come in with me, and I join the now dozen or more customers who dance around the idol as around a golden calf, but protest when the others set her on a table to make a meal of her. Chivalrous intervention becomes unnecessary when it turns out that the first attempted bite out of her loses the attacker most of his teeth, for she, or it, has indeed become a plaster work of pop art, like the sculpture hamburgers of yesteryear. But it retains this golden calf attribute, making Moses, when he descends from the mountain to behold the heathen sight, drop the tablets, which are in fact two aspirin somebody is trying to make me take. It's the strawberry blonde, her uniform and cap white as the pills in her hand. "These will bring your fever down, though we'll want an honest reading in the morning, without the symptoms masked. You're going to be all . . ."

"Call my mother and ask her what it is. Check with Mother. She'll know."

"There, there."

"She's in heaven, you know."

"I know."

"With Proust. He invested in American stocks. Railroads and things."

"Well, I hope the market's better there than it is on Wall Street."

"What people don't understand is that the stock exchange is simply an auction. A hundred and five, do I hear a hundred and six?"

"If we do we'll put you on an alcohol mattress to cool you down. Don't worry."

A hand on my brow again, no it's the damp cloth, cool as the drop of water the rich man in hell held his tongue out for, just a drop, please, Lord. "Draw me another beer, bartender?" He fetches up with a sketching pad and charcoal to do so, for he attends art school in his spare time, but the result is roundly criticized as proving his aspirations hopeless, and he returns to the trade on which he must settle as his permanent living. He'll never make a Matisse, or even a Bombois. Here Chirouble made a brief cameo appearance, long enough to drop one of his epigrams. "To have read nothing by Bulwer-Lytton can give a man a solid sense of accomplishment."

What was there to do but hold a wake for the bartender and his dead dream, but even that was a fiasco. The champagne glasses we threw into the fireplace to make the toast final, as they do, proved to be unbreakable acrylic rented from the caterer's, and instead of shattering on the hearthstone simply bounced back intact onto the rug, where they lay at the feet of the celebrants, mute testimony to the futility of their salute, and maybe to the vanity of all human endeavor. Reusable, scratch-resistant, top-rack-dishwashersafe. "I'll just throw them out," said the hostess on her hands and knees, gathering them up, "and it'll amount to the same thing." "No, no," said her husband, "I'll run out and get some glass ones, and then we'll do it over and do it right." All he had to do was dig some out of a forgotten corner of a cupboard, and they were beautiful hollow-stemmed crystal, but then there wasn't enough champagne left — the last of the remaining bottle dribbled into the third glass of the dozen outheld, and that was that. The rest were filled with ginger ale and the toast was offered, not to the bartender-artist at all. "To Eddie Teeters, may he rest in peace." The host himself gave the toast, a rangy man in tweeds whose teeth slanted, like the blade of a guillotine, and he wrote poetry which rhymed *laughter* with *slaughter* and *carousel* with *water ouzel,* and the end was not yet in sight. Threatening to read some, he was bound and gagged and delivered over to the Pharisees and Sadducees where he jolly well belonged, and the conversation flowed on to more important matters. "Do you realize that one out of every two marriages now ends in divorce," someone said, and another, "And three out of every four divorces end in marriages. So what the hell you gonna do." Nevertheless I wanted Madeline for my own, and we went apartment hunting in New York, where after scouring the city we finally found a flat, though it was on a back wheel of my car. According to my parents' scenario, I would own like a hardware store in our town and marry a nice girl who said "Likewise I'm sure." Though in a private room, I can hear a snorer across the hall, unless it's myself going "Smorgobliska eeeeem palimpsest." Mrs. Applewhite was the talk, if not exactly the toast, of the town back home. She married the owner of a furniture store, those ravishingly hideous borax parlor suits, and after two years together they have a retarded collie. Oh, Christ, I'm not eating pizza through a catcher's mask again, not that again. To get it through might be a relief, for I have a taste in my mouth like I have just drunk coffee dregs in which some cigarette butts have been doused. Like the cup on the counter at the Small Café where I first met Toby. I suspect her realtor is a chap who will tell you on short notice to pick a card, and who can twitch his necktie by bobbing his Adam's apple up and down. I can hear Mother Pickles exclaim, "Open marriages are bad enough, but open engagements!" She went back to a time when girls "puckered up" for suitors with clip-on bow ties, who rowed their "steadies" across the lake on Sunday afternoons. Ah, yesteryear, unrecallable time . . .

I remember a boyhood vacation on a lake where a band gave open-air concerts, but now I seem to be in a concert hall to hear the premiere of my symphony, a work of grinding cacophony entitled "Desperate Measures," and when I sit up to take a bow a nurse not Madeline is pushing me back. After rearranging the damp sheets she too mops my brow with a cool wet cloth preparatory to taking my blood pressure again. There's that somehow pleasantly tight feeling on your arm as the squeezed bulb inflates the cuff, and then the pulsations as the air is released. Delirium is a fine art, demanding the wildest transitions smoothly controlled, as witness how the sphygmomanometer becomes the tire inflators with which I helped Chirouble out the awful night he had two flats on the thruway. Then how the louvres on the dashboard heating ducts at which we warmed the Fix-a-Flats become the bars of my cell on death row. Little chance of a last-minute pardon as the governor is Frisch, elected on a Puritan ticket, who has been out to get me for some time, and will hardly mourn my demise. "So you finally fried him. That's what I call capital punishment." But there is a power failure, which being religious he takes as a Providential sign that my sentence must be commuted to life. I'm paroled into the custody of Mrs. Rampart, a climax of this particular installment of my nightmare from which I'm happily awakened by another nurse on fresh mission bent.

They're going to give me oxygen. How?

Dismiss from your mind the double Nebuchadnezzar wheeled in by the Reaper's sommeliers when you're plucking the sheets as the hour approaches. These are routine measures taken with the use of small containers hardly bigger than the Fix-a-Flat tire bombs, set into a fixture permanently installed in the wall over the head of the patient's bed. A rubber hose ends in a mask he can hold over his face, removing it from time to time to catch a breath of air if he wishes. No more dire than the use you've seen football players make of oxygen on the sidelines. But I found that the canister and the rubber tube between them produced two noises the phonetic rendition of which became an obsession that threatened to drive me crazy. Moisture gathering at a band, or kink, in the tube made a hideous lower-gut sound that went rhythmically on as "Gerburgle gerburgle gerburgle," while the canister, when it ran low, made a steady hissing racket I was powerless in my weakened state not to convert into "Dr. Needless costly tea, Dr. Needless costly tea." Amalgamated into a remorseless "Gerdocle burgless corstlug teagle," the refrain enters my hallucinations, so that a mob of seemingly antagonized tourists shout it as they chase me through the streets of Trieste to the little restaurant around the corner. A sympathetic headwaiter seats me at a secluded table, to which a phone is brought me, and when it rings I hear Cynthia's anxious voice.

"How are you?"

"Not so hot. I'm burning up."

A management apparently bent on appealing to American trade has some local variant of Muzak playing "Softly as I Leave You," and that has Cynthia in tears. I had not known she was so touching when touched, so moving when moved. Was this my aloof poolside patrician, first glimpsed in my already well-heeled but still yearning outsider days? The undulating piece who turned the paperback around as she departed, her hips swaying like a bell?

"Oh, no. Don't sing that song, please. In that voice."

Then it wasn't just Sinatra. I myself was croaking along with him? And the hallucination itself changed. Cynthia seemed to be here in the room with me, not on the long distance phone at all, bending over me, her cool hand smoothing the matted hair back from my brow.

"Let's pick it up from where we left off in the restaurant. About your proposing? The answer is yes. I'll marry you, Eddie, if, foolish boy, that's what you really want. O.K.? So it'll be us. Just don't sing that song anymore. No more stuff about softly as you leave me. I couldn't stand it."

Not to worry. The fever broke the next day, leaving me in the clear but, of course, limp as a dishrag. When I dragged myself out of bed to look in the bathroom mirror I had to laugh at the horror that confronted me. My neck was so swollen there was no neck. It came straight down to nearly my shoulders as hog jowls. And when I squeezed them, as the doctor had a few times, bending to listen, I heard the "crepitus" he commented on, a sound more popularly known in medicine as Rice Krispies. The faint but discernible snap, pop and crackle is an uncanny duplicate of that made by the cereal in a bowl of milk. It was fun to pinch your gills and listen, in the boredom of recovery. I was amusing myself with it when Cynthia came to call, her third visit in the two days since the infection had been routed by the antibiotics.

"I've brought you some fruit and another article I just got in. On prayer in schools. Does *this* woman take off on it! Could you swallow some grapes yet? Well chewed up, mind."

"I think. I'm off liquid and on semi-soft. You haven't lived till you've stopped eating custard." As though to prove my point, an aide came in just then to remove my untouched lunch tray. "I'd thank you for the lunch, but I haven't got it in me," I said to her. Exit laughing. Make that smirking.

Cynthia set the basket of fruit on the windowsill and the Manila envelope with the article in it on the vacated bed table.

"I'll take the other two manuscripts back. We can always use the Xeroxes. How did you like them? Have you had a chance to read them?"

"Yes, they're both terrific," I lied in my teeth. I couldn't have borne to read the one on stamping out smut, even knowing the other would cancel it out with the standard arguments against censorship. "They'll give a wonderful pro-and-con feeling that you need for the first issue. This, you're saying, is what *Overview* will be — a forum for all opinions. Now what was this about Cary Grant you were saying yesterday? The phone rang and you were interrupted."

"Oh, nothing. Your neck. Did you know he flunked his first screen test because the scout, or whoever, said his neck was too thick? Worse than Clark Gable's ears on the skyline. But yours is definitely receding. Be your old self in another day or two. The nurse out there, who's being a pearl about my violating visiting hours, says you may go home Sunday." Cynthia looked beat herself, and I wasn't surprised to see her fling herself into the room's single armchair and let out a long exhausted breath. "This has been some . . ." She broke off with a quaver in her voice and put a hand to her lowered head. "A hundred and five is a lot for a grown boy. No wonder you were delirious."

I had spoken of that adventure of mine before, telling a few of my mad dreams and waking fancies, and the inability to tell them apart. I now related one I had hesitated to before.

"You know . . ." I settled the pillow at my head and heaved myself up from the slouching position into which I had slumped. But I didn't look at her when I said: "There was one dream where I dreamt we were talking on the phone and you said you'd marry me. Isn't that a blast."

Without turning my head, I could tell out of the corner of my eye that she had remained in the position in which I'd seen her a few moments before, her elbow on the arm of the chair and her head lowered in her hand. Then she dropped her hand and settled her gaze on me.

"That wasn't a —" She broke off and before saying what she had intended she asked a question. "Did it seem in your dream that I was here in the room with you?"

"That's right! It wasn't over the telephone, or rather it stopped being over the telephone and seemed that you were actually here."

"I was."

"What?"

"It wasn't a dream. I was here, and I did say it. You see, Eddie, fearing you were going to die — or thinking that you might, because it was touch-and-go there, you know — that made me realize how much I cared, do care for you. Mixed up in it was this idea that you had lost the will to live. That sounds Freudianly corny, but one of the most touching scenes in *Buddenbrooks* is the death of poor little Johann for whom exactly that makes the difference between survival and departure. I realize it also seems egotistical of me to think my 'Yes' would tip the balance and bring you back, life hanging by a thread the way it can. But I'm not going to cop out by not mentioning this and so leaving everything the way it was, which I could now that I learn you didn't know it was actually me. You're on the mend now, and would have been none the wiser. But I remember how it absolutely destroyed me to think you might not make it. You with your ridiculous stretch limousine and your absurd —"

I never heard what was absurd about me, for as a welcome substitute for the information she burst into tears. I took note that she didn't rush over and throw her arms around me by way of clinching her avowal and sealing our union with a kiss, but was at the same time grateful that any such embrace was being postponed, an occupant of a sickbed being hardly the most savory thing in the world.

"God, Cynthia," I said softly, flinging a hand out toward her, which she didn't take, not having noticed the gesture. I shook my head in disbelief and emitted a long, low, one might even say reverent whistle, and then murmured gently, "I'm a sonofabitch."

"Probably," she said, and laughingly set about drying her tears.

EIGHT

⤫

Bomb in Gilead

SO THAT jelled us. It clarified and settled our relationship for good, right? Wrong. It left it more hopelessly confused than ever. Because look.

At least two previous visits had given Cynthia ample opportunity to inform me that we were to be wed. Why had she waited till a turn in the conversation appeared to leave her no alternative, except because she hadn't really wanted to follow through? *My* not blurting out something ecstatic like "Name the day!" had tipped her off that I'd been out to lunch in Cuckooland when I'd been "accepted," and therefore knew nothing about it. So she'd hesitated, my reasoning ran, weighing the wisdom of saying nothing about it now that her "Yes" had served the purpose of bringing me back from the valley of the shadow. The *Buddenbrooks* bit sewed all this up for me. I'd never even heard of the book till the dramatization on public television, of which I'd caught a few episodes including, by chance, the one in which this little Johann tells a schoolmate, "I want to die." So I understood the parallel she was trying to draw between his succumbing to typhus because life held nothing to draw him back from the brink, and my own near-tearjerker. My infection was something apparently called mediastinitis, which can be not only curtains but a rather nasty way to go, I later learned. But I'd made it and now we were both off the hook — me alive and kicking and she not *really* honor-bound to keep what had been a deathbed promise, sort of. She had after some supposed soul-searching "played fair" and come clean. Now the ball was in my court, and shouldn't I play fair by releasing her from the engagement? To deserve her, I ought to give her up. Such was the clump of ethical barbed wire in which I found my foot entangled. What to do? How to play this? That was when the light struck like it did Paul on the road to Jerusalem, or wherever he was headed. Of course. Where was I except at the exact point for which I had made provision in the scenario worked out as I lay beside the slumbering Toby?

You will remember that according to my timetable I would unmask myself as Monty Carlo the minute we were engaged, which would be cricket enough since it then would give her an honestly understandable out, while also retaining a little moral leverage for me. I would never hold her to it as I could fully appreciate how my way of life might be an embarrassment to her in the pursuit of her own. All right. We were engaged, by however unexpected a series of events. Now was the time to speak up. Any doubts she'd had before the big revelation could reasonably weigh in with her decision to break the engagement now, if she did. Whatever happened, we would both come out of it with honor, all demerits wiped away.

The plan, timetable, scenario and all blew up in my face with a force that singed these golden eyebrows to a crisp.

* * *

I made a date with Cynthia as soon as I could after getting home from the hospital, not neglecting to look in on Mother Pickles for a sec when I called to pick her up. Our arthritis was worsening and we were still getting punk rock on our teeth, but we were overjoyed that Cynthia and I were engaged to be married. (Cynthia's having broken it to her stepmother seemed to me a decided plus here.) "We're deliriously in love," I said, adding that I knew Mrs. Pickles had been rooting for me from the start and that I was grateful for it. Assurances of delight rained on me now, coming usually in the glossary of another day. I was a brick. I was true blue. I was all wool and a yard wide. Anybody could see that. "Perhaps not a yard," I demurred, simpering at my feet. Oh, yes, a yard. "No, no, a foot, possibly eighteen inches," I persisted, wondering if maybe the fever hadn't come back and I was going round the bend for good. "Absolutely — a yard." I shrugged helplessly at Cynthia, who was leaning against the doorjamb watching with her arms folded, expressionlessly waiting out another exchange between me and Mrs. Pickles. "Anybody who will make worms out of peanut butter and feed them to fallen birds is all wool and a yard wide." "Not maybe just a teeeeeny percentage polyester?" I went laughingly on with the bit. After recommending me to her stepdaughter for a while in this established vein, she asked, "How did you feel when Cynthia accepted you?" "They were words I was dying to hear," I said.

With a jerk of her head Cynthia signaled that we must now be on our way. Enough was enough, if not, as the fella said, too much. We were to meet up with Chirouble and Roxy, and after an early dinner head for a nearby town to take in a comedy at a summer theatre called the Whiffletree Playhouse, which if you really set your brains to the problem you may hit on the deduction that it was a remodeled barn. I suddenly regretted it was to be a foursome. That meant it would be hours before we were alone and I would be free to drop my appointed bombshell. I was impatient to get that over with and so clear the air between us and leave myself, so to speak, purged.

"I wish we weren't going to the theatre," I said as we went down her front stairs. "Or had any company tonight. We've loads to talk about."

"You said a mouthful — Monty."

"What?"

"I said I agree we've lots to talk about, Monty."

"Monty, who's Monty?"

"You know — Monty Carlo. *The* Monty Carlo. The porn king?"

We had stopped at the foot of the stairs and now faced each other with radically different expressions. Hers a taut, strained little smile, mine a stupid grin in an undoubtedly pale face. "Ah, come on, I'm no porn king," I said, simpering at my shoes as I had a minute before in denying to her mother that I was a yard wide. "I was going to tell you. Tonight. About my double life?"

"You don't have to, now."

"How did you find out?"

"You obviously haven't read this."

She drew from her coat pocket and unfolded a column-long story from the local *Advocate*, which she handed over to me. "Local Mystery Man Unmasked as Porn King," the headline read. The story ran like ice water into my veins:

Who is the young man seen riding about town in a 30-foot-long mauve stretch limousine flamboyantly dubbed his Land Yacht? Who is the originator, producer, and sometimes stud star of Sexucational Films, a series of pornographic shorts purporting to be counseling demonstrations on how to make love, thus fully realizing your carnal potential maritally or otherwise? Who is Monty Carlo, the mastermind behind it all? He — or they — are all the same person, and that person is none other than Edward Teeters, a newcomer to Merrymount currently residing at 217 Carmody Street. In addition to the above personae, he is also a stockholder in New Era Cassettes, the corporation selling and renting the films for video use. He is also incidentally one of the investors in *Overview,* a journalistic venture to be launched here in Sparta County.

Monty Carlo is the pseudonym he uses as producer and actor in the shorts which have come under increasingly fierce attack by the Citizens Against Pornography as well as by the Moral Majority, not because they are necessarily more obscene than the average porn flick but because by virtue of their masquerading as "educational" they are being widely purchased for the kind of home consumption that inevitably exposes children to them. In the studio where they are produced they are referred to, whether tongue-in-cheek or not, as "training films." Subscribe to the course and you will be a better bride or groom, or even adulterer.

She watched me as I refused to read any more, stuffing the clipping angrily into my pocket. "Well?"

"I'll sue the sonsofbitches. I'll sue the pants off them."

"My mother doesn't read much anymore because her eyes are so bad, and I haven't read this to her, or told her about it, or you'd have lost all the Brownie points you've racked up with her for God knows what reason."

"I'll sue them till they wish they'd never been founded in 1887."

"What's this about your acting in the things? You weren't in the one we saw."

"Yes I was, in the meat close-ups. I'm not an actor in the conventional sense, but the guy who played the part is no great shakes below the belt. Not enough staying power."

"So you're a stuntman." She seemed to be weighing it in

her own mind rather than addressing me. "He's a stuntman in skinflicks. My fiancé. My beloved."

"Does that surprise you?"

"No." She shook her head and laughed, but the laugh was of the nasally snorted kind. "So at the party we got turned on together by watching you."

"Don't blame yourself."

"He gets off on himself, then tells me not to blame myself."

"It was you excited me. You made me pop my tallow."

"Made you *what*?"

"It's jargon we use in the cinema of the erotic."

"Tell me more about the cinema of the erotic. What are some other terms for — that?"

"Well, Krumholz the director — of whose morals and language I do not approve, mind you — in filming a climactic scene —"

"Climactic scene he says," she murmured, as though wonders would never cease. "What else does this Krumholz of whom you do not approve say?"

"He'll say, oh, like, 'In this scene I want the tapioca. Let's go for the tapioca.' These are the people I have to put up with in order to produce something in good faith, of social value. I die every time he opens his mouth, but I bear it because I'm confident that what we're doing is worthwhile. I mean every time I die a little. 'I want the tapioca like they got it in *Deep Throat*.' Have you seen that by any chance, darling?"

"I refuse to believe this conversation is taking place."

"It isn't. Hold on to that. *It isn't taking place*. Hold on to that for dear life. It's a dialogue between two other people entirely. The other me who kept all this from the other you because he loved her and wanted to marry her the worst way —"

"What could be worse than this." To the heavens, the stars, she said it.

"Because he loved her and for that reason intended to tell her all in jew course — tonight, I swear! — so she could make up her own mind. At least there are two me's. The other me did this to pile up enough to finance his serious work, and in so doing ascend to a level that would put me in your class, so I could pop the question."

"At least we're popping questions. That's a relief." Again to the stars, the night. "What happened to tallow and tapioca?"

"There'll be no more tallow and no more tapioca. That I swear. It was one hand not knowing the other was washing it. You've heard of the expression robbing Peter to pay the piper."

"I have now."

"All right. So it's been a Gatsby sort of thing, worshipping the princess from afar, and him coming out fine in the end, though dead as a mackerel, that's the thanks you get. But by Christ I'll stack up my porn against his bootlegging anytime!"

Numerous cars were parked along the curb here so mine was waiting some distance down the block, and we made for it slowly as we talked, now and then pausing on the sidewalk to do so.

"Think what this will make *Overview* look like even before we're off the ground. A wholly owned subsidiary of Sexucational Films," she said, trying out what it must be assumed some people would think, human nature being what it is. "Where the hell did Tom Layton dig that up?"

"Where did he dig any of it up? Somebody in my company is a Judas, and I'll damn well find out who. And do you know what kind of a Judas? I'll tell you what kind. A Judas Iscariot — the worst kind!"

"Layton fancies himself an 'investigative reporter,' using pieces in the *Advocate* to tune up for the Big Story that'll win him the Pulitzer Prize."

"I'll Pulitzer Prize him. *Kapow!* Right in the kisser."

"Did you read his last line? His snapper?"

I fished the clipping out again to do so.

"Local residents treated to the sight of the Land Yacht cruising through our streets may have noticed it has a New York license plate. So our friend may not have intentions of permanently gracing our town with his presence." I crammed the clipping back into my pocket. "I'll sue the pants off him too. Him and the paper both."

"What for? I don't mean what for — I mean for what? What will you sue them for?"

"Libel."

"Is it?" Searching look.

"Well, slander then. For calling respectable and well-intentioned erotica pornography. That'll keep the courts busy with new definitions and precedents. Huh!"

"Sure, you can spend your arduously earned fortune taking it right up to the Supreme — Oh, my God, he's got the limousine! And that tableau again."

The sight of Meredith standing at attention beside the held-open door was undoubtedly what she meant by the tableau. It got to me a little too. I had been telling him to try to affect what they call a casual elegance, but no, he had to outdo the owner himself in putting on the dog. He stood stiffly at attention, with a kind of stern pride, like a man about to be executed declining a blindfold. A couple of urchins and even some adult passersby gaping at the scene didn't help the situation as far as Cynthia was concerned, though I must admit that in my heart of hearts I relished being the object of attention, one who could turn even people in this affluent community into rubbernecking yokels.

Sunk back in the upholstery, and humming along toward Chirouble's place, we resumed the argument.

"Layton must have run off all the films — twelve so far I gather. This one entitled *Foreplay* he says is two naked people simonizing each other for a quarter of an hour."

"Layton is not a dramatic critic," I said, reaching into my armrest for the intercom mouthpiece. "Meredith, hang a left there, and it's up four blocks."

"Where all them desirable homes are?"

"That is correct."

"Yes, sir."

Cynthia lowered her head in her hand and went into one of her laughing fits. "I'm sorry. This fire engine turn again. It's such a parody."

"Never mind the turns. The main thing is, will you believe I meant to tell you tonight?"

"I believe you."

"That would give you ample opportunity to back out of the engagement. Of course you will. I can see that now. I should have stood on my own side of the tracks."

"Don't be silly," she said, which couldn't weigh much as reassurance since, given her character, she'd have said it anyway, no matter what she secretly thought or intended. "I'm sorry," she then said, apologizing for a renewed burst of laughter. "But this 'ample opportunity' and these fire engine turns. He has to swing right to turn left. This 'Home, James' sort of thing. It really is such a parody."

That was exactly Chirouble's tack, only in a much more exuberant manner. Coming down the walk from his house with Roxy he approached me with his arms flung wide for an embrace. "Monty Carlo in the flesh! You old bastard, what a jape you've been pulling on us."

"I have?"

"Certainly. It's a gem of a put-on. A classic of its kind."

"It is?"

"What a send-up."

"You're not just saying that?"

"And this limo is the maraschino cherry on the whole caricature. I mean lilac yet! What color would a porn king choose but lavender. What playacting, old boy. As a satire on a certain kind of American vulgarity it's a priceless pastiche of the *arriviste*. Of course you had to personify it to bring it off."

"Bingo!"

To get a proper handle on what I was doing I would not only have to pay close attention to Chirouble's analysis but make a point of remembering all the words he was using so that I could look them up later. Let's see, jape, pastiche, *arriviste*. It would take a good hour with the dictionary to understand fully the sort of thing I was trying to do. Roxy chimed in with her own congratulations, though probably to some extent she was likewise taking her cues from Chirouble, who was just too breezy and good-natured to think ill of a friend. I also detected in Roxy's eyes a glint of speculative appreciation of a revealed stud. I was as glad she'd read the story as I was sorry Cynthia had. But that's human nature. What can you do?

The restoration of my spirits proved all too short-lived. The essential factor for me was still Cynthia, with this point as crux of the whole matter: Chirouble thought the parody conscious buffoonery; Cynthia, unconscious. And her intermittently glum mood at dinner argued poorly for her ultimate acceptance of my double life as one with social significance containing satire on bourgeois Americana. It looked less and less like we were heading for the old middle aisle.

If she'd been keen about it, why had she told nobody but her mother? It had taken her two days to tell *me* we were engaged, so to speak. Here it was two weeks and she clearly hadn't told Chirouble or Roxy the glad tidings. Tonight would be the ideal time to break them, say over a bottle of the bubbly. And she may very well have planned to, but the beans spilled about me had made her change her mind. No, she wasn't going to break the news, she was going to break the engagement. I had played my cards all wrong, or too late. It looked like Kaputsville.

I suddenly didn't want to be here in this restaurant, or going to the Whiffletree Playhouse. I wanted to be home alone with a wafflewich and a six-pack of Heineken, watching TV with my stocking feet up on another chair. I *had* been trying to step out of my own class (how could I ever forgive Toby for being right there?) and even now had to keep what little precarious footing I had left on higher ground by pretending that my erotica was a put-on, a jive of which the limo as a parody of bourgeois vulgarity had to be carefully sustained or it would really be Shambles Junction. If I needed any more proof that I was up to my gums in a mare's nest, the theatre still ahead of us supplied it.

The play was a drawing room comedy called *Baby Cakes,* and as you know drawing room comedies these days take place principally in bedrooms. I thought it was a howl, the jokes about "the bare necessities" and the double bed as "the workbench" pretty good, but apparently I was wrong. At the first intermission my companions exchanged looks that themselves sufficed, without Chirouble actually saying, "Well, have we all had enough of this piece of schnitzel?" Yes we had, apparently, so off we tooled. I wasn't about to cast a dissenting opinion that would brand me as a noodle-head, so I mumbled agreement with the rest, though really itching to go back and learn how the Merry Marital Mix-up came out, or failing that, slip behind the barn the theatre was a reincarnation of and dig up an old whiffletree to beat myself over the head with. To make matters worse, Meredith was nowhere in sight, being no doubt down in town lifting a few scuttles of suds, as was his want, so I had to drive our smart-assed little set home myself. I made a practice of carrying a spare set of keys on my own key ring for a contingency such as this, so there was no problem there. After dropping the others off I would go back around eleven for Meredith. Or let him take the bus home as a lesson well learned. One could see increasing point in taking a stern view in the master-servant relationship, if the social structure is to be preserved with the equilibrium it has always needed since the dawn of civilization. Communication with my companions was sarcastically maintained by talking through the intercom. I could easily enough have slid the glass partition down.

"In spite of all, I felt the piece had a certain belly naïveté in the main refreshing, and not to be entirely written off in an age of overintellectualization," I said through the chauffeur's mouthpiece, whipping around a poky motorist with the other hand on the wheel. Fishing the passenger, or boss's, mouthpiece out of the upholstery back there Chirouble replied, "So you could take it on two levels."

"Precisely."

"I see what you mean. But once you've got the idea, you've had it with that sort of thing. Sustaining it requires more brilliance than that."

"I suppose. Still, using the bedpost to pitch horseshoes with the Polish sausage was amusing, in a low sort of way."

Roxy reached over to take the mouthpiece from him. She'd overheard me.

"But the phallic implications we were supposed to see in it got to be so Freudian-labored, don't you think, Eddie?"

"I guess."

To hell with them, I thought. To hell with this whole place.

I might have stuck around to explore Roxy, but if she was hot to trot she wouldn't be needling me on the Polish sausage bit. Did any of them know it's called a kielbasa? Probably not, though if they ate one it would be "culinary slumming." No, my decision was made. To hell with the whole kaboodle.

I peeled around another molasses-in-January, telling him to get a horse as I shot by. No doubt venting on him the irritation I felt with Cynthia for having climbed in the back with the others when she'd sat up front with Meredith that time. Though it could have been instinctive, a reflex behavior that might have been true of anyone in the circumstances, it could also have unconsciously expressed her view of me at that particular time. No balm to my mood either way. The evening was a pile of rubble. The summer breeze meant nothing. The moon was a clot of phlegm. Parody of megabucks indeed. They had seen nothing yet. You want vulgarity, you got it. I would expand my porn empire and having done so supplement it with a string of brothels stretching to Timbuktu, a vice lord till I could buy and sell the lot of them. I would have them all on toast points. I might just damn *well* add onto the Land Yacht till she could seat ten and sleep four. I would welcome litigation, to show how money could scoff at the law, emerging from the limo picking my teeth with an old theatre ticket stub on my way to hear the Not Guilty verdict from a boughten judge, prior to snacking in the back seat out of the picnic hamper as I was driven out to inspect the site chosen by the town for the new band shell I was donating it. The Eddie Teeters Pavilion.

The Smart Set were still talking about the play.

"I've seen something of that author's before," Chirouble said. "His stuff is rather thin."

I lifted the mouthpiece up closer. "So are Hepburn, strudel crust, and gold leaf," I said. "They're thin too."

In the mirror I could see them exchange looks of consternation. Then in a conciliatory tone Roxy took the mike and said, "Which Hepburn, Eddie? Katharine or Audrey?"

"Jesus H. Christ, they're both skinny as a rail. Take your pick."

There was a puzzled silence back there you could feel up front, in the servants' quarters. Cynthia then said she did rather enjoy the scene where one of the characters in the farce, discovered under the bed, said he was looking for a cuff link. Some more talk about that which I didn't get clearly, since we weren't formally keeping up this conversation, only vaguely holding the mouthpieces in our hands. But I did hear Chirouble get off one of his own drawing room comedy kind of remarks. "I feel cuff links were invented in order that we might have something to give uncles for Christmas." Then the subject got into martinis, these having been heavily drunk in the play.

"I like mine with a whisper of Lemon Pledge on top," I said.

"Isn't that a furniture polish?"

"Yup."

"Of course the purists will insist — Hey, Eddie, for God's sake, you almost took that guy's fender off. Need we be driving all this brilliantly, old chap?"

"When it comes to chauffeuring," I said, "I don't take a back seat to anybody."

◈

Unexpected Kumquats

WHEN CYNTHIA discovered I was a hunk she stopped going to bed with me. That wasn't of course the way she put it, but it's what it came down to. After the exposé in the local rag it behooved her not to stigmatize her own paper by being seen in public with me too much until the scandal died down and *Overview* was successfully launched on its own merits. We trysted in out-of-the-way places to which we hied ourselves in separate cars, mine *not* to be the Land Yacht. Of course she did not lose her sense of humor (not necessarily to be confused with her laughing fits, which are crying jags turned inside out according to the shrinks).

"Hello, Mr. Macho," she greeted me once at a bar that smelled like a friendly old sock.

"Cut it out," I said. "Can I help this? We all have our own limitations."

"Like being a human jackhammer. How you must preen yourself on that shortcoming."

"You're a little old ball of fire yourself, you know, in that department. Not that you don't have your faults."

"Such as what?"

"Oh, you're so damn perfect. Everything is so precisely calculated. The way you mince around this damn thing, meeting away out here where Christ lost his shoes. Why don't you instead stick up for me, a martyr to Puritanic hypocrisy? Associate with me openly, like Jesus did with the Republicans and sinners, a living rebuke to the nay-sayers."

"I have a lot of other people's money riding on my venture, and the least I owe them is not to jeopardize it. You admit you're getting hate mail. 'Get out of town. We don't want your sort here.' For myself I couldn't care less. For them I have to wait at least till this cools down, or blows over, or see whether *Overview* gets rolling. I have to wait till I get the lay of the land."

"I thought you already had him. I know I have. We should be at my place now, rumpling the bedsheets, instead of sitting here like two conspirators."

"Spoken like a stud."

"How I hate that word."

"I'll bet. You wear it like a diamond stickpin."

I inwardly debated whether to tell Cynthia that hate mail was by no means the only kind I got. It was being outrun two to one by letters from ladies that sustained my faith in the fair sex faster than my respect for my fellow creatures as such was dwindling. They deplored my victimization by the life-deniers, and assured me that respite from the pack at my heels could be found in their arms, anytime I wanted to rest my weary head for a while on their breasts. Some of the writers said frankly that they wanted to test-drive this new sex symbol. Almost all included telephone numbers, specifying "the best hours to call," and two or three contained door keys. I had heard that a currently popular novelist known for his burly style was getting the same treatment from women readers, who flocked to his lectures, where they threw their apartment keys and in some cases silk underthings on the platform where he was trying to read from his stuff. I had doubted all that as P.R. copy from his publisher, or media hype blowing everything out of proportion, but not anymore. I quite believed it.

As more metropolitan dailies picked up the *Advocate* piece and publicity me-wise swelled, a duplicate of my story was being enacted in New York City, where Jack Sweeper was staying at the moment. You will remember him as the actor playing the lead roles as such. People ignorant of the fact that he had a stand-in doing the explicit sex for him took *him* to be the Macho Man of the hour, and he played it to the hilt, with many an assist from a P.R. firm of his own. He started pumping iron, the better to butch it up around the Apple as he went from bed to bed, to wrap in his bulging muscles the many starved women who sought his favors. That at least was beneath me — even playing the Midnight Cowboy at all.

I stowed the perfumed letters away in a drawer along with the we-don't-want-your-sort-here ones, but I never responded to any of them. One did tempt me, only because I was eaten with curiosity about any dame who would pen such a missive. Which ran: "Seven years ago I entered into a marriage of convenience. Relatives and friends warned me against it, but their prophecies of 'It won't last' fell on deaf ears. But they were right. It blew up in one tumultuous burst of passion, after which I now loathe the sight or sound of him, or even the thought. I need out — out I say — or failing the immediate realization of that, surcease in the arms of a man who *understands* . . ." I'm all for surcease, whatever that is. It was big this year, but I resisted sampling it with To-main Brewer, which was the name of the lady whose marriage of convenience one roll in the hay blew into splinters. God knew my relationship with Cynthia was complex enough without taking on anyone as twisty as Tomain.

Getting it together with Cynthia remained the be-all and end-all of my existence, but while that meant not feeding at the short-order trough with the kinky likes of Tomain Brewer, it didn't as I saw it in my needful condition rule out Toby Snapper. For Toby was a pre-existing infidelity, as the sociologists call it, or probably will when they find they've run out of jargon. You might even say I had been disloyal to her *with* Cynthia, when that got started. It was inevitable that I eventually run into Toby at the country club, whither I ofttimes wended my way as the most ideal place to conduct the parody of bourgeois vulgarity Chirouble must be credited as first having spotted that my life-style was. He had spotted it early on — even before I myself had realized my full potential by grasping the sort of thing I was trying to do. I suppose it had been subconsciously brewing all along, until recognition dawned that I was at bottom a smart cookie capable of doing things on two levels.

It is on two levels that we see me now tooling up the Rolling Acres driveway, all eyes agape at the sight of the youthful tycoon's famous Land Yacht; on two levels that we see me stopping to chat in the parking lot with Bertha the swillperson, by coincidence making her sanitation truck pickup at the back of the restaurant abutting there. I lean with the flat of my hand against a wall, one foot crossed over the other, having a word with our Wellesley girl as she dangles an emptied can by the handle — the true meaning of America. Let them all see the man of means passing the time of day with the poor student in a tableau of democracy at work.

"How's your dissertation on Proust coming, my dear?"

"I'm through *Swann's Way.*"

"Oh, yes. I keep promising myself to see the ballet Tchaikovsky made out of it but each Holiday season slips by without my getting to Lincoln Center. Tell me, was it we who were discussing Proust's fondness for American investments? I find that rather a scream for him, don't you? I mean an asthmatic nibbling on tea cakes buying into Standard Oil and the Delaware Lackawanna."

"Well, actually — My God! Who is that?"

I turned my head toward the spot at the pool where she was pointing. A sex kitten in next to nothing was churning her merchandise along the water's edge, swinging a bathing cap in one hand.

"Oh, that? That's my chauffeur."

A recent trip into New York aimed at learning who had spilled the story to the *Advocate* had netted me nothing, but I had run into Mea Culpa, very much at loose ends as she waited for the shooting on *Toot Suite* to commence. She had repeated her offer to drive for me, and this time I'd snapped at it.

"Is she naked?"

"No, no. It's a string bikini, and *made* of string. She crocheted it herself."

"It can't have taken her very long."

"It's Mea Culpa the film star. Would you like to meet her?"

"Thanks, but I haven't time. What's her real name?"

"No one seems to know. Would you like me to find out?"

"It's not important. I've got to be going. I'm behind in my rounds as it is."

I lighted an eight-inch cigar, and with a certain innate grace didn't toss the match into Bertha's can, but put it in my pocket after it cooled off, for future disposal. "I'm thinking I'd like to endow a scholarship for some worthy student of limited means, and I could fix it up so you'd get it.

Then you wouldn't have to take summer jobs to make ends meet."

"That's sweet of you, Eddie, but I don't mind this too much. It's good exercise for keeping the old avoirdupois down, and you have no idea how much fun I find it to be driving a truck."

I took a long drag and smiled at her through the cloud of smoke. "You're the goods, Bertha. There are no flies on you."

"At least not after five. So long, Eddie. See you around I hope."

"Tout allure."

I sauntered down to an empty table and sat there drawing on my Montezuma, the object of many eyes. Those, at least, that weren't watching Mea Culpa float on her back in the pool. It was a perfect day, not a cloud in the sky, except the possibility of her being arrested, and maybe me too. A voice behind me said: "Well, if it isn't 'im as has got the world by the tail. 'Im as has got the town split in two like a supermarket broiler. Wot'll it be today, kind sir? Wot's your elegant pleasure? Ain't we the toff now as well as swordsman. That your current squeeze? I saw you from the restaurant window."

"Hello, Toby."

She came around to my side, and stood there in her plum-colored house waitress dress, pad and pencil poised in mock servility, waiting to hear my pleasure.

"I've been looking for you. For the moment I just want that usual planter's punch we all seem to be addicted to this season, but how about dinner tonight? Anything to stuff that mouth long enough to keep it from spouting sass. I tried to call you twice but no answer. Not even your father saying how would he know where she is. He seems to have inherited your sarcasm."

"So did I try to reach you, but 'e's got an unlisted number now, wouldncha know. Does anyone know it but the ice princess?"

"Cut it out about her. She's about as cold as you, and we both know how cold that is. Things are in abeyance between us — means on the back burner — just now for practical reasons, and the fact that I got myself out of the book should be proof enough that I'm not a mattress bum. Calls I don't need on top of mail you wouldn't believe. Here's my number." I handed her a piece of paper on the back of which I had scribbled it. "I'm taking your word things have drawn to a close with you and the realtor."

She nodded toward the pool as she tucked the paper into a dress pocket. "Naturally I'm dying for a ride in your foot-long hot dog, but will the number in the G-string be driving us to wherever?"

"Suppose you let me worry about that. Pick you up tonight about sevenish then?"

"Saints preserve us, 'e's become one o' them ish people. Ain't we the quality though. Gettin' a piece o' chicken stuck in our throat and claimin' it's pheasant."

"The doctor was a snob. Just a little status game I played for his sake. And where did you hear this?"

"I have a friend who's a nurse there."

"A redhead named Madeline?" I asked.

"No." Toby's manner softened and sweetened, as it suddenly could, like a spring day when the sun reappears from behind a blowing cloud. She took me in with the most melting look. "I don't mean to be joking about it. I was scared stiff when I heard. I knew it was a close shave. I went to a church and prayed."

"My dear."

I watched her walk toward the restaurant with my order, those hips tolling in rhythm with the temple bells up front.

Halfway up the short flight of stone stairs, she turned and glanced at me. I made no effort to conceal my girl-watching. We exchanged grins and I swung back around in my chair.

Having uncraned my neck, I saw that my cigar had gone out. I stoked it up again, aware of being watched from all directions. I escalated the parody, picking my teeth with a corner of the matchbook flap as I slid down in my seat and gazed about me through smoked glasses. People digging me averted their eyes when I trained my own on them. One of the women held her gaze fast, and I wondered if it might be one of the letter writers. Maybe Tomain Brewer herself. There had been no picture of me in the local paper — yet — so people's familiarity with me was based on their seeing me get in and out of the stretch limo, and pointing me out to one another. Once in a while I removed or lifted the shades, so onlookers could see how bored was my hooded gaze. Mea floated on and on in the water. I had pumped her in vain for some clue as to who the Judas in the film company was. I believed her protestations of ignorance. I leaned my head back and closed my eyes, basking in the warm sunlight as I awaited my planter's punch and dreamed of my forthcoming evening — and night? — with she who was even now fetching it.

My reverie was shattered by a hideous racket. Up the drive roared the Devil's Disciples, nine strong, with the previously empty rear saddles now occupied by a women's auxiliary known as Hell's Belles. Avoiding them was out of the question as they made straight for the limo, which I didn't feel their obvious appreciation safeguarded from harm. Anything mechanized was sacred to these characters, which by the same token entailed the danger of bits being picked off here and there and retained as souvenirs. Nothing to do but edge over a little closer so I could keep an eye on my property.

They were circling it in dazzled awe as I approached, fondling and feeling it here and there. One of the Belles was stroking the radiator front, as though it was a prized horse's nose. "This yours?" she said. "Then you must be the hunk." I acknowledged as much with a modest nod. "Hey, here's the hunk, you guys. It's him."

Their bikes propped up everywhere, they swarmed around me. Of course the men had a bone to pick with me. Why hadn't I kept my promise to get in touch with them about a sequence in one of my pictures? I said there was a production hitch but that I hoped to get matters ironed out soon. The beef was forgotten in the general chorus of appreciation, the collective regard for me as a co-rebel. Nothing would do but that they stick around till I left, when they would salute my underground celebrity by providing an escort to wherever I was going next. I tried to aw-shucks it, protesting that I didn't deserve such a signal honor, but they persisted. We know that primitive man is easily and dangerously offended by any rejection of an extended courtesy, and these were nothing if not primitive. That included the Ladies' Aid.

In the midst of all this a security cop came over and conveyed the club's wish that they leave the premises as they were not now residents of the town, the most delicate way in which official revulsion at the sight of them could be put. A nasty hassle might have developed had I not hastily resolved the problem by saying that I was about to leave and would be honored to accept the escort. "Wait here just a second," I said, and in less than three minutes had paid for my drink, gulped standing up, got my chauffeur out of the water, settled her, still dripping, behind the wheel, climbed into the back seat, and made off, roaring down the drive with one Neanderthal leading the way and the other eight flanking me, four on each side. Fame can exact a stiff price, and the good life is often complicated.

173

The single most painful memory of my childhood was the discovery that my mother was paying the neighborhood kids to play with me. Fifteen cents an hour. Wouldn't that rock you? I mean to learn that you were regarded by your school peers as such a drip that they required remuneration to put up with you, to let you in on street games, neighborhood shenanigans, or just hang out and hack around with them. I was not on my own merits one of the bunch. That was the bitter pill to be swallowed. It must have hurt my mom as well to realize that her firstborn didn't fit in, to see him sitting on the doorstep alone or, hands in pockets, kicking a tin can as he trudged along the sidewalk. So she had to grease a few palms to buy him a chum or two. And you can understand that from the revelation she had done so stemmed my determination to belong, to ultimately fit into the picture, to *count*, which I have admitted is my consuming drive.

We see that I have fulfilled it, to no small degree. We see me being chauffeured in a stretch limousine with a convoy of motorcyclists you wouldn't ask to dinner with a ten-foot pole, true, but who will suffice as grown-up versions of the kids who wouldn't play with me without a fee but whom I can now buy and sell — as I can a lot of the country club set clucking their educated tongues and shaking their summer-tanned heads as I peel out of the driveway on two levels. Three, if you think of me thinking of myself operating on the other two.

We see me as a *cause célèbre*, to use the term the local *Advocate* did in the follow-up story depicting how I have split the town in two like a broiler, as Toby put it. We see the outraged half throwing ripe fruit at my passing vehicle, including, so help me, kumquats. The last thing you would expect being hurled as a sign of disfavor. Eggs, tomatoes, cabbages, yes. But kumquats. Of course this is a chic and affluent community. We see another element enjoying the spectacle I offer, waving at me as I go by to signify their objection to censorship in all its forms, the randier youths whistling at a chauffeur who is reminiscent of the Hollywood secretaries in bathing suits of yesteryear. We see me at the landfill, the town garbage dump ultimately to be paved over and landscaped for the band shell I offer to contribute, which again results in vociferous division of opinion.

We see me calling for Mrs. Pickles to take her to the Rehabilitation Center for arthritis treatments twice a week. Not only is her shoulder getting worse, but her sight is failing, so that the striped and checked suits I now sport are to her conservative dress. Dressed conservatively in the regular sense, I would be discernible to her as no more than a dim blob, poor thing. Cynthia, who has to read everything to her, including the *Advocate*, skips everything about me, for my sake and Mrs. Pickles' too, recognizing the value of my affection and friendship for a lonely stepmother who must, for me, replace the mother I have lost, and who once paid kids fifteen cents an hour to play with her loner son. We see Cynthia more and more reluctant to meet me even in out-of-the-way bars and restaurants, now that *Overview* is off to an auspicious start and must not be jeopardized by associations on her part which the jealous *Advocate* would unquestionably capitalize on.

"Is that a new suit, Eddie?"

"Yes. Do you like it?"

"Well, I have no objections to stripes that size, though I prefer them on awnings. Do you know they're calling you the Abominable Showman?"

"Oh, really? Barman, could you do this again?"

"Have you made plans to add onto the Land Yacht?"

"I'd like to install a Ping-Pong table. Also I was thinking of a rack on top, to carry a small job like a Volkswagen or Honda, like the dinghies they carry on yachts?"

"Are you rubbing salt into your own wounds or those of the town? Or the world?"

"Are you seeing Chirouble, as I hear?"

"Now and then. He's not only an investor — I finally got him to switch some of his money from that preposterous publishing house — but one of the directors of *Overview* too, you know. And you, do you like this Toby a lot? I can't imagine a man who wouldn't."

We see me in New York, shooting *Toot Suite* amid gathering rumors that the Citizens Against Pornography are ready to pounce with their class-action civil suit. The *Advocate* milks them for everything it can. Two teenage girls have allegedly become pregnant as a direct result of exposure to the cassettes. "Keep Porn out of the Home" becomes the war cry. Then the second shoe falls without the first having been dropped. CAP abandons plans for the civil suit when a process server slaps me with a summons to appear at a grand jury hearing on a federal criminal charge of transporting obscene material across state lines and through the mails. The hue and cry over X-rated videotapes for the home has brought us full circle, so that we are back to square one on the issue of censorship. It is a whole new ball game, and Eddie Teeters stands alone at bat, in a densely packed and brilliantly floodlit public stadium. At last he is somebody. He matters.

There had just been a news story about a process server getting into a cathedral communion line in order to hand a summons to a priest administering the sacrament. This one didn't have to do anything so drastic. He just gave me mine as I was climbing into my car one Sunday morning preparatory to a ride into New York on business. Meredith was holding the door open for me, which did add a little color to the occasion. I thanked the sheriff's minion, pocketed the summons, and off we tooled. Having perused its fully expected contents, I put it by and lit a Montezuma. Naturally I felt a great anxiety, yet flooding that emotion in at least equal quantity was a profound feeling of importance. People picketing the sidewalk in front of my place, brandishing signs reading "Merrymount is no Sodom and Gomorrah" and "Get out of town" and "Amscray!" and the like, only added to that feeling. So that as I was sped out of town toward the thruway, an occasional churchgoer thumbing his nose or shaking his fist at me, now and then an egg or tomato splattering the car, I experienced, more than ever yet, the most tremendous sense of belonging.

T E N

⌒⌒

Us Chickens

NOT ONLY were the judge's eyes too close together. They were themselves too close to his nose, which was in turn too close to a mouth of which the lips were as near to nonexistent as they could be and still have it rate as an orifice. They made the sort of tight seam that as kids we thought the dragonfly would sew our mouths up into, why we call them darning needles, and what it bespoke to me, seated at the defendant's table, was moral disapproval. The small face in which each feature fought for room made his ears seem huge when they were probably just normal size, though protruding a little, enough to make his head resemble a loving cup, of modest size. Say third-place trophy in a small-town bowling league. I suppose my observations were prejudiced because I feared this man, perched there at the bar of judgment, with the power to warehouse me. Should we after all have opted for a jury instead? My lawyer stuck to his story: it's easier to sway one man than twelve, any fanatical three or four of whom can swing any six or seven wishy-washy liberals into the current this-permissiveness-has-gone-too-far backlash. Rather than the other way around, he stressed. Fanaticism you can't wear down or win over. Where did Judge Brinkerhoff fit into this after all not very broad spectrum of opinion? I think my first impression was right. That *he* did not have a very good first impression of this clear-eyed, apple-cheeked, windswept American youth who would vend his training films down the eastern seaboard and into the midwestern heartland like an old-fashioned traveling salesman gone astray. But my lawyer, whose name is Wimbish, said not to worry. Which he also said just before the grand jury indicted me and bound me over for trial.

"Even if you get, say, three to five," he whispered in a mint-flavored breath of assurance, "we'll appeal this into your old age."

Plans for a short on "Sex After Sixty — and After" instinctively flitted across my mind, possibly guaranteeing some rosy sunset years even for myself after I got out of Ossining with a new suit and whatever the "gate money" is now. It used to be five bucks, but I imagine inflation has upped that too. The suit would be the Greater Dullsville gray the judge probably had on under his robe. Where was Toby? Working today or she'd have been in the front row among the spectators. Where was Cynthia? In New York trying to get the Civil Liberties Union to enter the fray for me and against this revival of the ogre, censorship, considered slain. This "cassettes crunch" did sound convincing. We'd got a whole new bucket of worms on the table.

"Do you have your Moral Majority membership card with you?" Wimbish asked in another peppermint zephyr.

I patted the wallet bulge of my coat, my other hand resting on the table, where my briefcase lay with the bumper sticker pasted on it: "Stamp Out Smut." I had them on my cars too, indubitable proof that no one was more opposed to garbage than I, a champion rather of true erotica. I had been advised against driving around in the limousine for the time being, as making me seem a scofflaw, so I had it stowed in the garage, or as much of it as I could get in there, and for public consumption had reverted to my old Buick. I was even thinking of getting a bicycle, and pedaling around on that as Simplicity itself.

The district attorney was making his opening statement.

The prosecution as you know takes the first hot solo, followed by a similar turn from the defense, each outlining what he intends to do. The D.A., name of Cutter, clearly intended to put me to work for a while turning out license plates, orating with such grippingness as to develop a genuine preparatory curiosity on my part how that's done in stir. Obviously on some sort of punch press, but how automatically? Mustn't you change the number after each pair stamped out, and for some states only one plate? The need to do so, to make the adjustment, might keep the job from becoming too monotonous, but on the whole I thought I would rather run the prison library. That would provide the chance as well as the leisure to steal a little time with the dictionary looking up the meaning of things he was calling me — lubricious, concupiscent, turpitudinous and the like — as well as to dip into a few of the authorities, literary and legal, he was citing against me. He even had my lawyer under his spell. Wimbish didn't seem to mind, the rain of invective disturbed him not. Was he what his very name seemed to conjure up — a wimbish? Cutter swung into high gear. "Has accumulated human genius produced the television set in order that our God-given airwaves may be polluted by the kind of visual abominations flung into them by the likes of *him?*" he said, pointing a finger at me.

"Why don't you object to something?" I said to Wimbish.

"I will. You'll see."

"What compounds his crime is the guise of 'education' under which it is committed." Cutter was really tuning up, conjuring now not so much the license-plate punch press but the rockpile on and from which the punch press and its lulling monotony would be wistfully dreamt of in the blazing noonday sun, as the library would be from the plate press. "What mockery! What perfidious sanctimony!" Two more words to look up in the library, if I made library. "This duplicity" — Christ another one, the Webster's would be in tatters before I was eligible for parole — "this duplicity might induce a tolerantly amused smile but for the damage it has done, does, and will do unless Your Honor renders a verdict running deliberately and courageously contrary to the current deplorable trend, one that somehow checks or limits the increasing latitude of First Amendment obscenity doctrine!"

Here Judge Brinkerhoff twitched upright in his chair. Was this the cunningly contrived pivotal point in the whole trial? The moment when the judge was inspired to see himself as handing down — at last! — a landmark decision?

Cutter modulated his tone, but in a way that produced an even more dramatic effect, as he went on to say: "We shall introduce a witness graphically demonstrating what the prosecution sees as the chief evil in X-rated videocassettes, one that did not obtain when these liberalizing court decisions were handed down, decisions that emboldened smut peddlers —"

"Objection!" Wimbish said, springing to his feet with a force that startled even me. "Prosecution knows full well that opening statements are restricted to what it intends to do, and are not to be usurped for the doing itself. The district attorney is pleading the case."

"Objection sustained. Strike 'smut peddlers' from the record, and while we are at it, 'visual abominations' as well.

Prosecution," the judge went reproachfully on, "is begging the case. It has not proved the material on trial is as claimed, and will have ample opportunity to do so at the legally provided time. Proceed."

Cutter did, pacing the courtroom floor while rolling a long sharp pencil in his two palms, a mannerism for which there might be plenty of psychiatric explanation available, what?

"We shall present as witness a teenage girl admittedly pregnant as a result of watching, with her boyfriend, one of these so-called training films allegedly designed to illustrate techniques of sexual intercourse of which the innocent might not have been apprised."

"Objection! 'Innocent' is a word semantically prejudiced, of which prosecution is taking unfair advantage."

"I meant it in the sense of 'ignorant,' Your Honor. Or 'uninstructed.'"

"Objection overruled. Court sees nothing reprehensible in that connotation, note of which is duly taken. Continue."

"Thank you, Your Honor. I mean to show by the introduction of the witness alluded to that she personifies the nub of the problem," Cutter resumed, "one which radically distinguishes it from circumstances given clearance by existing precedents. To a movie house showing such pictures my forthcoming witness would not have been admitted, being fifteen. At home, or her boyfriend's home, or at a so-called slumber party with a group of God knows how many tender contemporaries, in a jumble on the floor —"

"Objection!" Wimbish now fairly shouted. "Prosecution is extrapolating a use of the sex-counseling guides to which their author and producer *and* purveyor had no intention whatever of their being put. I cannot strongly enough protest this debauch of their purpose which exists solely in the district attorney's imagination."

"Your Honor, *I* object," Cutter returned with equal heat. "If counsel for the defense is insinuating that I have a dirty mind —"

"Hold it!" the judge said, getting into the shouting match with what was, for him, remarkable vigor. He lowered his voice to say, "Will prosecution and defense counsel approach the bench please."

The three huddled there in a supposed whispered consultation on the ground rules while I revolved in my mind fresh estimates of both Wimbish and Judge Brinkerhoff. The former had more fire than I had expected, and the latter didn't seem such a fuddy-duddy after all. They were both all right in there. Wimbish particularly looked good, also rolling out words I must look up, like *extrapolate,* and *debauch* used in a way I had never heard before, I must say.

"You were O.K.," I said when he returned to the table. "Going great guns."

But he was worried. "The sonofabitch is going to ring in one of the girls CAP intended to use against you in the class-action suit."

"They can't bring that against me while I'm in the clink, can they?"

He mumbled something I didn't get. He had problems of his own.

Cutter rumbled on in much the same vein, repeating himself to an extent that seemed to wilt the judge's briefly revived interest. A mist covered his gaze, as he probably wool-gathered about that landmark decision that would forever stop his wife's nagging him about never having handed one down in all his twenty, twenty-five years on the bench. Wimbish drew doodles on a pad of paper, of a kind that if analyzed would very likely show criminally hostile tendencies diverted into socially acceptable channels. My own mind wandered into furtively sidelong glances at the audience. Was Tomain Brewer here, or any of the other letter writers? Wimbish nudged me out of my reverie.

"He's rambled back into his literary authorities," he whispered. "Wait till he hears me quote Lawrence."

"Lawrence who?"

"His essay on obscenity nobody knows about. All they know is *Lady Chatterley's Lover,* and I'll be damned if I'll trot out *that* old wheeze one more time in an obscenity case. Or the steamy stuff in the Bible. Or Judge Woolsey on *Ulysses.*"

"Still, Homer would be good to have in our corner."

"Thank you, Your Honor."

Cutter had finished, and now Wimbish rose to tell what he intended to do.

I won't bother relating it in detail, because what he said he would do he did, and you'll get that in the telling.

The tide of battle seesawed for three days, during a lot of which I was sometimes bored so stiff I thought rigor mortis was setting in. I think His Honor was too, judging from how he constantly closed his eyes as if in deep thought but probably to catch a few winks behind the lowered lids, while the supposedly reflective nods once or twice broke with a snap you sorely feared might result in a whiplash case against himself. I took all this to be somehow in our favor, relaxing to such an extent that one afternoon following a heavy lunch I actually dropped off myself for a few minutes.

The two intellectual movie critics Cutter produced, one of whom I remembered seeing on television explaining the metaphysical implications of Laurel and Hardy, testified that Sexucational Films were not cinematic art, and to balance them off Wimbish trotted out two other intellectual types who said they weren't supposed to be art any more than *The Joy of Sex* and so on were supposed to be literature — they were just sex manuals projected on a screen instead of bound in a book. Each side quizzed the other's authorities, to what looked like a standoff, though one of ours drew a laugh when he called them illustrated lectures on the sacred art of love. Cutter himself contributed a horse yak by which he tried no doubt to leave the impression that he had now picked up all the marbles.

Wimbish jumped to his feet on the D.A.'s trumpeted laugh, denouncing the cheap attempt to color the testimony as tendentious, another word to look up if I made library, though I gathered from his speech that it means having, or pushing, a purpose. The purpose here being "to cynically impugn the defendant's motives, which there is not a shred of reason to consider suspect. And if the prosecution had sufficient access to my client's heart of hearts to justify the slur — and may the court note my resonant *if* — even then I cite William O. Douglas's recorded opinion that an author's motivation in producing something has no bearing whatever on its ultimate worth. He can be spurred by nothing more than the wish to make a pot of money — as Faulkner was when he wrote *Sanctuary* — and turn out a work of art — which *Sanctuary* is. He can have the most ulterior motive and still contribute something of redeeming social importance."

"Can counsel cite the case in question?" the judge asked.

"Yes, sir. I refer to Justice Douglas's dissent in the Ginzburg case of recent memory. His exact words were, 'A book should stand on its own, irrespective of the reasons why it was written or the wiles used in selling it.' End quote. What applies to a book can to a film — or an illustrated lecture."

Taking that trick wasn't a plus for long. The D.A. cleverly twisted the point around against us.

"Counsel for the defense cogently cites Justice Douglas's opinion. Indeed I was about to do so myself. Its gist is so valid that the reverse of counsel's application could be equally pertinent. Namely, that motives themselves unimpeachable may result in an end product not only socially worthless but permanently damaging. Which is precisely our contention these films are — damaging. As I hope to show with my next witness. I call to the stand Miss Cathy Cudlipp."

You could hear the neckbones grind, including my own, as we turned to watch the girl alleged to have been ruined by some Sexucational short or other rise from the back and make her way forward. There was no doubt some jock or other had got her pretty properly pumped up, all right. Under a blue skirt and matching worn-outside blouse with a Peter Pan collar was a billowing middle that spelled out: "License plates." She made her way demurely to the stand, where she sat in a tableau of trampled innocence, staring forward with great Bambi eyes. She laid her hand on the Bible I was thinking now Wimbish might have quoted a few of the bawdier passages from at that, hackneyed as it would be to ring in Holy Writ yet another time.

"Do you swear to tell the truth the whole truth and nothing but the truth so help you God?"

"I do. Kwee do this fast? Kwee hurry this up?"

"Of course, my child," said the D.A.

"Objection! The witness is clearly not a child, and the prosecution obviously uses the term in an attempt to smear my client by semantic implication."

"Overruled."

"But, Your Honor —"

"I must caution counsel for the defense that the bench has ruled on his objection."

"However, permit me to elucidate my reason," Wimbish persisted. "Prosecution is using the term in a, well, an almost priestly sense. A priest can employ the vocative in the case of an adult of even advanced years."

By this time Wimbish had hastily turned to the word in a dictionary he had handy on the table.

"But the district attorney is not a priest and this is not a church, but a court of law, which should, I submit, honor Webster's official definition of a child as one 'between infancy and puberty,' puberty in turn being defined as the age when one is capable of reproduction." And he slammed the dictionary shut. "The witness patently falls within that category."

I appreciated the way Wimbish (once, you remember, suspected of being a wimbish) could hot dog it when the occasion arose, though doubting that hot dogging it on this particular instance did us anything but harm. The judge looked very cross as he turned to the D.A. and said, "You may proceed." Cutter with a little smirk swung his attention back to the witness. He had taken the trick without playing a card.

"What is your name, my dear?"

Wimbish let out a whistled moan like the air going out of a rubber duck.

"Um, Cathy."

"Cathy what?"

"Um, Cudlipp. Kwee move this along?"

"Certainly. I realize how painful this is for you."

I could not help emitting the hoot that had all eyes turning reproachfully on me. The child, or dear, was so obviously enjoying her bit scene, right up to and including the bleated little pleas to hurry it along, that I guess I expected everyone to laugh as involuntarily as I had. The judge said, "I must ask the defendant to observe elementary courtroom decorum under pain of contempt judgment."

"Sorry, Your Honor." The first words I had uttered, except to my lawyer.

Cutter resumed his examination.

"How old are you?"

"Um, fifteen."

"You are plainly in a delicate condition."

"Yes."

"Do you wish to tell the court the circumstances under which this has come about?"

"Yes, if it will help society. My boyfriend and I went to a movie one night, and then had a hamburger and a side of fries at Goofy's Drive-in. Though of course we walked because he doesn't have a car. He can't drive because he's only fifteen too. Then he walked me, um, home, where we were as good as alone."

"What do you mean by that?"

"My father was in Brussels and my mother was asleep. So we had the living room to ourselves, and we turned the television on real low? It was a movie that my boyfriend said bored him, didn't we have a cassette we could put on. So I dug out this Sexucational short called *Adam and Eve,* which shows basic techniques of . . . of . . ."

"Of copulation?"

"Objection! Prosecution is leading the witness."

"Objection sustained. Prosecution is instructed to let the witness find and use her own words."

"Certainly, Your Honor. The film showed basic techniques of what, Cathy?"

"Of making out. Of doing it. Kwee hurry this?"

Cutter gave the court and audience ample time to observe the girl's modestly lowered eyes before crossing in front of her and taking another stance against the witness box. "Now I must ask you a most delicate question. What happened then?"

"We found ourselves turned on by the picture. I mean really, um, inflamed? My boyfriend came on real strong, and

I found I couldn't resist? So I gave myself to him. Gave him what he wanted at last."

" 'At last.' You mean by that you were a virgin up till then?"

"Um, yes."

"And you think you might still be a virgin were it not for that night?"

"Yes."

"So the film was directly responsible for your being deflowered."

"Absolutely."

"Your witness."

Wimbish rose slowly as Cutter took his seat at his own table, where he sat again rolling the pencil in his palms as my lawyer conducted what was certainly the shortest cross-examination of this trial.

"Cathy, I have no wish to prolong for you an ordeal through which I, myself, personally, would never put one of your tender years, however desperate I might be to grasp at every straw that might bolster however flimsy a case, given existing legal precedents."

"Objection!" Cutter yelped like a hurt dog. "Counsel is attempting to put the prosecution on trial with a tactic I myself would not hesitate to call dirty pool."

"Sustained. Counsel for the defense will desist from gratuitously maligning the opposition. Proceed with your questioning as such."

"Thank you, Your Honor. Cathy, I have only one question to ask. Perhaps two or three, only to establish a single point. We assume your parents purchased, or rented, perhaps regularly purchase or rent videocassettes of this kind which are popularly designated X-rated."

"Um, correct."

"That is not only correct, but perfectly understandable

and permissible. There is nothing wrong with it, for adults, or those come, as we say, to years of discretion. But what is their policy in the home? Isn't there one of those locks on your television set, by means of which children are prevented from watching certain things considered not suited to their years?"

"No."

"And aren't the X-rated films they buy or rent *themselves* kept under lock and key, or hidden from you somewhere, say in a chest or closet?"

"Sometimes, but not always."

"But this one was freely accessible to you on the night in question?"

"Yes."

"No further questions. Thank you, my child, and God bless you, and your own child, for all the years you may have together."

I've seldom heard anything like the hush that enveloped that courtroom as the girl stepped down and walked slowly out. Not a head turned, this time. Except possibly Cutter's. Without twisting to look in his direction, I seemed to sense him glaring fiercely at Wimbish, who, having waited till the witness made her exit, returned with the same deliberation to our table. He had planted a seed that must be left to germinate till his summation, the following day. For now, the court was adjourned.

Wimbish left open till the very last minute the question of whether he would put me on the stand. It affords you your day in court, but of course it also gives the prosecution a crack at you, and you never know how that might go. Everything your counsel extracts to your benefit might be more than offset by what the opposition will elicit to your disadvantage, especially a courtroom performer clever at using you as a foil for his own insinuations. Cutter was good at that. An ironic "I see" or a smirking "Is that so" and the effect of a supposedly favorable answer to a question is reversed. Considerations such as these made Wimbish finally decide against it. "I don't see what I could get you to say about yourself that hasn't already been said by our experts, and will be said by me when the time comes for my summation," he told me, "and who knows what that snake might twist out of you." He had even thought twice about my flashing my membership card in the Moral Majority (come in the mail unsolicited for God knows what reason) and he had asked me not to bring my briefcase into the courtroom anymore, at least not without steaming the "Stamp Out Smut" bumper sticker off of it. Both of these would have left the negative impression of a wiseacre. But I think his chief concern was that if called to the witness box I might make a fool of the D.A. by being clever like Oscar Wilde, and wind up where he did.

Why go to the trouble of even summing up the summations? Nothing was said for or against censorship that you haven't heard a thousand times. Nothing was said about me pro or con that had not been already anticipated in the crossfire of the trial itself. Our best moment came when Wimbish picked up the trick he'd won in his cross-examination of Miss Cudlipp. "Home video indeed introduces a new element into the problem," he said. "But are all adults now to have revoked the right of choice already guaranteed them by a succession of judicial decisions because a few are remiss in the discharge of their domestic obligations? The proper people to police the home are the parents — not the police — or we shall have a police state. Thus you cannot fairly penalize an entrepreneur for supplying merchandise already approved because a few adults allow it to fall into the hands of minors for whom that merchandise was never intended!"

But that was one trick, not the game. Or if the game, not the rubber. The real fireworks came during the D.A.'s rebuttal to Wimbish's summation — a second crack not allowed the defense by present practice, I was surprised to learn.

Going for healthy walks as he palmed his pencil, Cutter resumed enriching my vocabulary nineteen to the dozen. As he steamed up the stretch he pointed a rifle-length arm at me and said, "Here we have yet another opportunist disseminating his muck with the impunity putatively provided by increasingly permissive precedents, yet in fact far exceeding the customary limits of candor set by what the courts themselves call 'community standards.' A man who in the pursuit of his trade has contributed to the delinquency of a minor —"

Here Wimbish really blew a gasket. Slamming both hands on the table he got to his feet as though his arms were pistons heaving him erect and shouted, "Objection, Your Honor! Here the prosecution is committing an offense more detestable than any he accuses my client of. He is snidely attempting to draw into the circuit of considerations a crime of which the defendant is not accused, thereby with satanic subtlety expanding the gravity of the charges against him. But the charge has now been openly made and may be considered as tainting, however subconsciously, the deliberations of the court. Your Honor, I move for a mistrial."

His Honor was silent for some time as he pondered the outburst, looking straight at Wimbish. Then he leaned forward in his chair, resting folded hands on the desktop.

"May I remind counsel for the defense that he has committed a serious breach of courtroom etiquette."

"Not as serious a breach as his —"

Wimbish was silenced with a rap of the judge's gavel. "I warn counsel not to compound a contempt offense by similarly interrupting the bench. I was reminding you that one adversary does not explosively disrupt another's summation. You have had ample opportunity for your own."

Wimbish refused to be silenced. We were going for broke.

"Under pain of penalty for contempt, I must persist in decrying, not merely prosecution's act as such, but the format which makes it one against which the defense has now no defense. Time was when each had one summation. Now the prosecution enjoys the privilege of a rebuttal not granted the defense in turn. And the court well knows the crafty uses made of the new prerogative, namely, a prosecutor's frequently saving a particularly telling thrust the defense may not have anticipated, and against which by established routine he is now helpless. Illegitimate measures are therefore his own recourse. Thus while I apologize for the unorthodox nature of my retort —"

"Your Honor!" Cutter barked, but Wimbish raised his own voice and went uninterruptedly on, outshouting him.

"— I nevertheless offer it as a measure of my outrage at what is patently, if I may borrow the prosecution's own term, *dirty pool!*"

"Gentlemen! If such you are!"

It was above the gavel and Cutter's continued yelling both that Wimbish bellowed on.

"I have right on my side, and I make bold to flout courtroom etiquette because prosecution's thrust could well have planted a seed in the mind of the court that would sprout unfairly to my client's disadvantage in the final verdict. He is not being *tried* for the crime of which the prosecution has accused him. I would have been delinquent in my duty as a member of the bar if I had let it pass."

Letting drop the gavel, the judge now dismantled his previous pose and struck another. With the same leisure, he leaned back in his chair and laced his hands behind his head.

"Mr. Wimbish," he said, with a faint smile I didn't like,

"were this a jury trial, the fear that twelve good men and true, but unweathered in the nuances of courtroom procedure, would misinterpret these remarks might well have caused me to order the prosecutor's accusation stricken from the record and the jurors to ignore it, without a fulmination from the defense. Under the circumstances, however, one need have no anxiety about the bench's judgment being tainted or poisoned by accusatory elements gratuitously insinuated into a summary rebuttal, and well recognized as such by a judge not freshly graduated from law school. Court stenographer will strike from the record the statement about the accused's having contributed to the delinquency of a minor. And prosecution will kindly restrict his remarks to the charges under consideration. Proceed."

I had thought it had been just another piece of courtroom fencing, and was genuinely impressed by the near-apoplexy in which Wimbish plunked himself down, with a final muttered reference to dirty pool audible to Cutter and maybe the judge too.

It took the rest of Cutter's rebuttal for him to cool down and regain his natural color along with his composure. The expected request for a guilty verdict and the maximum penalty for obscenity brought the trial to an end. The judge set the date for his verdict, and possible sentencing, for five weeks from that date, which meant, according to Wimbish, that the judge was not going to make any snap decision based on private prejudices, but wanted ample time to review the precedents and ponder the problem in relative leisure.

"What, by the way, is the maximum penalty?" I asked Wimbish as we were about to shake hands and take leave of each other for the time being.

"Um, five thousand dollars or five years in prison, or both. Of course we will — we would appeal, and you'd be free on probably not much more than the twenty thousand dollars bail you're out on now."

"How does he strike you, all in all? The cut of Brinkerhoff's jib. What's your hunch?"

Wimbish shrugged. "You can never tell how these things will go. He might hit you with the fine, or some of it, but that's no problem with you. You can sell several feet of your limo. But I doubt he'll have your hide." He shrugged again. "You could draw some cell time."

You had to admire his stoicism. He was taking it like a man.

ELEVEN

Moanin' Low

THE SPECTRE of birdcage time, as we of the criminal element
call it, we with our picturesque jargon, that prospect naturally made me gather all the roses I could in the next five
weeks, despite Wimbish's assumption that I would remain
on the looserino while we appealed a conviction into my old
age. I backed the Land Yacht out of the garage and drove it
higgledy-piggledy through the now autumn countryside. It
goes without saying that I logged as much sack time with
Toby as I could, though in my present state of tension there
were occasions when not even my own pictures could have
roused the prurience the better element said they catered to.
But Toby showed herself to be as warm and understanding a
mainstay as any latent jailbird could have asked. In the hospital I had seen how sheer ministration could be sexual, at
least from the point of view of the recipient's sensations. Now
we had sex as a form of ministration. How she cradled her
crook in her arms, with what healing murmurs and caresses
soothed the poor bastard to sleep. She gave you a rose gar-

den without having promised it, inspiring the wildest promises in return.

The catering company she worked for was about to branch into the booming gourmet take-out business, with talk of her being taken in as a partner if she had any money to invest. Of course I would help her, as I had Cynthia with *Overview,* with one dark cloud hanging over that assurance: the possibility of federal injunction against Sexucational Films, and even, according to Wimbish, confiscation of existing materials as a condition of probation, or some such. That would mean the end of my income. "Well, we can always sell this," I said, meaning the limo in which we were spending the night together in a camping spot in New Hampshire, which was at the height of its foliage and not a motel with a vacancy. The back seats unfolded as a bed, have I told you? So there we were, snug under the covers listening to the falling leaves rustle down on top of the car. We had shot northward on a Sunday spur of the moment, and were obviously doing all this sans chauffeur. The countryside was full of leafers, as they call the fall tourists up there.

" 'Ow generous 'e is. Give you the shirt off 'is back, 'e would, if 'e 'ad one." So the cockney bit could be applied favorably as well as satirically, a welcome development. She fondled me experimentally, finding but a tassel to toy with. "Lover boy is worried stiff, except where it counts, I see. Ah, well. How about a little gentle music?" She switched on a radio embedded in a side panel and the strains of "Moanin' Low" enveloped us. A favorite of mine, especially these days. Soon Toby dropped off, and with that billow of a backside nestled warmly against me and a breast in my hand, I hoped it wasn't to my discredit that again I turned my thoughts to Cynthia.

If neither woman had attended every minute of the trial there were reasons. Both had work to do and the courthouse wasn't in Merrymount but a city twenty miles away. Cynthia had been a brick in her efforts to get the ACLU and other liberal organizations behind me, which hadn't paid off in connection with the trial but might prove valuable in the event of appeals, and in getting the intellectual community behind me if it turned out I was eventually warehoused. But there was a rub. Chirouble was likewise actively in my corner, and so the two had been thrown together in this worthy endeavor. Result, Cynthia saw him with new eyes as a man of genuine substance, not the charming dilettante everyone had thought him. *He* was all wool and a yard wide, tough darts for me.

So it turned out that it was her very love for me that had lost me the inside track — as it had lost it for Roxy with Chirouble, if indeed those two had ever been a real item. Ah, well, my quest had been misguided from the start. You couldn't expect Cynthia to marry a commoner.

It was on this note that I finally dropped off, grabbing a few Z's toward dawn and slipping without trouble into a dream featuring myself as the classic Laocoön, I believe he's called, only entangled in this case in yards of celluloid film.

Meanwhile I "did for" Cynthia's stepmother, as we said in Arkansas, taking her now three and even as much as four times a week to the Rehab Center for her arthritis therapies. Most of the outpatients there were elderly folks, many, as they hobbled on crutches or were wheeled in and out by friends and kin, looking already semi-departed in a way that naturally sharpened a chap's determination to gather those aforementioned roses whilst he might. I was inspired to fantasies featuring some of the young and more toothsome female volunteer therapists manipulating their charges, of whom I caught glimpses through an open door as I sat in the waiting room with a tattered magazine unread on my knee, in which, when the scene got really hairy, I fancied sympathetic twinges. "Pretty nifty that one," said a half-departed codger in a wheelchair, who had been watching me watch one of them, a small brunette with whom I could have had a lifetime of happiness. I gave a start, which was mostly a fresh spasm of horror over a jail term, ignited by the sight of the volunteer herself, a symbol of all that I would be denied while in stir.

Well, damn it, I was a volunteer myself, wasn't I, while sweating this out, and one thing Mrs. Pickles especially liked, for some reason, was our little trips to the dump. I had never yet got around to hiring a sanitation pickup, and when I mentioned incidentally that therefore I had to cart my own refuse out to the fill, nothing would do but that she accompany me so she could see the famous site on which my promised pavilion was to be constructed once the place had been paved over. That the Teeters Pavilion now looked pretty much to be deep-sixed I never mentioned. I took the stretch limousine, wedging the black Glad Bags full of garbage in front beside me, and stowing Mother Pickles in with the cartons of waste bottles and cans behind, in places where they would not discommode or offend. On our maiden run to the city limits where the pit was I explained through the intercom some of the merits of the polyethylene of which the bags were constructed, and their fitness for this purpose. She listened with her end of the intercom to her ear, lifting her bonnet slightly and drawing back some hair in order the better to wedge it in.

"Polyethylene, when properly incinerated, breaks down into harmless carbon dioxide and water vapor," I said. "When used as a landfill, it acts as a noncontaminating inert material."

"Well, now."

"Thus it is eminently suitable for the ultimate end in view:

199

a solid understratum for a surface on which safely to perform Tchaikovsky, Berlioz, and Debussy."

"And Hindemith?"

"Hindemith too." Who he?

"How proud you'll be at the inaugural premiere concert, where the pavilion in your name will be dedicated. What's the matter, Edward? You're coughing so."

"Just a little smoke seems to be coming from over there. My stars, is there one of those fires in the dump? They frequently arise, you know. No, I guess it's not so bad. Well, the thing is, we must have things that are biodegradable."

"Just listen to him."

Whenever possible I took occasions such as this to convey some idea of my excellence, in particular my conscientiousness as a citizen displayed in even such an environment as this, not generally matched by your garden-variety person.

"Note," I said, "how I first unscrew the caps from the bottles and throw them into the truck marked 'Metals' before pitching the bottles themselves into the 'Glass' gondola there. Watch."

Observing as I did just that, a detail most would shirk, she shook her head in appreciation. She could not believe such worth. Into the abyss of abominations I hurled the firmly trussed Glad Bags of garbage, flinging them with a gusto at which we both laughed, a shared moment of simple fun.

Tooling homeward, I segued smoothly into reminiscences of how commendably I had treated my mother from tenderest schoolboy days. "Like one time —" I paused till I had made sure in the rearview mirror that Mrs. Pickles had the intercom firmly to her ear. "Like when taking her fresh fruit to the hospital, or to her bedroom when she was at home convalescing, I always brought her loose grapes instead of in bunches, and one day she asked me about that, and I said, 'Mom, don't you realize these are the grapes that have fallen off the stems of themselves because they're the ripest and sweetest? Those are the kind I like to bring you.' "

Again the headshake, incredulity over such sterling merit in a world of petty self-seeking. I quite liked her. And motoring her about did take my mind off my current anxieties. But keeping the poor thing in this degree of public circulation bred a still further responsibility, namely that of safeguarding her from fortune hunters. That this was especially true in the case of the Rehab Center you can quite understand, or will after a word of explanation.

Though outpatients of all ages went there for physical therapies of all kinds, most, as I say, were in their sunset years, and of these not a few were widowed geezers able to see well enough in the gathering twilight the style in which she arrived. Moneylust gleamed in the eyes of more than one old goat as I maneuvered into a parking slot too short by half, sprang out to open the door for my passenger and then usher her on into the Rehab, prior to settling down in the reception room with one of those frazzled magazines or moseying back outside to wait in the fresh air. My instincts singled out a certain old duffer in particular as displaying more than casual interest. His name was Pewtersmith, and intuition told me there was more than coinkidinky in his appointment schedule suddenly synchronizing exactly with Mrs. Pickles' — Monday, Wednesday and Friday at 2:00 P.M. sharp. Once or twice I had glimpsed Pop, as they called him, being given some sort of shoulder workout by a young brunet therapist it would almost be worth having an infirmity in order to be manipulated by. Pop Pewtersmith had somebody or other's syndrome. I forget the name of the croaker his particular arthritis was named after, except that it was an unmistakably kraut moniker Pewtersmith enunciated with prideful impressiveness one day when, refreshed by an hour of the girl's half nelsons and hammerlocks, he shuffled over to the car against which I lounged with the tooth-sucking superiority of chauffeurs and engaged me in a conversation whose gist and purpose you could divine from word one. Dreams of ultimately sitting in the limo beside the newly wedded Mrs. Amelia Pickles Pewtersmith clearly danced in his head like the visions of sugarplums in those of kiddies on Christmas Eve. I sensed in a flash that I must give this codger short shift.

"Well, I did a complete external rotary today," he offered, demonstrating same by imitating a windmill with his right arm.

"That so." This without disturbing my slouch against the wagon he was drooling to own in joint tenancy with right of survivorship.

"Both arms, by gosh and by golly," and he repeated the exercise with his left. "Six months ago I couldn't even lift either over my head. To say nothing of developing the Groucho Marx walk through no wish of my own."

"I'm glad to hear that. I mean that you've made so much progress. This is one very good place."

"An absolute boon."

He wore a blue leather bow tie I would have laid fifty to one was a hook-on, a striped blazer and, to complete the re-creation of a bygone era, a straw katy tilted at a jaunty angle. He gave off a delicate aroma of good bay rum. He obviously figured me for a chauffeur much more casual in his grooming than is typical of the class.

"Why, how is Mrs. Pickles doing?"

"Well, you know how it is with her kind of trouble."

"No, what is it, if I may ask?"

I laid it on him with one of the many new words you know by now I carry around in my head for future looking up, being careful not to drop this one on my foot.

"*Weltanschauung.*"

"Can't say as I've ever heard of that one."

"It's a relatively rare orthopedic ailment. Not too rapidly progressing, but it is irreversible. She has it all through here."

"Really?"

I nodded, closing my eyes.

"They can't arrest it?"

Again with the shuttered glims, this time shaking my head.

"They can do wonders here," he said, threatening to repeat the full external rotary by way of communicating a ray of hope.

"Not for *Weltanschauung*, I'm afraid. Oh, ease the symptoms, sure, as to which thank God again for this place. But wonders in the sense of a cure, that's hardly in the cards. Thank God too for Medicare picking up most of the tab here, as you no doubt know for yourself. Lucky for those of modest means, or in danger of losing what they have, however much it may seem to the uninformed eye. Because ... Well, there have been some financial mishaps that are also irreversible, alas." I sighed and moved around to the front of the car, where I stood stroking its nose. "We may have to give up old Dobbin here."

"Really. I'm sorry to hear that."

"But" — another sigh — "we'll scrape along somehow." The plural was intended to convey the idea that these dire tidings were coming from a family retainer of unshakable loyalty, one who would be faithful to the end up to and including sitting together on the bare floor of a house from which all the furniture had been repossessed by loan companies, before a cold hearth, eating canned pork and beans off of paper plates by candlelight, the electricity having been shut off, while waiting for the sheriff to take the house itself away.

Pewtersmith heaved a sigh himself. "I'm sorry to hear all that. I've taken a bit of a shaking up in the market myself." This may have been a shrewd way of both expressing sympathy and indicating he had a few crates of lettuce himself to worry about. "I do wish the interest rates would go down and stay down. Mucks everything up. Lots of us are praying for the second leg of this bull market. The bull is coming mostly from the investment counselors you ask me." He glanced over toward the Rehab building. "I was wondering when your lovely lady will be finished. I'd like to buy you folks an ice cream soda."

"Oh, that's very kind of you, sir," I said, my alert if anything sharpened by the invitation, as coming from a foxy grandpa foxier even than I had surmised. "But Mrs. Pickles is always most fatigued after a physical therapy workout, and I must whisk her right home for her nap. But I will tell her of your kind invitation," I added, at the same time reminding myself that I must remember to forget it absolutely, also to make sure we made a change in her schedule so as to keep her clear of this operator — who probably, for his part, saw through my sob story as a ruse for discouraging his attentions. Given his way, he would probably have them both sporting about in the whirlpool tank, comparing incomes and Social Security checks. In any case the conversation was broken off by the reappearance of another of my current headaches.

There was a loud roar and the Devil's Disciples came barreling up the driveway. They had spotted the Land Yacht and me from the road, and dipped in to pay respects as well as offer me the honor escort home if I so desired. Most of them had one of the Hell's Belles sisterhood perched behind them.

"You'll have to excuse me. It's been nice talking to you," I said to Pewtersmith and went over to the newcomers. I spoke directly to the leader again, this Rock Bascomb cat, if I remember his name correctly.

"Look, you want to help me? Don't help me."

"Whassamah, man? Why not? We takin' your weight and you roundin' us."

Roughly translated, I figured this meant they were offering their moral support and I was trying to avoid them. It had the chilling ring of authentic slammer jargon. I answered patiently but firmly.

I explained that we were both alike victims of bourgeois bigotry, and however much I appreciated their consistent and unflagging show of support in my hour of ordeal, and possible martyrdom, too public identification with them would jeopardize my cause, even produce a guilty verdict and stiffer sentence than might otherwise obtain. He didn't know what *obtain* meant in this connection, and neither did I to tell the truth, but I had heard the word often drop from educated lips in such a context. He stroked the cactus on his chin and nodded. He understood. He ordered his cohorts to mount and disappear with him, all waving as they roared away with their chicks. "Good luck Friday," he shouted, that being the day he knew as an interested intellectual closely following the case to be the one set for the verdict.

The courtroom was jammed. Cameras flashed and TV crews followed me as I entered the building. Reporters asked for statements, were waved away with "Later." You sensed by a random sampling of expressions that the audience was equally divided between bluenoses and libertarians. Toby had got off work and rode up with me in the limousine I now saw no point in keeping from public view. She sat a couple of rows behind Cynthia and Chirouble. I took my place with

Wimbish at our table. In the silence there was a tension you could have bitten into with your teeth. The judge entered. "All rise." He sat down. "Please be seated."

The judge was an eternity getting to the point.

"This is a case in which I am particularly interested, not only for its own merits, if — ahem — such it possesses, but mainly because of the social climate in which it has arisen and has been conducted. The defendant has produced and distributed for public consumption certain films on which we are here to render judgment, but a radically tolerant contemporay atmosphere has produced *him*. He is a child of his times, and here I think I choose my words carefully."

Swell. This sounded hopeful. I was not responsible for my actions. I might be an idiot, but I would go free. The judge made a slight adjustment in both his glasses and the document from which he was reading, and continued.

"Successive court decisions, including some from the highest tribunal in our land, have precipitously relaxed moral standards that a few generations ago would have made anything like Sexucational Films unthinkable for distribution and display anywhere than among stag smokers."

Yes. So far so good. Moral standards were relaxed. So could I.

"For a time, the principle known as 'redeeming social value' made pornography legally palatable to any judge to whose satisfaction it could be demonstrated as containing that elusive quality, in however minuscle a degree. Latterly, the criterion of 'local community standards' has largely superseded that yardstick. But what does that any longer mean in an era when community distinctions are wiped out by a medium that has turned the world into a global village? And even if there were no television sets homogenizing us, but only books and movies to worry about, standards are everywhere disintegrating by virtue — if, again, that is the word —

ahem — by virtue of sheer continual exposure to what in a more disciplined day the average person would have been safeguarded against by a degree of censorship we now fancy ourselves as having laughed out of court, but which our best minds from Plato on have always deemed necessary to human welfare."

"I don't like the sound of this," Wimbish mumbled out of the side of his mouth. "This baby is oldfangled. He's going to steam-burn us."

"It has not been laughed out of this court. I am not one with the judge in the magazine cartoon who says to a colleague, 'I think the book is filthy too, but I don't want to seem square.' I do not mind seeming square, to use a word that has become totally turned around in meaning thanks to this vicious circle by which standards are relaxed by reason of exposure to something and the next 'something' becomes more obscene by reason of relaxed standards. I consider the pictures under review in this trial to be obscene as charged, and that their distribution across state lines is criminal as charged. I hereby issue an injunction against their further sale, and order confiscation of all obtainable samples of these mud pies."

"Oh, Christ," I heard Wimbish murmur with my sinking heart.

"Nor do I credit the pretense that they serve an educational purpose as instructions in the art of love — a pretense that seems to me rather to compound the main offense with that of hypocrisy. Incidentally —" the judge raised his eyes from his papers to look straight ahead out at the audience — "incidentally, I shall not multiply sanctimony by pretending that in viewing the films, as of course I had to, I myself did not experience the prurient ends to which it is my contention they were made. But hypocrisy," he continued, returning to his statement, "hypocrisy is not one of the charges here, and so I shall confine sentencing to the relevant illegalities on which by obvious implication I have already pronounced a verdict of Guilty as Charged."

Stunned gasps from my supporters expressed well enough what I myself felt, and these mingled with sounds of righteous satisfaction from the moral element, making for a hubbub which the judge silenced with a bang of his gavel. After which he said, "I have neglected to have the defendant rise to learn my verdict. I ask him to do so now to hear the sentence. I am waiving as quite unnecessary the usual period of presentence investigation. My mind is quite made up."

Sentence. The word was like a grenade exploding in my guts. Wimbish and I got to our feet and edged forward around the table toward the bench. I don't know whether I hated or feared the judge more as I stood there before him, a wretch. I hadn't seriously believed I would go to prison, even with the recent examples before me of similar offenders who had. It was only an intellectual concept. Now I tasted it as a hideous actuality. *Locked up.* I experienced a sudden swoon of fear of a kind I had heard tell or read about. I mean I had an orgasm, like your hanged man. What a fitting end to a career in erotica. In an insane writhing ecstasy I answered "No" when asked whether I had any statement to make before sentence was pronounced, and then heard somebody swimming in a mist up there say:

"I believe that 'permissiveness' and the plain salaciousness in which it has engulfed us have gone quite far enough. Resistance must be offered this contemporary shame of ours, and offer it I hereby do by invoking the sternest penalty provided by the law — five thousand dollars' fine or a maximum of five years' imprisonment, or both. I impose both."

The howls of mingled protest and approval from the spectators was such that for a time it even drowned out the sound of the judge's gavel. He rose to shout back, and by dint of this and banging as hard as he could he finally quieted the audience. "I have not finished," he called out through the finally diminishing din, "and unless I have quiet until I do so I shall clear the court."

He sat down in the returning silence, and continued.

"I am adding this, that the prison term is suspended —"

Sighs of relief and rumbles of protest, with the roles among the spectators now reversed. These were easier to quiet down.

"The sentence is suspended and the defendant is put on probation for a period of one year, accountable to a proper probation officer. As a substitute for the prison term, I resort to a current practice of which I do approve. I order that he devote a hundred hours to community service, performing good works of moral and humanitarian worth. I would be glad to hear from the defendant and his counsel what form these might take."

Wimbish stepped in here with commendable alacrity. "Your Honor, if the bench will give us a moment, in all gratitude I believe my client and I can make a suggestion wholly suitable to you." A sixty-second huddle was all he needed with me here. He emerged from it to say: "Your Honor, we might suggest a conscientious continuance of what the defendant is already engaged in. I speak of his present volunteer service in transporting to and from the Rehabilitation Center, of which Your Honor himself must be fully aware, elderly outpatients in need of the therapy provided there. I am sure a hundred more hours of that, or a thousand, would be happily spent by a client known for his kindness and consideration toward his fellowman, particularly the aged and infirm so dependent on humanitarian devotion such as he has faithfully —"

"That will be suitable to the court. There is no need to labor the point. I have one or two things more to say myself.

209

Chiefly this, that in imposing my original sentence, as well as that of it which remains in effect, I am deliberately striking a blow for the censorship whose passing I for one lament. I know I am going against the current stream, and knowing that, know also that in whatever appeals counsel and his client have in mind, somewhere in the chain my finding will be struck down. But make it I must, and made it I have. This court is now adjourned."

T W E L V E

Sixth Heaven

WIMBISH HAD little trouble talking me out of an appeal. What with the moral backlash that had already produced a Judge Brinkerhoff, we might well get another who'd impose a prison term he *wouldn't* suspend, and what was five thousand bucks in my young life. I remarked as much ironically after getting his bill, and in the cold realization that Brinkerhoff's injunction against Sexucational Films had dried up my source of income there, to say nothing of rendering my stock in the company worthless. The better element dropping the class-action suit was all the wind the good Lord tempered to this shorn lamb. I had to rescind my offer to donate Merrymount a band shell as well as sell the stretch limousine to the local livery, for which I went to work as a driver on hearing that Toby was pregnant, and that marriage seemed to loom ahead like an uncharted island toward which my battered vessel, rudderless, drifted.

"Sow 'e's gonna do right by the poor girl, is 'e? And 'im the one wot got arrested for makin' all them dirty moom pitchas.

Well, wot else can 'e do after gittin' the poor girl with one in the oven after makin' all that shame-shame 'isself?" What a lip on her. But what lips. And she looked and smelled like warm peaches, and her legs wrapped around you, till your spine threatened to snap in two like a stick of kindling, made the world go away. I have to report that on learning the situation my delight was as great as my dismay. I was only too glad to be tangled up with her, and not just on the rebound from Cynthia, who, as suspected all along, was going to marry Chirouble. Ah well, I guess in the long run you can't climb out of your social class. The jockey can't ever hope to marry into the horsey set. That's the last thing he could realistically aspire to. After this resolution of matters, though, Cynthia and I became faster friends than ever. With all bets off, we could express and enjoy our affection for each other freely. Indeed it was she who finally hit on a possible way out of the muddle toward which I had so long systematically been forging. She proposed her solution over lunch at the country club where it had all got started, what seemed both yesterday and a hundred years ago.

Only now it was getting on for winter, and we met at the restaurant indoors. With the case already fast fading from local memory, she apparently found no hazard in being seen with me in public, or maybe an open social engagement like this was her way of apologizing for the turn in our relations she had decreed when things were hot. The pool was empty now, the terrace furniture stored away, and past the window where we sat a sharp wind blew withered leaves like the carcasses of the long summer's butterflies. Of which the snowflakes when presently they whirled about would be the ghosts — or so ran my thoughts in a sadly poetic vein. Chirouble was to join us for a one o'clock luncheon, but Cynthia had asked me to come half an hour early to hear her proposition before he showed up, even though he was to figure in it later. Mine was a sneak preview. It was all very mysterious, and I showed all the suspense a woman likes to see in a friend on whom she is going to spring something, like a bit of gossip or a secret plot — or as in this case, a brainstorm. Toby of course no longer worked here, but a waitress every bit as *zaftig* brought our Bloody Marys. What beautiful music we could have made together. I spent a lifetime of happiness with her while waiting for Cynthia to pop her notion. We said our skoals, and then she unfolded her proposition, which I must say at first impact sounded like she had already had a few.

"I have this idea that will solve everything for everybody," came out at last.

"Shoot."

"*Well.*"

"Yeah, yeah?"

"You're broke and about to become a father, with all that implies in the way of marital burdens and responsibilities new to a blade past his first youth who has spent his salad years living it up to the hilt as a man about town."

"That's quite a sentence for all in one breath. Not to say funeral march."

"Amanda, with no close relatives, only some shirttail horrors I'll spare you hearing about, Amanda, seeing 'her line peter out,' as she rather sadly puts it, pines more than ever for a grandchild, which she will get neither from her stepdaughter nor the farthest-out adoption agency you could find. This is where my solution comes in."

"Which is? For Christ's sake are you going to light another cigarette while I sit here all ears?"

She waved the match out and dropped it in an ashtray while blowing out a cloud of smoke.

"Let her adopt you, and thus realize her fondest remaining wish. No, no, wait. Hear me out. I know it sounds crazy, but think of all the wrinkles it'll iron out. She and I have never been very close, as you know. Or rather we've been too close for two people not blood kin who have nevertheless been arbitrarily thrown together in a not even reasonable facsimile of a family, by force of a second marriage that was never so hot in the first place. I'm moving out, to our mutual relief, to marry a man now so rich — Chirouble has come into a chunk from another side of his clan, you know — so rich that I'll never need the money Amanda plans to cut me out of anyway. I have reason to believe she's changing her will this minute. She'll never forgive me for breaking our engagement, you know how she dotes on you, don't simper, to marry instead someone she doesn't really know and who is going to help me run a periodical she doesn't approve of, *and* for flatly announcing that I do not intend to have any children. All this makes you the poor orphan she'd be tickled to death to write into her will as an adopted treasure with a built-in guarantee of a grandchild."

"You're mad."

"So is the muddle it'll set to rights. As well as anything can be in this our cockeyed life."

"But Cynthia, I mean taking money rightfully yours —"

"Oh for Christ's sake. It's nothing *I'm giving* you, dumdum, only diverting from some shirttail clods on her mother's side it would kill me to see wind up with it otherwise. And disabuse yourself of the notion I'm 'above' money, or am being noble or anything. Money is one of the fondest things I'm of, but I won't be greedy. Jerry and I will have all we'll ever need. And as my dear friend I want you to land on your feet, Eddie, with that nice girl you're going to marry and have this wonderful baby with. How Amanda will dote on him, or her. Here's the scenario as I see it. God, I never thought that word would cross my lips. As her adopted son you won't have to live there with Amanda for long. Because you'll

214

leave to get married, like any normal son. See? Simplicity itself. You and Toby will be very happy together, she going back into the catering business after her maternity leave, you staying home and taking care of the kid while working on that script of yours about how money has nothing to do with happiness. Eventually a day-care center to leave you more time for revisions and all, then nursery school or whatever. Maybe a nursemaid as you get into the chips on your own, I mean if your inheritance itself turns out to be a long time in coming."

"I shan't want servants."

"Well there you are."

"I could even produce the movie myself."

"Of course! You mean if you should come into — And a bang-up job you'll do, with all the experience you've had. Explicit sex is bound to come back, after the setback you've so pioneered in giving it for the moment. So then. Let's drink to it. Cheers!"

"Cheers . . . Who, uh, who is going to put all this to . . . to Mom?"

"Chirouble. Here he comes now."

"But I gather he's in your stepmother's bad books because he's the one you're marrying after all," I whispered rapidly as Chirouble glittered along the tables past which he could be seen making his way to ours, absolutely the last word in his fawn checked tweeds. "Is he the best emissary to sell her on all this, which you'll admit is a trifle baroque?" Another of Chirouble's words which I hoped I was using right.

"Oh, none better. She hasn't even met him yet, so how could she dislike him. And this will be the ideal way for 'my intended' to get off on the right foot with her. So you see it serves its purpose the other way around too."

"But if she takes the shine to him you hope, won't it blow the other thing right up in our faces? I mean make her change her mind and leave the will as is, or put it back again the way it was?"

"Jerry darling."

As these two good-looking faces met in a kiss I realized what the term "beautiful people" should mean instead of what it's come to. Chirouble pumped my hand and said, "Eddie, Eddie, what a joy to see you, as against writing you faithfully in stir, or coming to talk to you through those glass partitions so woefully unconducive to conversation."

"Hi, Chirouble, old horse."

It was a pleasure to see him too, in this mood, after what had been rather a downer. You will remember him as a sort of dilettante sitting about the pool rejecting manuscripts, when not doing so in the better restaurants. *Playing* at being a publisher. Your typical young scion with a profession picked for self-enhancement. That had been all very well. Carried off with style. Then he had committed the boner of actually publishing a book, a slim volume of verse yet, and lost his shirt. Well, a button from one of the hundred or so custom-mades that composed that end of his wardrobe. That was all behind him now, he had learned his lesson, and now while he still played at being a publisher the game had some substance to it: he did it as titular head of the journal his bride-to-be actually ran and would continue to run. The world knows that anybody who is titular something is snugly niched.

Nothing could have delighted him more than the plan Cynthia now unfolded, except — the snapper — his own appointed role in it. It tickled him pink. He giggled with delight at the prospect of an operation than which he had never heard anything more baroque. So I had used the word right. I had thought it referred to architecture alone; now I gathered you could wing it to mean anything fancy or kinky at all. Again the terrific sense of belonging, what with terms like that issuing from my own lips. A little fresh Shakespeare presently to be thrown in redoubled my exhilaration. I frankly aired my doubts about this project he couldn't wait to try launching. And along with them the pessimistic view I took of my own present lot, to say nothing of a seeming blight on my future prospects as well.

"Nonsense!" Chirouble exclaimed. "What you've done, however a-gley it's gang, has given you a wonderful technical foundation for the more, shall we say, conventional efforts with which you're going to make us all proud of you. More's ahead of you than behind. I mean, old boy, the hand of your dial, as I believe Mercutio more or less puts it in *Romeo and Juliet,* is now upon the prick of noon. This is your life's meridian! Indeed you haven't even entered your prime. All's still to be, for you and that delectable Toby. Up with the cup!"

And so nothing would do but that we raise our glasses to my future with the peach tart.

I would have liked to be a fly on the wall not so much the afternoon Cynthia trotted out her intended for tea to meet Amanda, but during Chirouble's next ceremonial call alone, designed to make his future mother-in-law my adoptive mother, in what must stand as the baroquest piece of matchmaking ever. Toby said it was absolutely grotesque and I agreed. Cynthia reported herself hopeful, after the tea at which pinkies must have stood out like needles on a cactus. Amanda had liked Chirouble all *right,* without going overboard enough to jeopardize the adoption and the hoped-for change in codicils. That was how she read matters at that juncture. Chirouble struck her as the fancy-pants type not exactly her own, as against myself who had been firmly sized up as one the good Lord had thrown the mold away after making. So we waited in moderate hope for *this* verdict.

I absolutely couldn't resist driving past the house at the time I knew Chirouble was in there putting the case. It was dusk of a Saturday afternoon, and cruising by the place for the third time I saw the lights go on and caught a glimpse of Chirouble sitting on a sofa by the window, dimly discernible through the lace curtains, sipping what absolutely had to be a Presbyterian. Driving around to kill time, I wandered through a train of associations naturally getting me back to Toby, and I remembered we still hadn't located a pair of gloves she had mislaid several days before. Their disappearance and possible loss irked me no end, they being expensive pink ostrich-leather ones I had given her for her birthday. Nothing to sneeze at. Certain they'd last been seen in the Buick I was again driving, I began fishing in the crack of the seat, thinking they might have got wedged in there. As a result of poking first with one hand and then the other, my driving became a little erratic, and before I knew it I heard the siren of a prowl car and then there was a cop beside me waving me over to the curb. He climbed out and came over.

"Are you all right?" he asked after I had rolled the window down.

"Sure, why?"

"You been kind of wobbling back and forth over the yellow line. Are you sure you haven't had a few?"

"Positive. I was just —"

"Not to say weaving and wriggling around on the seat yourself. Could I see your registration?"

"Of course," I said, and as I reached in for it there were the gloves. In the glove compartment, for Christ's sweet sake. Who would ever put anything like that in a cubbyhole intended for car documents? The last place anybody would think of looking.

I sat there seething like a husband already as he looked

over the registration. He strolled around to check the license number then came back and returned it.

"Everything seems to be in order, but that wouldn't make me feel any better about letting you drive without a check."

"Kind of a check?"

"Breathalyzer. Station house is just a few blocks down there. Not too risky to let you do that, I guess. Just go nice and slow, and I'll follow you."

I explained about the gloves, concluding my tale with "Women," so that as men we might share a chuckle together over the fair sex. He seemed adamant. Then I explained that, in addition to fishing around in the upholstery for gloves all the while absurdly lurking in the glove compartment, I had also been feeling for the release latch to shove the seat itself back to where I needed it, the car having just been driven by the lady in question, who had shorter legs and required a corresponding adjustment the other way. "Damn seat sticks. That's why I might have seemed a little antsy to you, Officer. No doubt about it. I find it necessary to have two people on the seat, shoving *simultaneously,* to get this damn thing back. Well, so that's the story. As a citizen I commend you on your thoroughness, though."

"Nice and slow, and I'll follow you. Be right behind you."

Cursing a blue streak I started off again. On the way I passed a tavern, at which I looked wistfully. I could use a drink to see me through this. My temper flamed, and in what was probably an explosion of accumulated tension, frustration and anxiety, I jammed the brakes on, backed up a few feet, and swerved into an angled parking spot in front of the bar. I was out of the car before the cop pulled in beside me.

"What the hell is this?"

"I thought I'd have a quick one first. Will you join me, Officer?"

"Are you crazy as well as drunk?"

"It's so long since I've had a drink that my taking this damn Breathalyzer test is going to make somebody look like a damn fool, and it won't be me. How many is it you can have again before the alcohol shows up on the test? Two, isn't it?"

"That's right."

"O.K. So confident am I that this is ridiculous that I'm going, I'm willing to go in there and belt back two and *then* go on with you to the station house serene in the confidence that nothing will show up, except maybe the color of your face."

He had all this while been studying my own closely under the light from a nearby streetlamp.

"Hey, aren't you the hunk? Just had that trial?"

"Right."

He couldn't help grinning his appreciation. "What's it like to lay all that pipe and get paid for it too yet?"

"It ain't easy being a living legend."

"I've pulled in my share for an alky test, but I'm damned if I've ever run into this before. A suspect not only wanting a snort to do it, but brazenly offering to take the risk of two."

"A little baroque, eh?"

"What? Story's too fantastic not to believe." He laughed, shaking his head. "You do seem all right on closer look. But take it easy."

"Solemnly promised."

I thanked him and, cooled off, backed out and returned to my vigil. Chirouble was just emerging from the house when I got back, and though I was dying to hear how the visit had gone, I was by the same token nervous about learning its outcome, so with face averted I zoomed around the corner and out of sight. I didn't want to be seen spying either, of course.

So there was another verdict to sweat out. Except not for anywhere near as long. I got the news from Cynthia that very night. She telephoned to say Amanda was absolutely delighted at the prospect. Nothing could have pleased her more, given the facts (and continuing to conceal a few). The adoption papers must be drawn up and I must move in as soon as possible.

All this, mind you, without anybody inquiring whether the adoption of adults was allowed in the state, let alone the country. For the time being, all that was academic, as something happened that knit Mrs. Pickles and me together, by throwing us together, in a bond that was all but the equivalent of a mother-son relationship anyway.

Mrs. Rampart, no spring chicken herself, developed infirmities on her own account, gave notice, and moved west to Oregon to spend her remaining days with an also-widowed sister there, on a pension from Mrs. Pickles which I surmised to be handsome. Cynthia was already married to Chirouble when Mrs. Pickles, on the first day she was alone in the house, tripped on the stairs and sprained an ankle. Cynthia would have been glad to move back in and look after her till a "home visiting nurse" or some such was found, but we all agreed that this emergency offered me the absolutely ideal chance for a dry run as a son. All except Toby, who said she was buying Ivory Soap by the gross to wash her hands of the whole preposterous caper. She was not studying very hard to be a daughter-in-law, even with marriage looming on the horizon. Me her parents weren't especially keen on meeting either. They expected I'd be accompanied by my parole officer, I think. A big wedding was waived on both that general ground (the knot tied while the heat peered at the proceedings through the window) and the knowledge that it would cost the bride's father somewhere in the neighborhood of five thousand fish. In perhaps the single most money-saving word in the English language he cried, "Elope!"

This was how Mother Pickles twisted her ankle.

Faulty intelligence that I was an accomplished piano player, rather than just another guy who had picked up a little jazz by ear, had prompted her to have the piano tuned, as part of the preparation for my arrival. Among the superstitions she harbored was the familiar one that a piano should never be closed, and lying awake in the dead of night she began to worry about whether the tuner had followed her instruction to leave the lid open. "It's bad luck to close it, you know," she reminded him. It became an obsession, as things will at 3:00 A.M., and so she crept downstairs to check. Sure enough, the lid was down. That was probably all to the good, as it justified the trip. It was going back up that she stumbled, luckily on the next to the top step, which enabled her to hop on one foot back into bed. There she ended the night, wide awake but safe and not in too great pain, and phoned her doctor, whose home number she had, as early in the morning as one decently could. It was about nine-thirty when I got the news from Cynthia, who lost no time in emphasizing that this was my Big Chance. "Go in and win," she said. Toby's send-off was somewhat different. Watching from the bed as I dressed to hotfoot on over, she said, "What does it feel like to be the salt of the earth?" "I haven't time to explain it now," I answered. I bent to kiss her and dash. "Your father's the salt of the earth," she said, patting her swollen tum. "You won't find many like 'im, I'll be bound. I 'opes the nipper'll be arf the saint you are," she shouted as I disappeared through the door.

I did not get off on the best foot as a son apparent. My first domestic encounter was an argument. Of course there was the good side to it — it was a bona fide family squabble.

"Whatever possessed you to creep downstairs in the middle of the night for a thing like that, Mother Pickles?"

"Just what I said. See whether Mr. Bumbry had closed the piano, which it turned out he had — with the results we now see, by seeing me lying here. So I was right."

I paced back and forth across the foot of the bed, trying to get a handle on this thing, as well as keep a grip on my patience.

"What do you mean, you were right, Mother?"

"It's bad luck to leave a piano closed. He left it closed and I sprained my ankle." She spread her hands as if to say, "So there."

"But you sprained your ankle — and might have broken your leg, or a hip — because you went downstairs to *see* whether he had closed the piano, *not because he had done so.*"

"But he did leave it closed and the misfortune did happen."

"But if you hadn't crept downstairs in the dark because of this ab—— because you have this ridic—— because of this superstition I know a lot of people have —"

"What do you mean, superstition? Bad luck is bad luck."

"All right, Mother, O.K. Because of this quite charming folk legend. If you hadn't gone downstairs you wouldn't be lying here with a twisted ankle. You see, you're talking in non sequiturs we call them. Or it's what we call begging the question. Your reasoning is just as twisted as your ligament."

"*Well!* Is my own son accusing me of female logic?"

"No, no. I'm not accusing you of anything. I'm simply asking you to get your cause and effect sequence straight. Look. I'll explain it to you." I drew a long breath and let it out slowly, casting my eyes upward at the ceiling. "You had your mishap *because of what you believe,* not because Mr. Bumbry left the lid down."

223

She rolled her head to one side on the pillow and gazed out the window. "Our first quarrel."

"Oh, Mom."

I took the opportunity afforded by her averted gaze to move off a bit and beat my fists against the sides of my head, in loo of stepping out in the hall and banging my head against the wall. Suddenly dropping the subject, she said she found herself to be ravenous and would like some breakfast. I had it up in two shakes, bacon and fried eggs, toast and strawberry jelly, and a carafe of good hot coffee.

"We're out of oranges," I said, "so there's no juice."

"Fix me a Presbyterian."

"Isn't it a little early for Presbyterians, Mom?"

"Nonsense. I have to have my juice in the morning, one way or another."

I trotted down the fatal stairway again, returning with one Presbyterian and one backslider, which it wasn't too early for. I sat in a slipper chair sipping my drink while she had her breakfast, and together we went over the errands and other things to be attended to for the day. I would call the visiting nurses' service and, when help had arrived, go out and do the marketing. The doorbell rang, and thank God it was her doctor, a pleasant old gent bearing the wherewithal to tape her ankle up and even a pair of crutches, which he helped her launch herself with while I phoned the nursing service. Within the hour they had sent help over in the form of a plump little woman named Mrs. Duggan, who was so kind and efficient that I wished I was rich again so I could make a contribution as fat as she was to the agency she worked for. As she bustled about, she got on the subject of religion and asked me what I was. Now, church is something I stay away from in droves, but inevitably I said, "Presbyterian." Free association. She nodded approval as she rounded a corner of the bed with the speed of light. "I'm Episcopalian myself, but quibble about denominations is something we shouldn't do."

"We all worship the same God," I said, adding to myself, "Money."

That that got to be of consuming interest, in the first days of my tenure as a son-elect, was no fault of mine, exactly, though in my impoverished state it naturally remained a chronic consideration. It was mostly Mother Pickles' fault. I moved into Cynthia's old room, just across the hall and down a little from Mother Pickles', and when I wasn't salivating with thoughts of rolling about in the very same bed Cynthia had occupied for years, I attended to the noises coming from the other. After all, I must act in the capacity of nurse until a replacement for Mrs. Rampart could be found, through advertising and other channels being pursued. To that end both bedroom doors were kept open. I was thinking of my sister Petal one night when I heard from across the hall what were unmistakable sounds of a bedside telephone being dialed. Then they stopped and the phone was cradled. I returned to my musings about Petal. You will remember her as the kid sister with whom I'd had the near-incestuous relationship that accounts for my chivalrous worship of women. Should I call and tell her what was afoot? I decided against it. I never saw her anymore anyway, now that she lived in Rio de Janeiro as the wife of a South American branch manager of a California export company. I can testify that close childhood sibling intimacy can drive people apart in later life.

I was a little shy of reading matter. Cynthia had taken all her books with her and in Mrs. Rampart's old room were only a few she had left behind from her own library. *Problems of the Back, A Short History of Buttons, The Complete Book of Wading.* I was afraid the excitement of getting hooked on any one of them would leave me sleepless with palpitations, so that I would have to steal downstairs for a glass of milk, the desperate measure resorted to by people in movies. I was lying there imagining cracks in a ceiling I couldn't see, working up an obsession there out of whole cloth, and feeling my arms and chest for moles I could pick off and throw away (you will recall Toby's marking my resemblance to a Toll House cookie), lying there doing stuff like that when there were again the furtive sounds of dialing. I sat bolt upright to listen. There was no doubt of it. Was she trying to call her doctor? I put on a robe and switched on a hall light. That supplied enough illumination for me to dimly make out the figure of Mrs. Pickles in her bed, from the doorway where I stood. The telephone was on her stomach, the transmitter to her ear. She set it down when she saw me.

"Is something wrong?"

She smiled rather apologetically. "I was just calling the Dreyfus Funds. They have this eight-hundred number you can phone any hour of the twenty-four from anywhere and get the current yield? It sounds silly, but it gives you a sense of, oh, I don't know. Comfort. All you get is a recorded answer, running down the yields on all the funds, but it amuses me to do it all hours, especially when I can't sleep. Was I being naughty?"

"Not in the least." I came farther into the room. "Which fund do you have shares in, actually? Mom?"

"I have shares in two. The Liquid Asset, the interest from which is taxable of course, and one called the Intermediate Tax-exempt Bond Fund."

"Ah, yes." I strolled to the window, through whose lace curtains brilliant moonlight streamed, and stood gazing out over the rooftops. "Full moon tonight. What are the extent of your holdings?"

"I have about forty thousand dollars in the Liquid Asset,

which pays twelve point four percent. Of course that's tax-able."

"And the Intermediate?"

"Considerably more than that. More like seventy-five."

"Ah, yes. Naturally these are only part of your —" I checked the passage of "estate" across my tongue, and used a term I had noticed the genteel preferred. "Your means."

"Yes. That reminds me I —" She shifted around on the bed the better to face me, as she reached out to set the phone back on her cluttered night table. I sprang forward to help. "I must go to the bank tomorrow to see about some things — I'm sure getting down to the safe deposit box will be no problem at all with you to help me."

"No problem at all."

"And while we're there I'll have your signature authenti-cated as my deputy. I believe that's what they call a person who's empowered to open a box in your stead, in the event something happens and you can't get there yourself."

"I'll be glad to do everything I can. You know you can bank on me."

"Oh, you're so amusing."

"What? Oh, I see what you mean. No, it's you who are witty, in hearing it that way. Good night, Mom. Sleep tight now. The yields sound very soothing."

"Good night, Edward dear."

I fell almost immediately into a deep sleep. I dreamt of my old room in Backbone, of a particular curl of paper peeling off the wall in it, of "The Hound of Heaven" and the certifi-able teacher who expected me to memorize it in toto. Little did I dream of the turn our little trip to the bank was to give events on the morrow.

The safe-deposit box was a foot wide and half a foot deep,

and so heavy I almost dropped it on the way to the little private room into which I helped Mother Pickles on her crutches. There were two chairs in it, and I sat on one of them, half turned away from the sight of her going through the box's contents, a kind of compromise by which I could avoid the discourtesy of rubbernecking while yet catching sight of what she was pulling out of it. Stock certificates no end. There were nine hundred shares of IBM, worth almost a hundred thousand dollars alone. American Can, Pfizer Drugs, ITT, till my mouth watered. I tried to pull myself together by getting up and discreetly gazing out a small barred window giving on a back street with a bakery shop on it. We must have been there a quarter of an hour while she hauled things out and put them back. Twisting my head around the better to see something in the street, I was arrested instead by the sight of jewelry being extracted from the box. Out of the tail of my eye I made out rings, brooches, a watch. It was a heavy one in a gold case, some kind of initials carved on its lid. Obviously an heirloom, passed down from generation to . . . I willed my attention back to the street, to the walls, to a rack containing little envelopes and slips of paper of various kinds. Speaking of wills, that was what she finally kept out and stowed into her bag. I could see that was what it was when the sound of her finally closing the box enabled me decently to turn around. "Last Will and Testament" said the blue cover in which it was bound. "There we are. Now we can go. Thanks for being so patient."

"Not at all, Mom."

Our little adventure had at most, oh, thirty more seconds left to it. I helped Mother Pickles to her feet, got her settled again on her crutches, picked up the deposit box, and opened the door. In the narrow corridor between the cell blocks we had a little traffic jam. We bumped smack into an elderly gentleman emerging from his own cubicle, about whom at first I had a fuddled sense of half-recognition, which suddenly burst into full bloom. The *fin de siècle* straw skimmer tipped in courtly greeting to the lady did the trick. It was none other than old Pewtersmith, whom you will remember as the spiffy gink whose fortune-hunting attentions over at the Rehab I had felt it incumbent on me to snuff out. He was carting his own modest safe-deposit box back to the lockup, and a gander at the size of the one under my arm, followed by a sly look darted at me myself, told me the sob story about my lady's misfortunes had been seen through, and that I was forgiven. It was all in the game, as we men of the world knew, and we would both be good sports no matter who ultimately picked up the marbles.

"Ah, Mrs. Pickles. I'm so glad to see you elsewhere than at our mutual repair garage for a change. And to see you your old spry self despite the crutches, necessitated, I take it, by a purely passing misfortune. Or I should say your young spry self, 'tickly in that fetching print dress you're wearing. How did you know pink was one of my favorite colors? Makes you look *in* the pink, if I may make so bold as to opine." Jesus Christ, opine. Did people still do that? And how appropriate all the spry stuff was. It's also the name of a vegetable shortening, and this citizen sure could spread it. I saw it personally as a kind of treacherous underfooting on which I was skating for a real pratfall, both arms swinging in a full external rotary as I strove to keep my balance.

We inched down the corridor in single file toward a more open section, where he pulled out a few more stops while we waited for attendants to stow our respective treasure troves back in the catacombs.

"Glad to see it's a bit more warmish after that cool snap. Call me a cockeyed optimist, as well as an incurable romantic, but I make it a kind of rule never to put my straw hat away again till the first snow flies. Sort of personal declaration of mine. Do you approve, Mrs. Pickles?"

"I certainly do, Mr. — Porterhouse."

"Pewtersmith, and at your service." Again a doff of said skimmer, the kind delegates wear at political conventions you know, to say nothing of a bow from the waist, accompanied by a twinkle in the beady blue eyes that were reminiscent of the shoe buttons of yesteryear. They would never fade, they would always keep that glitter. "I'd say it's a perfect day for an ice cream soda. What say you?"

"Oh, it's always a good day for one of those."

"Then it's settled. You will join me for precisely such a libation in that new fountain around the corner, a stunning reconstuction of an old-fashioned ice cream parlor. Not just the marble-top tables and the wire chairs and ceiling fan. The ice cream's first-rate too. The invitation naturally includes your ever-attendant young Mr. Teeters."

I'd never told him my name, that I could recall. He'd obviously been casing me as part of the overall picture. The old duffer really did his homework, you had to give him that.

The two women attendants were finally free to put our boxes back in the mausoleum. I noticed that the plan to have me signed on as deputy with access to the container, just in case, seemed to have been forgotten in the stream of compliments under which Mrs. Pickles positively glowed, pinker than her dress. And by the time we left, nothing would really do but that we slip into the recently opened Gay Nineties confectionery shop just around the corner, for an old-fashioned ice cream soda "on him." To cap the nostalgia, he drew his money from a drawstring poke. What a treat. And the day still to be topped off with Presbyterians and cubes of cheddar on toothpicks. As we parted in the street he asked whether he might call one day soon and pay his respects. Where had I heard that one before?

I was on hand when he called to pay them, helping break in a permanent replacement for Mrs. Rampart supplied by a local employment agency. I even set a spell in the parlor with them. His beady eyes, ranging over the fine furniture and the glittering chandelier, left no doubt the old coot had matrimony on his mind. Somehow he engineered the conversation onto the subject of longevity. They were all Methuselahs in his family, so that "at seventy-two I still got a pret-ty good stretch to do." His father never had a sick day in his life and died at ninety-three. "And his father before him lived to be ninety-five," he told me.

"That so."

"Can't be too careful in your choice of ancestors. It's all in the genes."

That being the case, Mom was interested in what his own might have produced. "Do you have any children?" she asked.

"Four, and all the spit of me," he said. Which is after all one more than the number of perfect copies of the Gutenberg Bible in existence.

"All married by now I take it, and with children of their own."

"Oh yes. I have seven grandchildren, three girls and four boys. Most within vizting distance, thank God, and all cute enough to eat with a spoon."

That settled my hash. To my surprise, actually, Connecticut does permit the adoption of adults, and with no age limit. So that you could probably get the probate court to O.K. adopting somebody older than yourself, which should be baroque enough even for Chirouble's taste. Mom at sixty-nine could well have adopted old Pop Pewtersmith and at a stroke come by four grandchildren and seven great-grandchildren, eventually strewing IBM and Union Carbide in all directions. Even had she not dropped her interest in me as filial material, I myself might have boggled at having my name changed to Pewtersmith, Teeters being burden enough to carry through life.

For they were wed, as they put it, three weeks later, even before I was, after a courtship far more whirlwind than any I could have undertaken at the time. Their prospect of a long sunset happiness knocking back Presbyterians took the sting out of realizing our whole plan had been fool's gold from the beginning. Still, it had been rather exciting to hatch, and fun to watch run its course to its fizzling end. To this day I don't know what changes, if any, Mother Pickles made in her will. Whether I'm named in it or not. There's probably some sort of modest bequest for me, who can say, but it appears the whole ball of wax will go to the proliferating Pewtersmiths.

Toby and I slipped off to a justice of the peace to get married without any to-do, and then it was off on a working honeymoon to Los Angeles and working lunches with producers, a few of whom showed some interest in *Coin of the Realm*. No real nibbles, but some interest, predicated on changes I keep busy at. Tightening here, brightening up the dialogue there. I plug away at it in whatever time my work as a driver for the livery service leaves me, now that I'm back in Merrymount. Most of the trips are evening jumps into New York, people going to dinner and the theatre. They leave me hours of layover time, which I often kill at a corner table in a cafeteria, scribbling away at revisions over coffee and a roll. Now and then I draw my old Land Yacht for parties really splurging. Usually it'll be a foursome, now and then a sixsome. Often in full fig. One night I had occasion to use it myself with Toby and two other couples, to the Chiroubles' housewarming. They bought Greentop, wouldn't you know it, the estate high on a hill which I thought I was looking at for myself, but it turned out I was bird-dogging for them, unbeknownst to me. Sad. Yet jolly too, because what a bash! The ballroom that night! Between the lost limo and my unattainable mansion, how my heart ached. But dancing with the ever-fragrant Toby in my arms, now in her ninth month, kept it from breaking.

What a mainstay she has turned out to be. And what a bed partner, as I well knew. Today a marriage is often consummated with a handsome divorce settlement, but I trust that won't happen to ours. Toby never has a headache — even when she has a headache. I find that the premise of my screenplay, first tackled in something like calculated cynicism, turns out to be true. Money *is* unimportant. I know I'll get it produced someday. I figure it should cost around ten million five. Maybe eleven million. Somewhere in that neighborhood.